SUREFORCE

I motion the shoplifter towards the changing rooms. Once inside a cubicle, I turn to face him. 'Strip.' His jeans are so baggy he's able to pull them off over his trainers, exposing a pair of brand-new shorts. As he does so, I subtly stare at his physique from under the brim of my uniform hat. 'I think that piece of clothing belongs to us,' I inform him, nodding at the shorts.

He stares at me with his piercing green eyes. 'I'll give you a blow job,' he whispers, looking down the corridor to make sure nobody is listening.

'You bribing me?' I asked.

'Doesn't look like you need bribing,' he says, nodding down at the growing bulge in my uniform trousers.

SUREFORCE

Phil Votel

First published in Great Britain in 1999 by
Idol
an imprint of Virgin Publishing Ltd
Thames Wharf Studios,
Rainville Road, London W6 9HA

ISBN 0 352 33444 4

Cover photograph by Trademark

Typeset by SetSystems Ltd, Saffron Walden, Essex
Printed and bound in Great Britain by
Mackays of Chatham PLC

For Hally,
the inspiration behind the words.

SAFER SEX GUIDELINES

We include safer sex guidelines in every Idol book. However, while our policy is always to show safer sex in contemporary stories, we don't insist on safer sex practices in stories with historical settings – as this would be anachronistic. These books are sexual fantasies – in real life, everyone needs to think about safe sex.

While there have been major advances in the drug treatments for people with HIV and AIDS, there is still no cure for AIDS or a vaccine against HIV. Safe sex is still the only way of being sure of avoiding HIV sexually.

HIV can only be transmitted through blood, come and vaginal fluids (but no other body fluids) passing from one person (with HIV) into another person's bloodstream. It cannot get through healthy, undamaged skin. The only real risk of HIV is through anal sex without a condom – this accounts for almost all HIV transmissions between men.

Being safe
Even if you don't come inside someone, there is still a risk to both partners from blood (tiny cuts in the arse) and pre-come. Using strong condoms and water-based lubricant greatly reduces the risk of HIV. However, condoms can break or slip off, so:
* Make sure that condoms are stored away from hot or damp places.
* Check the expiry date – condoms have a limited life.
* Gently squeeze the air out of the tip.
* Check the condom is put on the right way up and unroll it down the erect cock.
* Use plenty of water-based lubricant (lube), up the arse and on the condom.
* While fucking, check occasionally to see the condom is still in one piece (you could also add more lube).

* When you withdraw, hold the condom tight to your cock as you pull out.
* Never re-use a condom or use the same condom with more than one person.
* If you're not used to condoms you might practise putting them on.
* Sex toys like dildos and plugs are safe. But if you're sharing them use a new condom each time or wash the toys well.

For the safest sex, make sure you use the strongest condoms, such as Durex Ultra Strong, Mates Super Strong, HT Specials and Rubberstuffers packs. Condoms are free in many STD (Sexually Transmitted Disease) clinics (sometimes called GUM clinics) and from many gay bars. It's also essential to use lots of water-based lube such as KY, Wet Stuff, Slik or Liquid Silk. Never use come as a lubricant.

Oral sex
Compared with fucking, sucking someone's cock is far safer. Swallowing come does not necessarily mean that HIV gets absorbed into the bloodstream. While a tiny fraction of cases of HIV infection have been linked to sucking, we know the risk is minimal. But certain factors increase the risk:
* Letting someone come in your mouth
* Throat infections such as gonorrhoea
* If you have cuts, sores or infections in your mouth and throat

So what is safe?
There are so many things you can do which are absolutely safe: wanking each other; rubbing your cocks against one another; kissing, sucking and licking all over the body; rimming – to name but a few.

If you're finding safe sex difficult, call a helpline or speak to someone you feel you can trust for support. The Terrence Higgins Trust Helpline, which is open from noon to 10pm every day, can be reached on 0171 242 1010.

Or, if you're in the United States, you can ring the Center for Disease Control toll free on 1 800 458 5231.

One

Interviews! I bloody hate them. Still, now I've been kicked out of the army I need some sort of income. I've been blowing my dole cheque in a night. My mate Gazza, that I used to be in the army with, told me nearly all the bouncers in Manchester are ex-squaddies. It was him who sorted out this meeting with the Boss, the head of the security firm he used to work for. Reckons the Boss will think I've got what it takes.

It's not really the sort of job I want to end up in, but I may as well take it until I've decided exactly what I do want to do. I'm twenty-six next month, so I should have my feet on the first rung of some sort of career ladder by now.

It's a scorching evening for September. I undo the top button of my shirt and pull down the window of the cab. Don't want to leave a sweat stain under each arm. This shirt cost me an arm and a leg. Still, it was worth every penny: I've copped off both times I've worn it. My mum reckons it's nothing to do with the shirt, though. She says it's the good looks I got from my father that get them flocking. A handsome face is one of the only things he did give me. Haven't seen the bastard in twenty-two years.

I rub my hand over my newly cropped light-brown hair, making sure all the bits of shaved clippings have completely

1

disappeared. I never usually have it this short, but I can't be arsed gelling it any more.

'Come on!' I mutter impatiently.

This cab is taking for ever. I'm ten minutes late already.

I suddenly spot some bright lights up ahead. The cab pulls up outside a modern-looking bar. Four neon letters sit above the door, spelling out the word ZERO.

'That's five sixty,' the driver grumpily announces.

As I wait for my change I notice three stocky bouncers stood laughing and chatting at the door. They are all wearing black bomber jackets with the words SUREFORCE SECURITY printed on the back. I jump out of the cab and slam the door closed. All three bouncers turn round to face me. The biggest one takes his fag out of his mouth and aggressively throws it down on the pavement in front of me. He leans against the doorway, trying to look frightening.

'I'm here to see the Boss,' I say in my deepest voice.

They all check me up and down, realising I could be competition. The biggest bouncer folds his meaty arms menacingly.

'Ain't here yet, mate,' he grunts as he nods at the door. 'Better go in and wait.'

I slowly walk towards the two other bouncers who are standing in front of the doorway. Just as I think I'm going to have to stop before I bump into them, they stand aside. As I walk through the middle of them, the shortest one knocks his shoulder into mine. They're going to have to try a lot harder if they are trying to frighten me.

As I disappear into the bar, I feel their eyes staring into my back. I hear one of them make some sort of snide comment. The other two break into exaggerated laughter. If I wasn't wearing a short-sleeved shirt, I'd be rolling my sleeves up by now. I'm sure they wouldn't be so cocky if they were on their own. I'd sort them out, no trouble. Still, don't want to be kicked out of this job like I was the army. I know I've got to learn to control this temper.

I sit at a table in the corner of the packed bar. Dance music pounds out of the tiny but powerful speakers. Young men and women stand around the shabby bar drinking, all dolled up for a night on the town. Two women, both old enough to be my mum, sit at the table next to me sipping cocktails. They immediately begin to stare over at me, winking and giggling. I noticed the dirty old buggers clocking me as soon as I walked in. Shouldn't complain: I'm lucky really. I always seem to get loads of attention. My meaty, lad-next-door look seems to work every time. Don't even have to work at it. I have a naturally good physique. My mate Gazza curses me. Says he has to pump iron four times a week to get pecs as defined as mine. I hope the Boss gets here soon: those two wrinklies are starting to do my head in.

Through the open bar door, I notice a silver BMW pulling up outside. The biggest bouncer opens the passenger door, and a young, bleach-blonde bimbo steps out on to the pavement wearing next to nothing. She kisses all three bouncers and totters into the bar on her five-inch heels. I lean forward to try to get a glimpse of the driver, but one of the bouncers is blocking my view. The blonde teenager kisses one of the barmen and climbs on to a bar stool. She arranges her skirt, making sure she's displaying plenty of fake brown leg. I glance back over at the door. Suddenly the bouncers part to reveal a big beefy guy wearing shades. It's the Boss. I know it's the Boss because of my mate Gazza's perfect description of him.

'Someone you wouldn't want to get on the wrong side of,' Gazza had warned me.

Looking at the thickness of his neck, I pray to myself that I never do get on his wrong side. Jesus, he's big. He towers over the other bouncers, and they're not exactly small. I'm sure most of it is real, but I can't help feeling he must have been helped on by steroids. No one is naturally that much of a brick shit-house.

One of the bouncers suddenly nods towards me. The Boss looks over in my direction. I quickly turn away, embarrassed by the fact he had caught me staring at him. After a while, I subtly look back in his direction. Although I can't see his eyes through the blackness of his shades, I know he's staring directly at me. He thumps one of the bouncers playfully on the shoulder and struts into the bar.

From the corner of my eye, I can see him walking slowly

towards me. He acknowledges the bar staff and winks at his giggling doll of a girlfriend. As he gets nearer, I'm able to get a closer look at him. I reckon he must be in his mid-thirties. If he took his shades off and revealed his eyes, I could be more sure of his age. His dark, receding hair is cropped short, and a perfectly trimmed goatee beard covers his chin. His tracksuit top is slightly unzipped to reveal the chunkiest gold chain I've ever seen in my life. (With his money, I can imagine it's the real thing as well.) His tracksuit bottoms must be the largest size, but they still cling tightly to his tree-trunk thighs. Boy, he looks nasty. If my mate hadn't told me he's harmless unless you cross him, I would be out of here by now.

As he gets nearer my table, I get to my feet. The older women on the next table spot him and nudge each other, obviously a pair of his many admirers. He stops right in front of me and holds out his huge, meaty right hand. I stare at the solid gold signet rings that cover his fingers. I reach out and shake his hand as firmly as I can, but it's nothing compared to his crippling grip. (And I thought I was strong!) His rings begin to dig into my palm, and I start to lose the feeling in my hand. He lets go just as I'm about to show I'm in pain.

'All right,' he bellows in his Mancunian accent. 'You must be Matt.'

I nod, trying to get a glimpse of his eyes. Unfortunately all I can see is my reflection in the dark glass.

'You've come highly recommended,' he says, checking me up and down. 'I can see why!'

I grin, pleased that he thinks I'm physically up to the job. He nods over at a door marked STAFF ONLY at the back of the bar. 'Right, let's see if you've got what it takes.'

He struts slowly towards the door, taking a bunch of keys from his pocket. I nervously follow him, wondering what sort of questions he's going to ask me.

He unlocks the door and pushes it open. He stands in the doorway holding the door open for me. I walk into the room, feeling his hot breath on my neck as I pass. He walks in after me and closes the door firmly behind him, plunging the room into darkness. The loud music from the bar outside fades to a muffled thud. He flicks a light switch on, and a dim, wall-mounted work lamp lights up the room slightly. As I look around, I realise that I'm not in an office at all. Metallic barrels of beer line one side of the room and crates of designer lager are stacked on the other. The electronic pumps attached to the barrels make a loud whirring noise every time a pint is pulled at the bar outside. Why has he brought me into the stockroom?

The Boss notices me looking round at the filthy stockroom. 'My right-hand man's in the office doing some paperwork. Didn't want to disturb him.'

He walks over to a waist-high stack of crates and sits on top of them. His thighs press against the empty bottles, making them look even chunkier than they already are. He reaches over for an empty crate and sits it on its side in front of him.

'Sit!' he growls, nodding at the crate.

I walk over to the crate and lower myself down on it, making sure it doesn't topple over. I look up at him, waiting for him to take his shades off. He smiles at me, his face losing its harshness and looking quite handsome.

'You're a good-looking lad,' he says, leaning back against the painted brick wall. 'You'll certainly pull more punters into this place if we stick you on the door.'

I smile nervously, not knowing exactly how to take his compliment.

'So, reckon you can handle yourself then, do you?'

'Always managed up to now,' I answer confidently.

'Gazza said you were a cocky little shit,' he says, grinning to himself. 'Do you work out?'

I sit upright and push my chest out, making sure I look as big as possible. 'Now and then.'

He looks at my meaty forearms that stick out of the bottom of my short-sleeved shirt.

'Let's have a look at the rest of you, then.'

I frown at him, not sure what he wants me to do.

'Go on, take your shirt off,' he says seriously.

I stare at him in disbelief. He leans forward to within a few inches of my face.

'This is an interview for a job as a bouncer. I'm here to test your brawn, not your brain. So, take your fucking shirt off!'

Realising I'm going to have to take it off if I want the job, I slowly begin to untuck my shirt from my trousers. Noticing I'm a little nervous, the Boss tuts and shakes his head.

'Jesus, you're a shy little fucker, aren't you? Look, I'll take mine off if it makes you feel any better,' he says standing.

His gigantic hand reaches for the zip on his tracksuit top. His massive signet rings sparkle in the wall-mounted light. He begins to slowly pull down his zip to reveal two huge, hairy pecs. He notices me staring at them in awe.

'Your tits as big as these then, boy?' he asks, proudly flexing his huge chest.

I shake my head sheepishly. I know I've got a good body, but next to him I'm going to look like a right wimp. I undo my shirt buttons and slowly pull my shirt off my shoulders. I throw it on to a stack of crates and sit upright, subtly flexing my muscles to look as toned as possible. As I look down at my smooth chest, I remember that I've got quite a good colour on me from the summer. This makes me feel a little more confident. I look up at the Boss. His face is looking in the direction of my chest. I can't actually see his eyes, but I know he's staring at my compact, hairless torso.

'Quite a muscly little fucker, aren't you!' he says, grinning to himself. 'You're right, looks like you can take care of yourself.'

He takes his unzipped tracksuit top off completely and throws it on top of a barrel. He puts his hands on his waist, displaying his near-perfect body. His huge chest and arms look like they are about to burst at any minute. His rock-hard nipples point directly at me. I notice he's got two huge tattoos on the top of each arm. I lean to the side to try and get a glimpse of what they are of.

He suddenly moves, drags another barrel over and stands it between us. He rests the elbow of his right arm on top of it, indicating that the next test is an arm wrestle. I lean forward and grab hold of his sweaty hand. I move my fingers to get a firm grip.

I realise I'm probably not going to win, but I know I've got to put up a good fight to impress.

'Go!' he suddenly yells.

Within a fraction of a second, he bangs the back of my hand down on to the barrel.

He grins at me mischievously. 'Don't worry, you haven't failed your interview yet.'

He jumps to his feet, towering over me like a flesh-covered skyscraper. He gestures with his head, indicating that he wants me to stand in front of him. I slowly get to my feet. My eyes reach the same height as his huge, thick neck. I stare at my reflection in his chunky gold chain. He begins to pace up and down in front of me.

'So, it's a busy Saturday night. There's just two of you on duty. A big group of lads come walking up to the door.' He continues to pace up and down. 'They're all lagered up. When you tell them they can't come in, they start getting aggressive. The gobby ringleader starts mouthing off.'

He starts to bang into me as he paces around the stockroom. My skin tingles as his flesh comes into contact with mine.

'The gobby little shit starts giving you hassle. He starts pushing and shoving you.'

He starts banging into me even harder. I know it's some kind of test, but I don't know exactly what he wants me to do. As he continues to bang into me, I feel my fists naturally clench. Shit, what am I doing? I've got to control this temper. I can't smack the Boss one: he'd bleeding put me to sleep.

Right, think straight. I couldn't lay a punter out, or I'd be charged. I've got to try and restrain him, that's what I've got to do. I suddenly make a grab for the Boss's wrists. I clench hold of them as tightly as I can, but in one simple move he rolls his hands around and grabs hold of mine. He grins at me and suddenly twists one of my arms over my shoulder. He holds it halfway up my back in an arm lock. I stand in front of him, helpless. I feel his breath on my neck.

'You lose,' he whispers in my ear. 'But don't worry, you shouldn't have to contend with anyone as big as me on the door.'

He loosens his grip slightly, but keeps me in an arm lock. We stand in silence, apart from the thud of bar music rattling the crates.

'I think I'll give you a go,' he suddenly says to the back of my head.

I smile to myself, trying to free my hand from his arm lock. He quickly tightens his grip.

'Wait!' he says sternly. 'You've passed the interview, but now it's time for your induction, lad.'

He continues to grip me in an arm lock, our sweaty skin occasionally meeting. He stands nearer me, and I feel his hard nipples digging into my back. His free arm reaches around my waist, and his hand begins to undo my belt. I pull his hand from my belt buckle and look over my shoulder, trying to face him.

'What the fuck you doing?' I ask angrily.

He tightens his arm lock even more. 'It's OK, mate, all my lads go through this little job induction,' he says, with a snigger in his voice. 'It's sort of my way of welcoming you to Sureforce.'

He puts his hand back on to my buckle and begins to slowly undo it. This is mad! Surely he's too bleeding straight to swing both ways? I mean, I've met some real straight-acting bi-guys in borstal, but Jesus, he's just too bloody laddy.

'Don't worry, you'll be getting bonuses for extra duties,' he mutters in my ear.

Once he's finished undoing my belt, he starts ripping open the button fly on my jeans. Shit! He really does want me. I begin to relax, and my cock starts twitching in my pants at the thought of going down on the Boss. He slightly loosens the grip on his arm lock, hoping that I'm not going to try and get out of his hold any more.

I can see now why my mate Gazza recommended me. We had been fuck buddies in the army. If we were away on service, and he hadn't shagged his bird for a few months, I sort of helped him out. When all the lads were out of the barracks, I'd pretend to be his bird and let him fuck me like he would her. My cock starts to pump with blood just thinking about it. I imagine Gazza and the Boss talking about my arse.

The Boss suddenly pulls my jeans down to my knees. He looks over my shoulder and notices my rock-hard cock bulging through my pants. I've not only been lucky enough to be blessed with a good body, I've got quite a big, thick cock as well.

'You're a big boy in lots of ways, aren't you?' he says, obviously impressed. 'Looks like you're ready for me.'

He starts to grope my arse through my pants, his huge hand fitting perfectly round my pert cheeks. He slowly pulls them down, still holding me in an arm lock. My bulging knob falls out of them and springs up and down in front of me. He grabs hold of my bare arse with his manly hands, and I feel the cold rings on his fingers digging into my flesh.

'Nice tight cheeks, mate,' he says appreciatively.

His hand leaves my arse, and I feel him begin to pull down his tracksuit bottoms.

'So you gonna help me out like you did Gazza?' he asks.

He obviously does not care if my answer is going to be yes or no. I know he's determined to take me whatever happens.

'My bird's got her period. Haven't had it for days. Got a fucking gallonload stored in here,' he says, matter-of-factly.

Once his tracksuit bottoms are around his ankles, he stands upright. I feel his rock-hard meat rubbing against my arse cheeks. I look over my shoulder slightly and catch him looking down in the direction of my smooth arse. He's still wearing his shades, but over the top of them I can just about see his eyes transfixed on my crack.

My dick really begins to throb now. It's about time I got serviced by a real man. Whenever I cop off with a lad, they usually want me to do the fucking. He stands close to me and sticks his hard cock between my legs. It's so long I can see the head of it peeping out from under my balls. I know he's really getting off on staring at my cute arse. I clench it to try and get him even harder. He suddenly grabs hold of it like an animal and begins to rub his hand up and down my crack. I clench my arse muscles even tighter, jamming his fingers in my vicelike grip.

'Come on boy, let the Boss in,' he demands. 'I wanna feel that juicy hole.'

I unclench my cheeks slightly, allowing him to get his hand nearer. As his fingers find my twitching hole, he moans in delight. My cock throbs harder, knowing that he really wants to get inside me.

He slowly sinks a finger into my pink hole, breathing heavily on my neck as he gets more and more turned on. I look down at his purple helmet poking out from in between my legs. I wish I could see the whole of his beautiful piece of meat. I know it's huge because I can feel it rubbing against my arse cheeks. I move my right arm to see if he'll let me out of his arm lock. He tightens his grip even more. Guess I'm going to have to imagine what his huge stabber looks like.

He begins to dig another finger roughly into my dilating hole. 'Feels like you're ready, lad.'

He pulls his throbbing cock from between my legs. I hear him tearing something open, and an empty condom pack suddenly falls down next to my trainers. He gobs in his hand and then places his moist, rubber-covered bell-end at the edge of my man-cunt. He slowly starts to move his thick meat inside me. I reach for the stack of crates in front of me and steady myself. He kicks my legs further apart and grabs hold of my waist with his free hand. Once he's sure that the tip of his cock is safely in, he rams the rest of his length straight up inside my juicy hole. I throw my head back, groaning in pain and pleasure, unable to conceal how much I'm enjoying my induction. I picture the Boss looking down at the base of his cock disappearing up my arse. Wherever he's looking, I know he's really turned on, as I can feel his meat throbbing inside me.

He lets go of the arm he was holding behind my back, knowing he's now got hold of me in another way. He pushes me down over the crates of empty bottles in front of me. Both of his huge hands grab hold of my waist as he slowly pulls his fat meat out of me. Just as I think he's about to pull out completely, he shoves his throbbing tool back even further up my arse. As he tries to get it as far up as he can, he leans over me. His huge chest touches my back, and I feel his rock-hard tits digging into my flesh. I want to wank my cock, but know I would come in seconds with this horny bastard riding me. Getting a firm grip of my waist, he starts to pump me hard and fast.

'Got a nice juicy arse, boy,' he shouts, as he slides in and out. 'It's just like fucking my bird's cunt!'

His balls start to bang against my arse as his rhythm gets faster. I lift my cheeks higher, letting him get even further in. It really turns him on, and he begins to hammer it up me even harder. The empty bottles in the crates start to rattle as he bangs me against them. He reaches under me and places his hand against my flat, muscly stomach. He pulls me back on to his cock as far as I'll go. His other hand reaches round the side of my leg and grabs my smooth, meaty thigh. He starts to really fuck me fast, like a dog.

Suddenly the stockroom door opens. The deafening music from the bar floods into the room. The Boss carries on pumping me, not letting anything get in the way of his pleasure. A black guy sticks his head round the door. A lit cigarette hangs out of his mouth.

'Boss, I just –' he stops in mid-sentence, staring at what is going on.

'Get in and shut the bleeding door,' the Boss shouts over the top of the music. He continues to ride me.

The bloke walks into the stockroom and slams the door behind him. He's a little shorter than the Boss and looks about the same age as me. He wears a basketball vest and shorts that show off his well-toned arms and legs. The sides of his hair are cropped short, and he is extremely good looking, in a mean and moody sort of way. He stands watching the Boss working my arse, taking a drag on his fag and blowing the smoke out between his full lips.

'This is Twinny,' the Boss informs me. He continues to stab me with his hard knob. 'He's my right-hand man.'

Twinny grins down at me, his face lighting up. Shit! He's cute.

'Fancy helping me with Matt's induction?' the Boss asks him.

'Whatever you say, Boss,' he says, grinning over at him.

Twinny walks around to the other side of the crates and looks down at me being fucked like a dog. He sticks his fag back into his mouth and begins to untie the cord on the waistband of his shorts. He slowly pulls down the shiny white shorts and reaches in

11

for his weapon. I lift my head to get a good view of his dick. He watches me, knowing I really want to be fucked in the face as well as the arse. He slowly, teasingly yanks out his semi-erect, black cock. My mouth starts to salivate just looking at its juicy length. As he begins to jerk it, it starts to grow fatter and longer.

'Will this black dick do for you, white boy?' he says, as he begins slapping it around my face.

Once it's fully erect, he aims the fat, purple bell-end at my mouth. I open up wide, welcoming his throbbing flesh. Once I've got it inside, I work my tongue round it, tasting his manhood. He groans and starts to jab it in and out of my mouth.

The Boss carries on banging me from behind. My cock starts to throb, getting turned on by two big men working on me. I know I'll be wanking about this one for years to come.

'Give us a drag,' he grunts at Twinny.

Twinny hands him the lighted cigarette. Once the Boss has taken a long drag, he grabs hold of my waist again, still holding the fag in his mouth. He pulls me back on to his thick length as far as I will go. I can really feel it throbbing inside me now; I know that huge daddy dick is on the verge of exploding.

I grab hold of Twinny's knob and start wanking him, making sure his shiny bell-end stays in my mouth. I feel the ash from the Boss's cigarette drop on to my back as he starts to bang me even harder. Through the walls I hear the muffled thud of the music, and voices shouting and laughing as if they were egging the Boss on to fuck me harder.

I start wanking my cock with my free hand. I know I'm going to come in seconds with these two rough fuckers using both my holes.

'If he's gonna work for me, we've got to keep his strength up,' the Boss shouts to Twinny. 'He needs plenty of protein. You got any protein for him, Twin?'

'Oh yeah, Boss,' gasps Twinny, starting to fuck my face really fast. 'Got a load that'll keep him going for a week in here.'

'Fill the little fucker up then,' the Boss yells, as his balls start banging against my arse.

Turned on by what the Boss is saying, Twinny begins to groan, and I suddenly feel a spurt of hot spunk in my mouth. I start to gag as he keeps squirting more and more man juice down my throat. I start to choke, but he grabs hold of my head, making sure he's emptied every last drop inside me.

I feel the Boss pull his shaft out of my loosened hole. I feel his dick knock against my cheeks as he tears the condom off and begins to wank it furiously.

'Shit! Shit! Here we go,' he yells aggressively.

He begins to groan, and I feel a hot jet of spunk land on my arse and back. I begin to get up, but he pushes me back down, releasing jet after jet of thick white cream over my smooth cheeks. It feels like he's never going to stop coming. His spunk starts dripping down my crack and thighs. It feels so good it makes me release my load. I pull Twinny's dick out of my mouth and stand upright, wanking my dick hard. The Boss puts his firm hand on my arse and begins to rub his hot spunk into my cheeks.

'Come on, boy, show us what you're made of,' he says, encouraging me to shoot.

At that point, a flow of thick white come shoots out of my throbbing end and flies over the crates. I keep wanking it, knowing there's plenty more where that came from. Four more jets of cream cover the crates, sliding down the sides of the empty bottles.

Once I am completely empty, I stand in the middle of the stockroom panting.

'Nice one, kid,' says the Boss, as he slaps my spunky arse.

He starts pulling up his tracksuit bottoms. I quickly turn to try and get a glimpse of his beautiful piece of meat. Too late: he's already stuffed his semihard cock down inside them. I pray that I'll get a glimpse of it one day.

He puts on his tracksuit top, and I watch his huge, hard nipples disappear as he zips it up. I hope I get to have a taste of those as well. Twinny shoves his still hard dick back into his shorts, grinning at me cockily. His knob bulges against the white, shiny fabric, wanting to get back out for more.

The Boss opens a cupboard in the corner of the stockroom. He takes out a black bomber jacket with the words SUREFORCE SECURITY printed on the back. He throws it over to me.

'Welcome to the club,' he says, grinning. 'Think I'll get you working closely with me.'

I catch the jacket, beaming proudly to myself. He was obviously impressed with my performance.

The Boss opens the stockroom door and walks out into the noisy bar. Twinny follows him, turning around to give me a threatening look before the door slams closed. What's his problem? I pull my jeans up over my wet, spunky arse. I pick my shirt up off the floor and button it up. Throwing the Sureforce bomber jacket over my shoulder, I walk confidently out of the stockroom.

As I walk across the bar, I notice the Boss standing with his blonde girlfriend. He notices me looking over and winks at me when he knows his girlfriend isn't looking. As I head towards the door, I stare at his huge hand that's grabbing her pert arse cheek. I smile to myself, confident that it'll be grabbing mine again soon.

Two

———————

Turns out the Boss was so impressed with me he wanted me to start right away. He has sent me to one of those huge, out-of-town sport stores to work as a security guard. Apparently, Sureforce Security have the contract for the whole chain in the Northwest. He told me all I have to do is stand around looking mean. The Boss says there won't be as much physical contact as there is on the nightclub doors. Says he wants to break me in slowly. Could have fooled me.

My first day is going pretty well: no major incidents so far. The only thing that is giving me any hassle is this bleeding uniform. I really want to undo the top button of this shirt and loosen my tie, as the collar's digging into my neck. The peaked hat isn't any more comfortable either. I'm just going to have to suffer. I can't leave the floor until my replacement turns up. Can't even walk round much as these trousers are so bloody tight. Must suit me though: one of the cashiers hasn't kept her eyes off my arse all day.

My security radio starts bleeping. 'Damn,' I mutter. Looks like there is going to be some action after all.

I start walking towards the exit. The manager has somehow spotted some scally ripping a security tag off a pair of football shorts in the changing rooms. I'm only allowed to grab him once

15

he's stepped out of the store. I walk through the rows of tracksuits and sweat shirts and eventually reach the exit.

I hover near the metal strips that are situated either side of the door. I try to look inconspicuous, but it's a bit hard when you are wearing a full security guard's uniform.

A young lad suddenly walks out of the changing room carrying a pair of football shorts and looking extremely shifty. He must be in his early twenties, with his hair cropped at the sides and a natural blond, centre-parted fringe hanging over his forehead. A large red scar runs down his right cheek. I'll have to watch this one, could be a rough little bleeder.

As he walks towards the clothes rail that displays all the football shorts, I notice that he has quite a stocky frame. He must be a few inches shorter than me, though, so I reckon I could pin him down if I have to. He puts the shorts he is carrying back on the clothes rail. The manager is sure he has nicked a pair, though. He must have taken two in with him and stuffed one of them down those baggy jeans. Oldest trick in the book. No matter how much you've stuffed up your jumper, always put something back on the shelf. The assistants are less suspicious of you then.

I'm not letting this one get away with it. It's my first day: got to impress the manager. Apparently he's a good friend of the Boss. He's obviously going to report back to him to remark on my performance.

As the lad turns around, he looks either side to see if anyone is looking; he doesn't notice me watching his every move. As he moves from behind a clothes rail, I look him up and down. Christ, he could have a duvet down those jeans for all I know. His shirt is so baggy it almost comes down to his knees.

As he quickly heads towards the exit, he suddenly notices me stood next to the metal security gates. He slows down, scowling at me cockily. He begins to strut confidently through the gates. The alarm remains silent, and he grins to himself as he walks straight past me and out through the electronic doors. He saunters across the car park, whistling happily. I'll soon wipe that smile off his face, the cocky little sod.

I rush out through the sliding doors and sprint across the car park. A family loading shopping into their car stop what they are doing and look in my direction. I catch up with the lad and grab him by the shoulder. He turns around snarling.

'Get your bleeding hands off me!' he spits through gritted teeth.

'I've reason to believe you're concealing a stolen item of clothing,' I inform him, gripping him even tighter.

'Says who?' he snaps, aggressively shaking my hand off his shoulder.

'Says the manager who was watching your every move in the changing room,' I state, grabbing him by the shoulder once again.

'That's illegal; I know my rights,' he yells, shrugging my hand off his shoulder once more. 'And touch me again and I'll have you for assault!'

I grab him tightly by the scruff of the neck, getting fed up with his cockiness. 'Look, you little shit, you're going to walk back into that store before you have a nasty accident in this car park.'

Realising I'm not going to put up with any of his nonsense, he pulls my hand off his collar and adjusts his shirt. He glares at me with his evil-looking green eyes, chewing on a piece of gum ferociously. He slowly turns and begins to walk back across the car park towards the store. The group of spectators that has formed begin to cheer and whistle. He sticks a V-sign up at them as he passes. I follow him towards the store.

Once inside, I motion to him to head towards the changing rooms. He saunters across the shop floor, doing the Salford Shuffle (a walk adopted by every scally in Manchester). He keeps his head lowered, embarrassed by all the attention he is getting.

The manager of the store is waiting for us at the entrance to the changing rooms. He's a tall, wiry man in his early forties who wears an ill-fitting suit. His receding hairline reveals his red, shiny scalp.

'We have to find the hidden security tag and retrieve the stolen goods before I can call the police,' he explains.

'You go and finish cashing up, Mr Asprey. I'll sort him out,' I suggest, being as overhelpful as I can.

The manager nods and pulls a floor-standing CLOSED sign in

front of the entrance to the changing rooms, then heads off towards his office.

I lead the shoplifter into the changing rooms, constantly checking he's not about to do a runner. I walk past the row of empty cubicles, looking at the floor of each one. When we reach the final cubicle, I stop and turn to face him. A huge wall-mounted mirror covers the back of the small changing room, and a ledge-type seat is fixed to the side wall. A pair of flimsy curtains hang on either side of the doorway.

'So, which one did you hide it in?' I ask, wanting to get it over with as quickly as possible.

He stares at me with his huge green eyes, looking quite cute in this light. 'Hide what?' he says unconvincingly.

I undo the top button of my shirt and loosen my tie, knowing that this little shit is going to give me a painfully hard time.

'We're gonna be here all night at this rate,' I remark, not amused by his attitude.

'Suits me,' he grunts. He walks into the cubicle and slumps into the plastic seat, moodily crossing his arms.

'Yeah, well, it doesn't suit me,' I inform him sternly. 'Get those football shorts out of your trousers, now!'

'You've lost the plot, mate. No bleeding shorts would fit in these,' he says, shaking the legs of his jeans.

I stand in the doorway, completely blocking his exit. I look down at his fringe-covered face. 'You leave me no option, mate. I'm gonna have to strip-search you.'

He suddenly looks up at me, scrunching his whole face up as he frowns aggressively. 'You bleeding ain't. I want a solicitor,' he demands.

'What?' I lean against the doorway, laughing. 'If you think I'm gonna wait here until a duty solicitor decides to show up, you're stupider than you look. I've got football tonight, and I ain't going to miss it for a little scally like you.' I push my chest out, looking as big as I can. 'Now, you're gonna get your clothes off before I dye 'em red.'

He lowers his head, realising I'm not going to put up with the shit he probably dishes out to all the other security guards. I walk

18

out of the cubicle and lean against the wall opposite, giving him room to undress.

He reluctantly gets to his feet and slowly begins to undo the buttons on his Ben Sherman shirt. I look at my watch, eager to release my tension at football practice. He eventually undoes the last button on his shirt and it falls open to reveal a muscly, bronzed six-pack. He obviously isn't working, so he's had plenty of time to ride his mountain bike around bare-chested this summer. Got a nice bit of colour on him.

He begins to peel off his shirt begrudgingly. It slowly falls off his shoulders and down to reveal two meaty little arms. If I had realised he was so beefy, I might have thought twice about coming in here alone with him. Too late to worry about backup now though.

As he hangs the check shirt on the hook in the cubicle, he subtly flexes his biceps, as if to warn me he's certainly no pushover. A tattooed heart on the top of his arm grows with the bulge of his muscle. I notice the name KIM badly hand-rendered underneath it. He turns around to face me, holding his arms down at his sides. I cannot help staring at his perfectly bronzed chest that's covered in wisps of blond hair. His brown nipples temptingly protrude from the centre of his hard pecs. He catches me staring at them and grins over at me cockily, knowing I'm impressed by his horny little body.

'Told you I had nothing on me,' he says, trying to wind me up.

I look at my watch, making sure I don't miss a minute of football practice. I've only got half an hour. Right, I'm getting pissed off with his cockiness. I'll show this little shit who's boss.

'Look, just get your fucking jeans down before I rip them down!'

Realising he's not going to get out of here unless he does what I say, his chunky hands slowly move towards the button on his jeans. Luckily he's not wearing a belt, so he's not going to take for ever getting them off. As he slowly begins to undo the button, I notice that the washed-out denim waistband makes his flat stomach look even browner than his chest.

He stares at me as he pulls the button through the hole and the top of his jeans flap open. He tilts his head to the side and reaches for his fly. The jeans are so baggy, they begin to slide down his hips as he slowly pulls down the zip. Once his fly is completely unzipped, the jeans immediately fall to the ground, revealing the nicked pair of white football shorts he is wearing underneath. Sticking out of the shorts are the most perfectly formed pair of male legs I've ever seen. They are the same colour as his stomach, and contrast beautifully with the shiny white material that stretches round his meaty thighs.

His jeans are so baggy he's able to pull them off over his spotless trainers. He kicks the last leg off and stands up straight, wearing just his trainers, white socks and football shorts. Fuck! He looks cute.

I subtly stare at his physique from under the brim of my uniform hat. I suddenly notice him watching me. He grins, knowing I'm impressed with his meaty body. I start to feel embarrassed, but then realise that I'm the one in control here; he's the one who should be embarrassed.

'I think they belong to us,' I inform him, nodding at the shorts he's wearing.

He stares at me with his piercing green eyes and slowly reaches for the elasticated waistband of the shorts. Still staring at me, he begins to slowly pull them down. As the shiny material moves down to reveal his cropped, blond pubic hair, I realise that he isn't wearing any underpants. The material slides down past his small, but perfectly formed cock. What it lacks in length it certainly makes up for in girth. In fact, I bet it's a fat little piece when it's hard.

He continues to lower the white shorts temptingly down over his smooth bronzed thighs. Once they pass his knees, he lets go of them, and they fall to the floor. He kicks them high into the air with his foot and catches them as they start to descend.

He stands in front of me, naked apart from his socks, trainers and cocky grin. My dick begins to stir in my tight uniform trousers. He tosses the shorts over to me, and they land on my shoulder. I lift them off, smelling his crotch on them as they pass my face.

20

'Right, get your clothes on,' I order him. 'I'll be waiting outside.' I begin to walk along the corridor of the changing rooms.

'Wait!' he shouts, sticking his head round the cubicle.

I stop in my tracks and turn around to face him.

He looks at me sheepishly. 'Look, mate, I'm on a caution. If I get nicked for this I could get sent down.'

'Should've thought about that before,' I shout as I turn around and continue walking towards the entrance.

'I'll do you a deal,' he shouts in desperation.

I stop once more and turn around to hear what this scally has got to say this time. He looks over at me with a puppy-dog expression on his face.

'Come on, I haven't got all day!' I snap, wanting to get to football practice.

'I'll give you a blowy,' he quietly mutters.

I slowly walk back to the cubicle he is standing in.

'A what?' I ask, pretending not to understand the meaning of the word.

'A blowy,' he mutters once again.

I frown at him, still pretending not to understand.

'A blow job,' he whispers, looking down the corridor to make sure there is nobody listening. 'I'll suck your cock if you let me off.'

My dick begins to twitch with the thought of having this rough beauty on his knees in front of me.

'You bribing me?' I ask.

'Doesn't look like you need bribing,' he says, nodding down at the growing bulge in my uniform trousers.

I stare at him, my mind in a whirl. He's really cute. But it's my first day. Still, I can just tell the manager I didn't find anything; he's not going to know any different. But what if someone comes in? Sod it. I haven't emptied it in a while, and he has got a beautiful pair of fat lips. Bet he knows how to give a really good suck after all the practice he gets in the nick. He'd be the pretty boy in there. Bet the older inmates have a field day. No, what am I thinking? I can't fuck his face here: I could get the sack.

I begin to walk away, but he's obviously sensed that I could be persuaded. His strong, firm hand makes a grab for my bulge. He stares at me with his bright green eyes, slowly rubbing my growing knob. I guiltily look away, knowing that this shouldn't be happening. My head's saying no, but my dick is definitely saying yes. He begins to rub it even harder. It looks as if it's about to burst through the thin material of my uniform trousers.

'Get a kick out of strip-searching young lads then, do you?' he says, grinning down at my massive hard on.

These trousers are really making it look bigger than it already is.

Unable to stop myself from touching his smooth skin any longer, I make a grab for his bare arse. Although he's a rough-looking fucker, his arse cheeks feel like pure silk. Now he knows I'm definitely up for being bribed, he begins to tug at the belt on my uniform trousers. Once it's unbuckled, he quickly begins to pull open the buttons on my fly, eager to get the job over with. He roughly pulls the last fly button out of its hole. He tightly grabs a belt loop on either side of my trousers, and pulls them down to my knees with one firm yank.

Staring me in the eyes continually, he slowly kneels on the floor until his beautiful red lips are directly in front of my hidden cock. He stares at the outline of my hard meat that is straining against the fabric. He slowly leans forward until his mouth is touching my white Calvin Y-fronts. His saliva-drenched tongue creeps from between his lips and starts licking the contours of my throbbing meat through the material. More blood begins to pump into my dick at the thought of that hard little tongue working round my fat bell-end.

His hands suddenly grab for the elastic waistband of my Y-fronts, and he pulls them down, stretching the elastic forward so my hard meat can easily be freed. My juicy, throbbing cock springs out, already oozing with pre-come. It comes to rest an inch away from his wet lips, still twitching and growing. I look down at it proudly, wanting to thrust it between his lips straight away. He stares at my pulsing bell-end, realising there is no going back now. I know he would rather be licking his girlfriend's vagina, but I don't give a shit, I just want this meat sucked.

He cautiously moves his tongue towards my sticky, purple

helmet. As his wet flesh comes into contact with mine, my whole body spasms slightly. He begins to slowly lick off the pre-come that dribbles from my slit. Once he's mopped it all up, he begins to move his mouth slowly around my rock-hard dick. I look down as his beautiful lips start to engulf my veiny cock.

He suddenly looks up at me from under his blond fringe. His eyes pierce into me, trying to make me feel guilty for what I'm making him do. It suddenly brings me back to reality, and I realise where we are actually performing this act.

The outcome of being caught suddenly dawns on me, and I begin to have second thoughts. He continues to suck my cock into his mouth. The further my meat disappears into his warm orifice, the harder it gets to pull out. I'm just going to have to get it over with, and get him out of here as fast as I can.

I grab hold of the back of his shaved neck and force him right on to the full length of my shaft. He gags slightly as my fat helmet hits his tonsils. I begin to shove it in and out of his mouth, really fucking him selfishly. He suddenly grabs my dick with his right hand and begins to wank it, still holding the tip of it in his mouth. Shit, that feels good. He obviously knows what he's doing. I knew he had probably given head before. I bet he gets out of trouble by doing this all the time. Probably sucked off most of the coppers in Manchester.

He really starts to eat my meat now, wanting to get the sentence over as soon as possible. I look down at his face; he's deep in concentration. I suddenly get the impression that he might have started to enjoy his punishment.

I reach down towards his muscly pecs. I fumble through his thin, blond chest hair for his nipples. It doesn't take me long to find them as they are now rock hard and protruding from his firm pecs even further. I pinch his erect tits with my fingers. Boy, they feel good: haven't felt a pair as hard as this in ages.

He starts to suck even harder on my cock, obviously turned on by me playing with them. He wanks my juicy dick even faster, his lips making sure my throbbing bell-end doesn't leave his warm mouth. I think this little fucker's tricked me: I reckon he was hungry for some spunk all along.

I pull my cock out of his mouth and lift it up, indicating that I want him to give my balls a good licking. He nuzzles into my crotch, practically getting both my balls in his mouth at the same time. His wet tongue works its way round every inch of my bursting sack. I quickly shove my cock back down his throat, not sure how long I can keep this gallonload in.

I grab hold of his blond hair and start to really fuck his face. He reaches round and pulls my bare buttocks towards him, urging me to stab him even harder. As I start to pump his mouth deeper, my uniform hat slips down over my face. I reach to take it off. He suddenly grabs my arm to stop me and pulls his mouth from around my cock.

'Leave it on,' he whispers in desperation.

Boy, got a right kinky little scally here. Obviously got a thing about security guards. I lift my cap from over my eyes, until I've a good view of this beauty kneeling in front of me. I grab hold of my cock and start to slap it around his face. Each time it hits his chin, he opens his mouth wide in the hope I'll give it back to him. I look down at his face staring at my dick, desperate to eat it again.

'You're not off the hook yet, mate,' I warn him. 'You gonna suck even harder this time?'

He nods his head obediently. I ram my cock down his throat and start pumping hard. I notice his hand disappearing between his legs. I move my head to get a glimpse of him beating his young meat. I was right: what it lacks in length it certainly makes up for in thickness. He tugs at it with his chunky hand, while his other hand grabs my length and starts wanking it furiously. Christ, I'm really going to shoot it today with the help of this dirty little scally.

I grab hold of the cubicle curtains to steady myself. I start pumping my hips, making sure my knob goes right to the back of his throat. He lets go of both our cocks and moves his hands up under my shirt. His fingers reach for my rock-hard tits, and he starts pulling on them roughly. Shit, that's making me come; I'm nearly there now.

I start to bang my meat into his gob even harder, not caring if it's choking him. My balls tighten and my spunk begins to rise.

My knees weaken, and I grab the cubicle curtains even tighter. They are the only things that are keeping me standing.

He starts to suck me really hard now, eager for some spunk. My body is like jelly, and the curtains take the whole of my body weight. Suddenly, the plastic rings holding the curtains on to the pole begin to snap, one by one. The curtains fall to the ground, and I begin to lose my balance. The shoplifter lets go of my tits and grabs my waist to steady me. He turns me round with his strong arms and shoves me against the cubicle mirror. As my back and arse come in contact with the cold glass, my whole body tingles.

Once he's sure that I'm leaning securely, he grabs hold of both our cocks again. His stubby hands begin to pump us ferociously, his hand moving back and forth like a piston. He notices the pre-come dribbling out of my dick and clamps his mouth firmly around my helmet. I look down at him gnawing on my dick.

'Yeah, eat it, you fucking scally. You're still not off the hook,' I remind him.

I grab hold of his blond head and pull him right on to my meat for the final few thrusts. My balls feel as if they're going to burst. I've two days worth of semen ready to escape. This little piece of jail bait is going to choke.

He feels my body shake and grabs hold of my bare arse, making sure I pump every last drop down his throat. I feel my hot spunk being released and shooting through my shaft. I pull his head right on to my dick as it begins to squirt into his mouth, covering his gold fillings. I thrust my hips back and forth as I watch my throbbing meat spurt stream after stream of thick cream on to his tongue. He tries to swallow it all, but some of my thick white juice dribbles out of his mouth and down his chin. I reach down to his face and wipe it off with my fingers. I push them into his mouth next to my cock, and watch him greedily suck the last trace of fuck juice off them both.

Once my cock and fingers are completely clean, I grab him under his armpits and lift him up. I position him in front of the mirror, so he has a perfect view of his own reflection. I stand behind him and reach under his arms. I grab hold of his chest and pull him tight against me, letting my wet cock slap against his smooth arse. I start playing with his hard tits and stare at his reflection in the mirror.

'Shoot over it,' I instruct him, nodding at the mirror.

He grabs hold of his rigid cock and begins jacking off, staring at his own reflection. I feel myself getting hard again, watching this cocky little lad turning himself on. I hold his smooth brown back tightly against my hard chest. I start to feel his whole body tremor like a volcano.

As I give his tits a good hard tug, he suddenly releases a load of healthy, young spunk. It slams hard against the mirror as if it were being fired by a gun. My cock starts twitching again as it reaches its full size. He continues to aim his cock at the mirror and squirts the rest of his fresh cream over it. The hot, white liquid slowly begins to trickle down the glass.

Once he's finished emptying his tight little balls, I feel his body relax in my arms. If I were to let him go, he would simply slump to the floor. I slowly lower him down on to his knees and stand over him, his head between my legs. My hard cock slaps on the back of his head. He looks at me from over his shoulder, wondering what I'm about to do.

I grab hold of the back of his head and push it towards the spunk that is trickling down the mirror. Realising what I want him to do, he slowly sticks out his tongue and reaches for the hot come with it. He starts to lick it off like a dog, spreading the slimy substance further up the mirror. I start wanking my cock again, turned on by the sight of him eating his own spunk. I push the back of his head closer to the mirror, making sure he laps up every last drop.

'Eat it all up, boy,' I order him.

As he laps the spunk up off the mirror, I tug on my cock even harder and release another stream of spunk over the back of his head. As I continue to wank it, more spunk streams out, landing on his smooth, brown neck and back.

Once my balls are completely empty, I wipe the end of my dick on his fine blond hair. I lean forward and check that he has left no trace of spunk.

'Good boy,' I say condescendingly, once I'm happy the mirror is completely spotless.

I step out of the cubicle and pull up my Y-fronts, stuffing my spunky, semi-erect cock inside them. I pull my uniform trousers up over the top of them and begin buckling up my belt.

The shoplifter gets to his feet and starts to put on his clothes. I stare at his smooth, muscly arse. I'm going to help myself to that the next time I catch him nicking from the store. He stares at me with his big green eyes as he buttons up his shirt.

'I'll have to nick something else soon,' he says, reading my mind.

He grins at me cockily. I straighten my tie and stare him right in the eyes.

'The punishment will be a bit more severe next time. Get out,' I order him.

He brushes past me flirtatiously and saunters along the changing-room corridor. I notice a patch of my white spunk on his shaved neck. I stare at it, wondering if I'll get the chance to breathe on it again. As he walks through the exit, he looks back and winks cheekily. He slowly walks through the store and disappears out of sight.

Back to reality. Better go and lie through my teeth to the manager. I reach down to pick up the football shorts but suddenly realise they are nowhere to be seen.

'Little bastard!'

I feel like I'm standing in front of the headmaster at school, waiting for a telling-off. The manager leans back in his office chair and looks up at me.

'So you're telling me you couldn't find the shorts on him anywhere?' he says, obviously not believing me.

'He must have dumped them when he saw me waiting at the door,' I murmur unconvincingly.

He gets up and walks over to a row of security monitors. 'So how come I saw him change into them on these?' he asks, nodding at the monitors.

He presses a button and a picture of the changing room appears on each of the screens. Shit! He has even got security cameras in the cubicles. This is where I lose my job.

'Do you want to know what I've just been watching?' he asks, raising his eyebrows.

He presses the play button on the control panel, and a snowy haze appears on the four monitors. As the interference begins to clear, I realise he's playing a video of me fucking the shoplifter's face. Each of the monitors shows me pumping him from a different angle. The end monitor has a close-up of my meaty arse as it thrusts back and forth into his face. The manager presses the pause button. On screen, my cock is held in freeze-frame as it's about to slide into the lad's mouth. I look down at the floor, not believing how badly I've screwed things up.

'The cubicle cameras aren't really for security,' he says, with a smile in his voice. 'They're for me.'

I raise my head and look over at him, not really understanding what he's saying. He slowly walks towards me, grinning seductively. He stops in front of me, his body uncomfortably close to mine.

'Don't worry, I won't let your boss know what you've been up to,' he says, looking down at my packet. 'On one condition.' He reaches for the fly on my uniform trousers. 'You give me a repeat performance.'

Shit! The dirty bastard wants my knob. Who'd have thought it? He's as ugly as fuck, but I'll let him have a lick if it means keeping my job.

I stick my crotch out, indicating that I'll let him suck it. His face lights up, like a cat that got the cream. Bet he doesn't believe how lucky he is to be sent a security guard like me. He reaches for my fly once again and hurriedly begins to unzip it. The pervy little git drops to his knees and yanks out my flaccid dick. He shoves it into his hungry mouth and begins sucking on it, probably enjoying the fact it's still cheesy from my last encounter.

I look down at his balding head, praying I'll be able to get it up for the old tosser. I wonder whether all my jobs are going to be as demanding as this. I close my eyes and start to fantasise about the

Boss's hard tits digging into my back, trying my best to get my cock hard. Blood instantly begins to pump into my knob. The manager starts groaning in delight as my meat begins to balloon in his mouth. Sorted!

Three

Another bleeding uncomfortable Sureforce uniform and another shit-boring security job. Shouldn't complain though. It's earning me good money and keeping me out of mischief. The Boss has moved me to one of those fancy office blocks in the centre of Manchester. Says I should look at it as a sort of promotion. Apparently, guards usually have to have been with Sureforce for years before they get placed somewhere as prestigious as this.

I spent the whole of this autumn at the sports store, reprimanding shoplifters on a regular basis. The manager didn't want to let me go. Told the Boss that he was impressed with my technique and that I was indispensable. The Boss eventually persuaded him that all Sureforce security guards could do as good a job as me. At my leaving do, the manager said in his speech that he was going to miss the store feeling so secure. Yeah, right! I know the only thing he's going to miss, the dirty old bastard. I bet he's praying that my replacement will be as generous with his knob as I was.

Anyway, I'm out of there now. The Boss was keen to get me here for some reason. Been at this place for three weeks now, and it's a doddle. Easily beats rugby tackling scallies who have four pairs of trainers shoved up their puffer jackets.

Christ, it's dragging tonight though. There isn't even any talent to gawp at through the huge reception windows. This part of the city is like a ghost town in the evenings.

I swivel round in my chair and glance at the huge clock that hangs behind the reception desk that I am sitting at. Seven thirty. Another six and a half hours to go. The only thing that is keeping me awake is the string of flashing lights draped around the tallest Christmas tree I've ever seen in my life. It's another world in these advertising agencies. The pretend presents at the bottom of the tree remind me I haven't bought one present yet. Only two days to go. I had better get my act together. I'm going to have to get the Boss something: he's been really good to me.

I spin round childishly in my chair. I come to a stop directly facing the marble lift that is situated to the side of the reception desk. I bet I'm going to see some tottie walking in and out of that when I work my first day shift.

The night bell at the reception door suddenly rings. Sounds like I've got a visitor. I pick up my huge bunch of keys from the reception desk and walk across the gleaming, marble foyer. As I reach the huge double doors, I peer through the tinted glass. Stood on the pavement outside is a courier leaning on his highly polished mountain bike. He wears a helmet and full cycling kit, including tight-fitting cycling shorts. He must be bloody freezing in this weather. He notices me and holds a small package up to the window. I unlock the double doors and hold one open for him. He wheels his bike closer and hands me the package.

'For Mr Paul Cheadle at CWP,' he states, in a well-spoken accent.

Must be a student making a bit of spare cash. I take the package from him, and he pulls a clipboard out of his courier bag. He rests it on his handlebars and hands me a pen. I take it off him and begin to sign my name on the dotted line. Once I've finished, I look up at him and catch him staring at my meaty forearms. Randy little sod. He quickly looks away, embarrassed.

I hand the pen back to him with a grin on my face. As he tries to take it off me, I grab hold of it tighter. He stares at me with a furrowed brow. I wink at him and let go of the pen. He sheepishly puts it back into his pocket and quickly turns his bike around.

31

'Happy Christmas,' I shout mischievously.

Ignoring me, he mounts his bike, and I get a good glimpse of his pert cheeks that are packed inside his cycling shorts. My knob begins to stir. He cycles off along the road, desperate to get away from this embarrassing situation. He obviously wants to taste a piece of cock, but just won't admit it to himself yet. Oh well, hopefully I'll be around when he does.

As he disappears into the distance, I make a mental note of the logo on his courier bag.

'CCT,' I read aloud.

I lock the door and walk back to the reception desk. Suppose I'd better stick this package on the owner's desk. They are not going to get it until after Christmas now, though: everyone finished for the holiday today. I reach for the phone on the reception desk and dial a number.

'Joe, it's Matt,' I shout loudly, making sure he hears. 'Can you cover for a while? I've got to take a package up to the fifth.'

I put down the phone and walk over to the lifts, carrying the package under my arm. I press the button, and the machinery behind the closed lift doors begins to whir into action. The numbers of the floors sit above the lift in a metal strip. The number fourteen is illuminated. As the lift slowly descends, each number lights up separately. It finally reaches the ground, and a large letter G at the end of the strip is illuminated. The lift pings and the doors slide open.

Behind the reception desk, the door marked PRIVATE creaks open, and Joe walks through it, carrying a mug of tea. He is Sureforce's oldest employee. No one knows exactly how old he is, but he's old. The Boss can't bring himself to sack him. Reckons this job is all he lives for, poor old sod.

'Won't be long,' I call, as I step into the lift.

He nearly jumps out of his skin: he obviously hadn't realised that I was still there. I press the button marked five, and the lift doors slide closed.

I stand in the lift as it slowly begins to climb. I take the package from under my arm and begin to inspect it. I definitely reckon it's a Chrissy pressy that's arrived late. Maybe it's a book. I shake it, and it rattles slightly. Sounds more like a video.

The lift reaches the fifth floor and grinds to a standstill. The doors ping open to reveal a long corridor with plush red carpet on the floor. I suddenly remember that the fifth floor is where all the bigwigs' offices are. I step out of the lift and look up and down the corridor, not sure which way to go.

I suddenly hear a whirring noise coming from the office that is directly opposite the lift. I look at my watch – seven forty-five. Shouldn't be anyone left in here at this time. Certainly not two days before Christmas, anyhow.

From my position outside the lift, I can see part of the office through the open doorway. I notice that the main lights are on. Still, that's nothing unusual: all the lights are on a timer switch anyhow. As I lean to one side, I can see a large leather office chair sitting behind a very elaborate desk. The whirring noise begins again and I slowly walk towards the open door, determined to discover what it is.

As I move nearer and nearer the door, my heart begins to pound. A Sureforce security guard got knifed the other week, when he stumbled across a gang who were nicking a load of computer equipment. There must be thousands of pounds worth in this place. Wouldn't be surprised if it was the same gang.

The strange noise is still going on. Christ, this is all I need. I look down at my walkie-talkie on my belt. No, I can't use that: you can hear it a mile off.

I eventually reach the office and take in a huge breath of air. I slowly peer round the doorway. I sigh with relief as I see a man cycling on an exercise bike on the other side of the office. Unaware that I'm watching, he continues to pedal like mad. He wears a smart shirt and tie, loosened at the neck. He's quite tall and stocky, to the point of being fat. I'd say he was in his late forties. Not bad looking for a wrinklie. His head of grey hair makes him look very distinguished. Sweat begins to soak through the back of his shirt. He's really giving that bike some. He must be pretty fit for his age.

I knock on the door. He suddenly stops pedalling and turns around to face me.

'Mr Paul Cheadle?' I ask, holding up the package.

'Ah, bloody marvellous,' he shouts in an extremely posh accent. 'I thought the damn thing was never going to arrive.'

He jumps off the bike and walks over towards me. He grabs the package out of my hand and rips it open excitedly. He pulls out a video with a note attached to it and begins to read it.

'Dirty bugger,' he says, smiling to himself.

He takes the cassette out of the case and slides it into a state-of-the-art video machine that sits under a wall-mounted TV.

'Just a little stocking filler for the wife,' he says, slightly slurring his words. 'Want her to get a little more adventurous, if you know what I mean!'

He picks up a glass from the desk and knocks back its contents. He's obviously had a few at the lunch time office party. He walks over to what looks like an ornate filing cabinet and pulls open one of the mock doors. As the door swings fully open, I notice a fully stocked drinks cabinet inside it. He picks up a bottle of whisky and tops up his glass.

'Join me?' he asks, holding the bottle up for me to see.

'Umm . . . I'm on duty, better not,' I reply sensibly.

'Sod it. It's Christmas!' he announces. 'Old Joe's down there, isn't he?'

I nod. He begins to top up the other glass with a generous measure of whisky. He takes a tray of ice out of the minifridge and puts some into the glasses. He hands me one of the glasses and raises the other in the air.

'Merry Christmas, umm – what's your name?' he asks, realising he doesn't know me.

'Matt. It's Matt, sir.'

He clinks his glass against mine before taking a huge swig from it. He picks up a remote control from the desk and points it at the TV and video.

'Just want to check it before I wrap it up,' he remarks. 'The wife's picking me up in a minute.'

The video machine clicks into action, and an American copyright warning fills the screen.

'Hope you're not too squeamish?' he asks.

He quickly polishes off another glass of whisky.

The credits start to roll, and I realise that his wife's stocking filler is in fact a hard-core porno movie. He tosses the plastic case over to me. On the front cover there is a naked woman sat on top of a half-naked man. The words REAR ENTRY are written above them.

'My chum recommended it to me. Said it should really get the missis going.'

He knocks back the contents of his glass and takes the whisky bottle back out of the cabinet.

'She's a bit of a prude, you see,' he informs me, as he tops up his glass. 'Won't let me go anywhere near her arse.'

Boy, this guy is really pissed. I can't believe he's telling a total stranger about his sex life. He pours some more whisky into my glass.

'Come on, drink up. You've got some catching up to do.'

I knock back the whisky in the glass, and he pours another measure into it.

'The wife's driving,' he slurs. 'It's the one night of the year she lets me get totally bladdered.'

He remembers the video is playing and starts watching it again. On screen a man and a woman sit on a sofa kissing.

'Sod the boring bits,' he says, pointing the remote at the TV.

The video begins to fast forward, and the speeded-up man and woman undress each other like they are in a scene from the *Benny Hill Show*. The woman's head begins to rapidly bob up and down on the man's dick, giving him a speeded-up blow job. The woman starts to climb on to all fours, and he points the remote at the TV once more.

The video resumes normal play just as the man starts to shove his cock up the woman's arse. Paul stares at the video engrossed, forgetting that I am still in the room. I notice a bulge appearing in the front of his pinstriped trousers. He lowers himself into the office chair, not taking his eyes off the TV for a second.

35

'Wish I was married to her!' he says in utter wonder. 'You ever done your girlfriend up the . . . you know what?' He suddenly looks over at me apologetically, realising what he's just asked. 'Shit, sorry, mate. Don't mean to be so personal. Must be the drink talking.'

'It's OK, mate, I'm not exactly shy,' I reassuringly tell him. 'Yeah, I've done a bird up the arse.'

'Really!' he says in disbelief. 'How did it feel?'

'Brilliant,' I enthuse, wanting to get him aroused. 'It's nice and tight up there. Bit like doing a virgin every time.'

'Lucky sod,' he says enviously. 'Wish I could find someone who'd let me fuck them up the arse.'

He stares at the TV, mesmerised by the woman being butt-fucked. I notice his cock swelling under his suit trousers. He knocks back his whisky and reaches for the bottle again. He is getting pretty pissed, and I am getting pretty turned on by the porn. Do I push it? He's in good shape and looks like he's got a bit to offer downstairs. I'm sure the Boss wouldn't sack me if he was to report me. I'm his blue-eyed boy at the moment. Sod it! Let's go for it. It is Christmas.

I knock back the contents of my glass. The bloke notices and leans over the desk to pour me another, still glued to the TV. On screen, the man continues to pump the bronzed woman.

'What about a bloke's arse?' I ask cautiously.

'Nah, they're too hairy,' he answers, without even flinching.

It almost sounds like he's considered it already.

'Mine isn't,' I say brazenly.

'Your what?' he asks, totally engrossed in the film.

'My arse. It's nice and smooth,' I say temptingly.

'What, as smooth as her gorgeous behind?' he asks, nodding at the TV.

'Yeah,' I say confidently, not quite believing how easily this one's going to swing.

'I'll bet you a tenner it's not,' he jokingly teases.

'OK,' I agree, calling his bluff.

I place my glass down on the desk and unbuckle the belt on my uniform trousers. He is so pissed and engrossed in the film he doesn't even realise what I am doing. I walk round the desk to where he is sitting. I unzip my fly and lower my trousers and underpants to my knees. I turn my back to him and slowly lift my creased shirt-tail, revealing my tight, muscly arse.

'What do you think?' I ask, stroking my smooth cheeks with the other hand.

I look over my shoulder and catch him staring open-mouthed at my arse crack.

'Looks like I owe you ten pounds,' he says in disbelief.

'I haven't won the bet yet,' I respond. 'I've got to prove it feels smooth as well.'

I stick my arse out further, encouraging him to touch it. He nervously empties the contents of his glass, continuously staring at my cheeks. His rock-hard cock strains against his fly, fighting to get out. I bet he can be a right dirty sod. He puts the empty glass on to the desk and puts his hands on his lap. I reckon he's going to need some encouraging.

'Go on, it won't bite,' I say, temptingly stroking my cheeks.

He sits uncomfortably in his chair, obviously not knowing what to do. I had better get this sorted before he sobers up. I want a bit of cock – haven't had any in weeks.

Realising that he's going to need some coaxing, I reach for his hand and slap it on my right arse cheek. 'Smooth enough for you?'

'Yes, you win,' he says, quickly taking his hand off my arse. He begins to rummage around in his jacket pocket. 'I'll find that tenner.'

'Wanna fuck it?' I ask shamelessly, fed up with his little guilt trips.

He looks up at me, half shocked, half turned on. 'But I've never . . .'

'It's OK,' I reassure him. 'I'll do all the work.'

He pours himself another whisky to steady his nerves. I pull my uniform trousers down completely and kick them off over my steel-toecapped boots. I lean across the desk and pick up his phone, lifting my shirt to ensure he gets a good eyeful of arse.

'Joe, it's Matt. Just checking all the floors. I'll be down in a bit.'

I put down the phone and sit on the edge of the desk in front of his chair. My shirt-tail hides my cock and balls. The only flesh that is exposed is my smooth brown thighs and calves. I place my boot on the office chair and swivel it round until he's directly facing me. Leaning forward, I start to undo his tie. He frowns at me, feeling uneasy about what I'm about to do.

'Just borrowing it for a minute,' I inform him.

He suddenly grabs my arm with his hand, stopping me from going any further.

'What are you doing?' he slurs.

I shake his hand off my arm and continue to undo his tie. 'You'll see!'

I yank the tie through his shirt collar and carry it round to the back of the chair.

'Give us your arms,' I say.

'What?' he replies.

'Stick your arms back here!' I order.

He slowly stretches his arms round the back of the chair. I pull his wrists together and begin wrapping the tie around them. He tries to pull his arms away, but (thanks to my army training) he doesn't stand a chance.

'What are you doing?' he asks nervously.

I ignore him and carry on knotting the firmly wrapped tie. Let's see him try and get out of that. I walk round to the front of the chair and stand in front of him, my purple helmet poking out from the bottom of my shirt-tail. He stares at my smooth thighs, still sporting a bulging packet.

I suddenly reach forward and rip open his shirt; buttons fly in all directions. He moves his arms to try to free himself but eventually gives up. I stare at his large manly chest that's covered by a forest of grey hair. Two huge pink nipples protrude from the thick, dense growth.

I reach over to one of the whisky glasses on the table and take out an ice cube. He looks at me with a puzzled expression on his face. Shit! He really is naive. I straddle the chair, my shirt-tail acting as a curtain between my cock and his face. I place the ice cube against one of his nipples. As the ice makes contact with his fleshy pink lump, his body tenses, and he lets out a breathless groan. I move the cube slowly around his hardening tit.

Once it is fully erect, I move the ice cube to the other nipple and lower my mouth down on to the hard one. I poke at his protruding hard lump with my tongue. He thrusts his chest out, clearly getting aroused by what I'm doing to his hairy tits. I move my tongue through his grey undergrowth, wanting to check that his other nipple is as hard. I find the rock-hard lump instantly and throw the unwanted ice cube across the office. My cock twitches into action as I continue to bite and lick his manly stumps. He groans in pleasure. I bet his wife's never eaten his tits as well as this, if at all.

I reach down and start to unfasten his trousers, still sucking on his nipples. I quickly unzip him, eager to see exactly how much he's got for me. I pull his hard knob out of his trousers and kneel on the floor in front of him, wanting to get a bird's-eye view.

I stare at his circumcised dick. What it lacks in thickness it certainly makes up for in length. He watches me staring at it, desperate to get it wet. I reckon he would shove my head down on it if his hands weren't tied together.

I take some more ice cubes out of the glass and put them into my mouth. I grab hold of his meat and lunge my mouth down over it, dying for a taste. As the ice comes in contact with his cock, he groans loudly. He throws his head back, obviously never having experienced anything like this before.

As I pump my mouth up and down, I reach up to find his hard tits again. His body begins to shudder as I really start to pull on them. It's now obvious that his wife has never played with his chest like this. Shame. He probably would have given her the fuck of her life if she had.

He arches his back and starts to groan even louder as I circle his bell-end with my tongue. I look up to get a glimpse of his ecstatic face, keeping his cock firmly in my mouth. He glances down at me, probably wanting to see his saliva-soaked dick disappearing into my face. Our eyes meet, and he looks away quickly, embarrassed by the fact he's got his cock in a bloke's mouth.

I move my tongue to his hairy balls and manage to pack them

both into my hungry mouth. I start sucking on the sweaty sacks. My arse begins to twitch. Fuck, I really want this old geezer up me. I reach into my trousers that are on the floor, still sucking on his testicles. Once I have found what I am looking for, I release his balls from my mouth and tear open the condom I'm holding in my hand. I stuff the rubber in my mouth and begin to roll it down over his long knob.

The condom unravels fully just two-thirds of the way down his dick. Christ, I didn't think he was that long. I stand over him and spit on my hand. I start rubbing the saliva round the entrance to my arsehole. I spit in my other hand and clasp my dripping palm round his knob.

'Look, my wife's going to be here any minute,' he says, realising what I'm about to do.

'I'd better get a move on then,' I say, smirking cockily.

I slowly lower my arse on to the tip of his cock. I reach under my arse and guide his circumcised dick into my hole. Once I'm certain his helmet's safely inside me, I lower my arse cheeks down on to his long length of shaft. He throws his head back as he feels the sides of my man-cunt engulf his veiny length. My cock hardens as I feel the tip of his knob slide right up inside me. I don't think any meat has ever gone that far into my passage.

As I feel him getting harder and harder inside me, I begin to move my cheeks up and down. I grab hold of his hard nipples and start to ride him even faster, my cock flapping back and forth under my shirt. He stares at me in ecstasy, clearly forgetting all about his embarrassment and guilt. His wife doesn't know what she's in for now that he's been introduced to the joys of anal sex.

He tries to free his arms, wanting to touch my young flesh. I look at him sternly and shake my head. I bet he wants his arms free so he can force my arse all the way down on to his meat. But I'm in control here. Even though he's got his cock up my arse, I'm the one doing the fucking.

I grab hold of my hard cock and start to tug on it. I'm really going to cover this dirty old fucker's chest with come. He stares at my youthful thighs. He thrusts his pelvis up each time I lower my arse, making sure he gets his knob as far inside me as he can. My arse really starts to relax, and I sit all the way down on his meat. The tip of his cock knocks against my internal G-spot, and I yell with pleasure. I pull my arse back off his knob, my thighs bulging with the strain. When I feel my entrance has reached his helmet, I jam my cheeks back down on it.

Boy, this is really dirty. Two guys shagging in an office. My tits go hard just thinking about someone finding us. If old Joe stumbled across us it would surely finish him off.

I pull on his tits hard, wanting to feel him come inside me.

'Like fucking arse then, do you?' I yell.

He nods his head, concentrating on thrusting himself right up me. I yank on both of his nipples.

'Didn't hear you,' I shout aggressively.

'I love it,' he whispers.

I start to ride his cock faster, my calves bulging out of the top of my boots.

'Bet your missis couldn't ride you like this!' I say through clenched teeth.

My arse grinds up and down like a piston. He begins to groan louder and louder. Suddenly the phone begins to ring. He stops thrusting his dick and freezes. I carry on riding his meat and tugging my knob, just wanting to shoot.

'Shit! She's here,' he shouts.

I continue to grind down on his cock, totally ignoring the phone.

'I've got to answer it,' he shouts, getting in a real panic.

I pick up the receiver and hold it to his ear, still wanking my cock with my other hand.

'Hello,' he says, trying to disguise his panting. 'Right, could you tell her that I'll be down in a minute?' His expression suddenly turns to horror. 'She's what?'

He begins to struggle maniacally to get free.

'Put it down!' he yells.

I put down the receiver and grab hold of his tits once again. He distorts his body, trying to get up off the chair.

'My wife's on her way up. Bloody well untie me!'

'Not until I've come, mate,' I say, making him even more on edge.

The lift opposite the office pings, and through the doorway I notice the doors slowly slide shut. He quickly turns his head, thinking that she's arrived. The floor numbers above the lift light up individually as it begins to descend to the ground floor. I start to really ride his cock again, jamming all the way down on his length. I've got to bleeding come after all this.

'Come on, mate, make me shoot it and I'll untie you,' I inform him.

Realising that I'm not going to get off him until I have spunked, he begins thrusting his meat deep inside me. I grind down on every thrust, feeling his bell-end knock against my insides. I notice the letter G above the lift is illuminated.

'Let countdown commence,' I say breathlessly.

I grab hold of the back of the office chair with one hand and start to pull myself up and down on his dick. My balls tighten as I begin to wank my cock furiously. The illuminated letter G suddenly goes out.

'One!' I shout loudly.

The figure one on the metal strip over the lift suddenly lights up. After a few seconds it goes out. I feel his cock start throbbing inside me, ready to explode. He throws his head back against the leather chair, his pleasure taking over from his concern.

'Two!'

The figure two over the lift flashes on and off. I let go of the chair and pull on one of his nipples, wanting to feel him squirt it up me. As soon as my fingers come in contact with a hard tit, he groans loudly. My arse clamps itself round his knob, as he pumps his man juice up inside me.

'Three!' I groan, yanking back my foreskin aggressively.

As the figure three lights up over the lift, a long jet of spunk suddenly squirts out of my cock. It shoots through the air and slams into the grey hairs on his chest. The figure three goes out, and my cock continues to fire jet after jet of creamy come over his hard tits. Thick white semen dribbles off his erect nipples.

I wipe my cock on my shirt-tail and slowly pull his semihard knob from my arse. I pull my leg over the chair and quickly pick up my trousers. As I pull them on, I notice the number four light up over the lift.

'Get me out of this,' he begs, struggling with the knotted tie.

The figure four goes out, and a few seconds later the figure five lights up. I reach for the knot of the tie and pull it undone. The lift in the corridor pings and the doors slowly slide open. He pulls his shirt around his chest and begins to do it up. Realising most of the buttons have been ripped off, he holds the shirt together and leans forward across the desk.

A smartly dressed woman in her mid-forties walks out of the lift and into the office. I presume this must be the frigid wife. She walks over to him and plants a kiss on his forehead. He smiles at her guiltily. She looks down at his ripped shirt.

'Not another riotous office party?' she asks.

As she turns around, she suddenly notices me. She looks me up and down quizzically. I smile at her, subtly tucking my shirt-tail down the back of my uniform trousers.

A loud groan suddenly fills the room. We all turn our heads to the other side of the office. On the large TV screen, a man thrusts his cock up the arse of a petite blonde. She throws her head back, groaning in pleasure. Realising the video is still playing, Paul quickly reaches for the remote control. He aims it at the TV, and the room falls silent. His wife looks over at him in disgust, and he lowers his head in shame. I quietly begin to back out of the office.

'Sorry, Joe,' I say apologetically. 'Took me a bit longer than I had planned.'

I take my seat behind the reception desk, and Joe plods off into the back office, still holding his mug of tea. I pull at my cock through my trousers, making sure the spunk doesn't stick to my underpants.

The lift doors suddenly glide open, and Mrs Cheadle marches out across the foyer. Paul Cheadle sheepishly follows behind her. I jump off my chair and unlock the main door with my keys. I hold open the door, and Mrs Cheadle waltzes through it.

'Good night,' she says angrily.

Mr Cheadle follows her through the door, not able to look me in the eyes.

'Hope you get what you want for Christmas, sir,' I call loudly.

He carries on walking briskly towards the car parked outside. I pull the door closed and turn the key in the lock, grinning contentedly to myself.

Four

'Drip, drip, drop, bleeding April showers!' I grumpily sing to myself.

I'm bloody drenched, and it is absolutely freezing. Thought the weather was meant to improve in the spring. Thank God I clock off in a minute: I've been traipsing round this muddy building site all day. And the Boss calls this another promotion. Could have fooled me! I'd much rather be sat back in the warm reception of those poncy offices.

Still, got to do as he says if I want to remain his blue-eyed boy. And this place is nearer the Sureforce office, so I can pop in and see him more often. Apparently, he wants me here because the foreman of the building contractors hasn't been happy with the other Sureforce security guards. He says they just sit in the builders' Portakabin and sleep all night. He reckons one or two of them have even nicked pieces of machinery.

The Boss says it is a job for his number one guard. He is sure I'll keep the foreman happy. Certainly kept that bloke at the advertising agency happy. He soon got over his guilt trip and came back for more. Started working late a few nights a week. He couldn't get enough of my arse. Married men, they're the worst. Poor old Joe ended up having to cover for me quite a bit.

Anyway, turns out this Mr Cheadle was only the vice president of the whole bloody company. He signed another two-year contract with Sureforce, and the Boss gave me a bonus. Don't suppose the Boss would be too happy if he knew it wasn't just my security skills that persuaded him to continue using Sureforce. I'd probably get the sack if he knew I was fucking the clients.

I shine my torch around the deserted building site. The beam is so bright I'd spot a robbing scally a mile off with it. Satisfied that the site is secure, I head towards the builders' Portakabin, eager to knock off. I shine the torch down at my muddy boots and notice that the mud has even travelled halfway up my trouser leg.

'Shit!' I say, realising I'm going to have to take a shower before I can get in my car.

In the distance I can see the lighted windows of the Portakabin. As I head towards it, I make out a dark shadow walking in my direction up ahead. Suddenly someone bangs into me. I grip my torch tightly and hold it threateningly above my head. The beam of light shines directly into the person's eyes.

'Shit! It's you, Pete,' I say, relieved.

Stood in front of me is my replacement Sureforce guard. He is a tall guy in his late thirties. He wears a Sureforce bomber jacket and uniform trousers, tucked into a pair of Wellington boots.

'Sorry Matty, did I scare you?' he asks. 'Thought I'd better get straight out here. Apparently that little shit of a foreman is still around.'

I lower my torch, my heart still racing. 'What's he still doing around?' I ask, looking at my watch. 'It's nearly midnight.'

'He has to check the electrics. Plasterers get in tomorrow. Look at the state of you,' he says, looking down at all the mud on my trousers.

'Yeah, you've got it all to come, mate,' I happily inform him.

'Right, better start patrolling,' he says, turning on his torch. 'I'll say my goodbyes. You'll probably be gone by the time I get back to the hut.'

'Yeah, see you tomorrow, mate.'

He walks off into the pitch-black building site, the ray from his torch slowly fading. I briskly head towards the Portakabin, eager to get out of the rain.

I reach the Portakabin and burst through the door. I close it tightly behind me, making sure the cold and rain stay completely outside. I lean against the door and sigh with relief, happy to be back in the warm cabin. A Calor Gas heater burns at one end of the room, and a table and chairs stand in the middle. Torn-out pictures of naked page-three girls cover the walls. A pile of power tools sit under them. I take off my saturated Sureforce bomber jacket and throw it on the back of one of the chairs.

I walk through a door into a connecting Portakabin. The walls of this space are completely tiled. Along one side of the cabin are three toilet cubicles and a washbasin. A large mirror is screwed into the wall above the basin. Along the opposite side are three wall-mounted communal showers, hanging over a tiled floor. I feel the wet fabric of my trousers clinging to my thighs. I've got to get out of these trousers before I catch pneumonia. This cabin is freezing. Unfortunately, the heat from the Calor Gas heater doesn't travel this far. Still, at least the showers are scalding. They'll soon warm me up.

As I kick off my muddy boots, I pull my soaking Sureforce sweat shirt over my head. I pull down my sodden uniform trousers and throw them on top of my sweat shirt. I catch a glimpse of my muscly torso in the mirror.

'Looking good, Matt,' I say to myself as I flex my muscles.

I'm really lucky I don't have to pump iron to keep in this shape. I even drink loads of lager. Must burn it off in other ways.

I turn the knob on the nearest shower, and a jet of scalding water floods out of the shower head. I adjust the knob to a bearable temperature and step under the hot stream of water. My body relaxes as the spray of water massages my back. Boy, that feels good! Just what I need after wandering around in the freezing cold for eight hours.

I pick up the cheap bar of soap that rests in a soap dish hanging from the shower. I begin rubbing the soap all over my body, paying particular attention to my sweaty bollocks. The soap begins to form a thick, white lather. I scoop some of the lather off my cock and start to rub it up my arse crack. Once my arse is nice and clean, I move my hand to my flaccid dick and begin to rub the lather up and down my shaft.

I put my head under the hot jet, and warm water begins to slowly wash away the thick, white lather. The creamy lather is forced down my torso and disappears down the plughole. More and more of the lather is washed away, revealing my smooth, semihard cock.

I suddenly hear a thud coming from the other cabin. I stop stroking my knob and stick my head out from under the jet of water. I hear the sound of footsteps on the plywood floor. Shit! There's definitely someone in there.

'Pete? That you?' I call out hopefully.

The person doesn't answer. That means it isn't him. What the hell is Pete doing out on that site? I bet a scally has sneaked in behind his back. Dozy sod.

A heavy pair of footsteps approaches the shower room. I clench my fists, ready to teach the robbing scally a lesson. As the footsteps get nearer and nearer, my body tenses. Suddenly, a bloke sticks his head around the door of the shower room. I jump.

'Don't panic, Sureforce boy!' he says, grinning from ear to ear. 'It's only me.'

I suddenly realise that it's the foreman of the building site. The bastard obviously enjoyed giving me a good fright. He stands in the doorway laughing to himself. Cocky fucker.

He takes off his hard hat to reveal a thick, black flat top. A red line runs across his forehead where the hat has been digging in. He pulls off his heavy waterproof coat and hangs it over one of the toilet cubicle doors. He's a cute-looking guy who I reckon is in his late twenties. He has a thick, black moustache and hypnotic blue eyes. He has a plaster on his right eyebrow. I can't tell if it is an injury from the building site, or whether he was out scrapping last night. He looks about the same height and build as me. But then again, he could be a lot more beefy under those work clothes. He wears a pair of those dodgy beige builders' boots, with a pair of cement-splattered tracksuit bottoms tucked inside. On his top half he wears an old sweat shirt that has a gigantic hole under the arm. His thick, black underarm hair peeks out of it.

I stare at him. I have always wondered what it would be like to shag a builder. You get some well cute ones on a lot of the building sites in Manchester, especially in the summer when they have got their chests exposed. It makes walking around town a lot more interesting.

He begins to take off his sweat shirt and lifts it over his head. As it covers his face, I sneak a good look at his chest. His pecs are really pumped up from all the lifting he must do on site. A few strands of thick, black hair stick out from around his nipples, but apart from that he's completely smooth. His nipples stand out like buttons, obviously rock hard from the freezing weather. His skin is still quite brown from the previous summer. Just one of the perks of the job. He's got a bit of a beer belly on him, but the rest of him is so stocky he can get away with it.

He pulls the sweat shirt from over his head, and I quickly look away, pretending I'm busy washing. He kicks off his cement-covered boots, and they fly across the shower room. He pulls down his tracky bottoms to reveal a chunky white arse – there's only so much flesh you can expose when you're on site.

As he turns round and heads towards the furthest shower, I get my first glimpse of his dick. It's only about average size, but it has a huge, ridged head on it. I can't keep my eyes off it: it's so unusual. My cock starts to stir, and I turn away from him, not wanting to get a hard on. Can you imagine: it would be all over the building site if he caught me with a stiffy. I hear a jet of water hit the tiled floor as he turns on his shower.

'Shouldn't you be on duty?' he asks suspiciously.

'Pete's taken over,' I answer. 'He's out there patrolling now.'

'I didn't see him,' he snaps. 'Sure he's not just in one of the other cabins having a nap? It seems that's what they train you to do best at your head office.'

I continue washing, determined not to rise to the bait.

'We've got rid of the lads who were taking the piss,' I say, doing my best to stand up for Sureforce. 'The boys you've got protecting your building site now are topnotch.'

'Top-bleeding-notch!' he exclaims. 'Doesn't look like half of you could stop a bunch of poofs breaking in.'

Sounds like he really has got it in for Sureforce. I'm not going to let the grumpy bastard get away with that. I turn round to face him, still soaping myself down. He stands under the jet of water, laddishly scratching his balls. The soapsuds gathered round the crack of his arse begin to trickle down his chunky thighs.

'You saying I can't look after myself, mate?' I ask aggressively.

'All I'm saying is, God help us if some scally does break in one night,' he says, looking me up and down. 'He'd have you tied up in seconds.'

'Look, mate,' I say, angrily. 'I take my job seriously. I can take care of myself and this place.'

'Yeah, right,' he mutters under his breath.

This cocky little shit is really getting up my nose. I want to smack him one. I step out from under the shower to confront him.

'Wanna see for yourself then, mate?' I challenge him.

'Wouldn't waste my energy,' he replies, continuing to soap himself down.

'Well, you're fucking going to have to!' I yell, reaching breaking point. 'I'm not having you going round slagging off Sureforce.'

'Fuck off. I've had a long day,' he says, turning his back on me.

'Then a few more minutes aren't going to hurt, are they?' I say, grabbing his arm and pulling him round to face me.

'Right, Sureforce boy, you want it, yeah?' he asks, threateningly.

'Yeah, come on, you gobby fucker,' I answer, through clenched teeth.

He suddenly flies from under his shower and dives on top of me. His smooth, wet chest rubs against mine as he grabs my arm and tries to topple me over. I grab hold of his chunky neck to steady myself. He sticks one of his huge hands under my crotch and tries to lift me into the air. His palm rubs hard against my wet balls.

I grit my teeth and grab hold of his head, trying to push it to the floor. He flings his arm over my back and takes a firm grip of my shoulder. He starts to grunt as he tries to force me down with his huge weight. My feet begin to lose their grip on the slippery floor, and I eventually topple on to the floor tiles.

We start to wrestle on the wet, tiled floor, getting covered in soapy lather as we roll around over each other. We both grunt loudly as arms and legs fly in all directions. As we're pretty much the same size, it's an evenly matched contest. We take it in turns to take control of the battle.

Eventually, I notice that he is beginning to weaken. Seizing the opportunity, I muster enough energy to sit firmly on his chest. As I'm about to pin him down completely, he grunts loudly and rolls round on top of me. His wet flesh covers every inch of my body. The jet of water from the shower beats down on to his back and rebounds off into my face. I quickly rub the water out of my eyes, eager to see ways of getting him off me. Before I'm given the chance to wipe my face, he grabs my arms and pins them to the floor. I try to free them from his grip, but he turns out to be a lot stronger than I had originally thought. He moves his knees on to my arms. Once he's sure he has pinned them down, he removes his arms. He sits back on my chest and wipes the water from his face. His soapy cock hangs down the side of my neck. We both remain still, panting loudly. He looks down at me, grinning triumphantly.

'Thought you said you could look after yourself, Sureforce boy,' he goads.

Determined to teach this wanker a lesson, I subtly take in a deep breath of air. I quickly raise my legs into the air and wrap them around his neck. I yank him off my chest with all my might, and he falls to the side of me, completely startled. I push myself up off the floor and jump on top of him. I sit myself down firmly on his chest with my back to his face. My knees and calves pin his arms down on either side of him. He tries to kick me off with his legs, but I lean forward and hold them down firmly. My face hovers over his knob, and I get a closer inspection of his abnormally fat bell-end. I push my arse back a few inches from his face.

'Who did you say couldn't look after themselves?' I ask, panting from the wrestling.

'Get off me,' he demands. 'You've proved your fucking point.'

I feel his cold breath on my arse as he speaks. My knob begins to twitch. 'I'll get off when you give Surefore Security an official apology for undermining their skills,' I reply smugly.

'Just get off me, or I'll get you fired so fucking fast,' he threatens.

'I'm really scared,' I say, sarcastically. 'I want an apology.'

'Eat my arse!' he responds.

'You'll be fucking eating mine if I don't get an apology,' I shout, digging my knees deeper into his arms.

'In your bleeding dreams,' he says, still trying to free himself from my grip.

'Right!' I exclaim. 'Hope you're hungry, you cocky little shit.'

With that, I lower my arse right down over his face, and I hear him spluttering for breath.

'Was that an apology?' I ask, slightly raising my arse from his face.

'Fuck you,' he spits.

I slam my arse back into his face and rub it around, until I feel his lips make contact with my hole. 'Eat it, fucker!'

I continue to grind my twitching hole right in his face. I stare at his cock, wanting to take it in my mouth. Suddenly, I notice it growing slightly. As I convince myself I was seeing things, I suddenly feel the tip of his tongue searching for my entrance. Jesus! Wonders will never cease.

I realise he's on for a bit, and blood starts pumping into my shaft, which slowly starts to raise itself off his chest. His tongue finds my soapy hole and begins to creep up inside. I stare at his cock growing before my very eyes. The helmet begins to inflate to twice its flaccid size. I move my arse slightly, allowing his hard tongue to venture further inside. My knob reaches its fully erect size and hovers in midair. I slightly lift one of my knees off his arm to see if it is a con. He immediately pulls it free, and my body tenses, ready for another battle. Instead, he slaps his hand down on one of my firm buttocks and pulls me further on to his tongue.

I pull my knee off his other arm, and he quickly grabs hold of my other buttock. Assured that the struggle is over, I let go of his legs. I sit up fully, my cheeks parting down either side of his face.

The shower of water rains down heavily on my chest, bouncing off my hard nipples. He begins to really stab his tongue up me, pulling my cheeks further apart to get even deeper. I feel my arse muscles relaxing, encouraging him to dig as deep as he can.

Not being able to stop myself from sucking his cock, I lunge forward and stuff it into my mouth. His fat helmet fills my mouth, and I work my tongue round its defined ridge. Turned on by this, he starts fucking my arse with his tongue, plunging further into me with every poke. As he digs deeper and deeper, my arse opens wider and wider. He starts to slap my firm, smooth buttocks with his chunky hands.

I start to wank his shaft, making sure his fat bell-end stays firmly in my mouth. I suck on the throbbing purple end, still running my tongue around the hard ridge. He grabs hold of my waist and pulls my arse right down on to his face. I groan in pleasure. My cock throbs just thinking about how dirty it is shagging in a builders' cabin.

I pull my mouth off his cock and start licking his hairy sack. My tongue burrows through his thick, black curly hair and reaches the flesh of his testicles. I wank my cock to make sure it's fully erect. I kneel up slightly and push my now throbbing meat back under my legs. I feel his hot mouth engulf my meat and start sucking on it. I move my knees back even further and start moving my arse up and down. I move my head from his balls and look underneath me. I watch my juicy cock slide in and out of his mouth, his fat red lips fully stretched round my meat.

I move my mouth back down over his dick, and I begin wanking him with my mouth. I feel it getting harder and harder, and I suck like mad, wanting to taste this cocky bastard's spunk. I hear him gag on my cock as I ram it further down his throat. His meat begins to pulsate, and I grab hold of it tightly. I clamp my mouth firmly round his massive bell-end, ready to catch his fuck juice. Just in the nick of time. He starts to groan loudly, and his cock suddenly explodes in my mouth. Squirt after squirt of salty semen is unloaded down my throat. I really start to pump his mouth, ready to empty my man juice down his neck. As he releases more jets of thick spunk into my welcoming gob, I feel my balls tighten. Shit, I'm really going to spunk up my cock tonight; I'm feeling so fucking horny.

Suddenly I hear the main door of the cabin opening.

'Shit, it's Pete!' I whisper.

Footsteps begin to approach the shower room. I pull my dick out of the foreman's mouth and jump up. I hold my hand out and pull him up off the floor. I dash under one of the showers and chuck him a bar of soap. He quickly makes his way to the other shower and begins to innocently soap himself down.

The door to the shower room is pushed open, and Pete walks in carrying a spanner. I quickly turn my back on him to hide my still fully erect knob.

'Oh, you're still here,' he says, sounding relieved.

'Yeah, I was filthy,' I lie.

'Anyone want a brew?' he asks.

'Yeah, OK,' I answer, desperate for him to leave us so we can get back to what we were doing.

Pete walks back into the adjoining cabin, and a radio is switched on. The foreman quickly turns his shower off and walks over to take a towel off one of the shelves. He's not getting away with it that easily. I haven't bleeding come yet.

I turn round to face him, indicating that I'm still rock hard. He shakes his head at me, gesturing that Pete is only next door, as if I didn't know. I raise my fist threateningly and nod down at my throbbing cock. Realising that I'm not going to take no for an answer, he looks through the doorway of the cabin to see where Pete is.

Once he's happy the coast is clear, he walks back into the communal shower. He falls down on his knees in front of me, eager to get it over with. I start slapping my moist weapon across his face. He moves his lips towards the tip, looking up at me. Water splatters down on his face as his mouth moves slowly around my cock. I grab hold of his flat top and pull him all the way down on my meat. I thrust my hips, making sure my cock is knocking on the back of his throat. I start to groan, and he quickly stretches his hand up over my mouth, not wanting to get found out.

Pete clanks around in the cabin next door, the thought of him discovering us making it all the more exciting. I pull my throbbing dick out of the foreman's mouth and start to beat it right in front of his face.

'Stick your tongue out, wanker,' I whisper.

He obediently opens his mouth and slides his hard tongue under my dick. My wrist jacks my foreskin back and forth repeatedly. My balls really start to tighten. I haven't had a wank for a few days, so I know I've got a good load stored up. He's going to be in for a surprise when I completely coat him with spunk.

'Brew's ready,' Pete shouts from the other room. 'What you fucking doing in there?'

If only he knew! I continue wanking my cock. The foreman stares at it, waiting for it to start firing. I give it a few last almighty tugs, pulling on one of my hard tits with the other hand. I groan loudly, and he presses his hand harder against my mouth. I look down at my cock just as my piss slit opens. Squirting out of my end comes a long spray of white come. It lands on his red tongue and gets washed down his throat by the spray of water. My dick continues to squirt spunk until my balls are completely empty. The final large squirt misses his mouth and lands over his face and hair.

I pull my cock out of his mouth and turn my back on him, hopefully making him realise he's just been used. I start rinsing my spunky cock off under the shower. He jumps to his feet, and I hear him gather together his clothes. One of the cubicle doors bangs shut, and the lock is pulled across.

I turn off my shower and grab a towel from one of the shelves. I wrap it around my waist and pick up my clothes. I walk through into the other cabin, my still slightly erect dick banging against the towel.

Pete is sitting at the table drinking his tea and reading a paper.

'Thought you had fallen down the plughole,' he says sarcastically.

I walk over to the Calor Gas heater and start drying myself off.

'How's misery guts?' he whispers, nodding through to the shower room.

'Fine,' I answer.

'Fine?' he says in disbelief.

'Well, put it this way,' I say loudly, making sure the foreman in the next room can hear. 'I think he now realises that us Sureforce boys aren't going to put up with any of his shit.'

Pete looks over at me with a puzzled expression on his face.

Five

Business must be booming. The Boss has sent me to pick up his brand-new car. I'm sure he just wants to rub in the fact that I'm still driving round in a Mini Metro. Oh well, at least I'll get to drive his new BMW back to the office.

'It's that showroom over there, mate,' I inform the cab driver.

Sureforce have won another contract, so the Boss is splashing out. He says he even has a surprise in store for me. (I bet it's not what I'd like it to be, though.) Told me it is his way of showing how grateful he is to me for putting in all those extra hours – if only he knew what I was doing for most of those hours.

The Boss reckons I played a big part in securing this new deal. The contract is to man another site for the building contractors I'm presently working for. Turns out the grumpy foreman hasn't moaned about us Sureforce boys in weeks. In fact, it was him who asked his bosses to consider us for the other site.

I think I've got a good idea why he's being so nice. Bet he is shit scared I am going to blab about our little confrontation in the shower room. Suppose he's got a lot more at stake than me. He'd be out on his ear if his bosses found out he'd been sucking off one of the security guards. Pete, my Sureforce colleague at the building site, keeps asking if I slapped him round a bit that night. To shut him up, I eventually ended up telling him I did. Little does he know it was with my dick and not my fist.

I can't believe I've been with Sureforce for eight months already. It's a shame I don't get to see the Boss that often. I'm running out of excuses for visiting the office. Whenever I am in there, I always catch him staring at my arse. Just wish he would do something about it.

The other reason I love going into the office is to wind Twinny up; he can't stand the sight of me. Wish I knew what his problem was. Anyway, I'm even prepared to put up with Twinny, I'm enjoying the job that much. It's not exactly what I had planned to do, but the Boss gives me really good bonuses, and I get some excellent perks. Besides, what else would I be doing? My only qualifications are a cute face and a fat cock.

I want to stick with Sureforce; reckon I could go a long way. I was reading that the security industry is one of the most rapidly growing areas of employment in Britain. This could be where I make my millions.

The cab pulls up outside the car showroom, and I jump out. I walk along the long line of spotless, flash cars, thinking to myself, one day. I walk through the gliding electronic door and into the minimalist showroom. An elderly car salesman pounces on me, probably thinking I'm casing the joint. Well, I don't suppose they have many customers wearing tracky bottoms and puffer jackets.

'Can I help you, sir?' he asks, looking me up and down.

'Yeah, I've come to pick up the Boss's – I mean Mr Groves's new car,' I reply aggressively, pissed off at being treated like shit.

'Oh yes, we've been expecting you,' he says, his whole manner towards me changing. 'Mr Mitchel's dealing with that; I'll just go and get him.'

Smiling at me politely, as if I had just turned into the prime minister, he walks into a glass-walled office. Through the louvre blinds, I watch him chatting to a suited young lad. The lad suddenly turns and looks at me through the blinds. Fuck! He only looks about eighteen. I hope I'm not getting palmed off with the Youth Opportunities trainee.

The young lad struts out of the office and walks towards me with a cheeky grin on his face. He has a short back and sides with one of those floppy fringes hanging over his forehead. He's clean-shaven and is very boyishly good-looking. He is probably a little shorter than me and wears a suit that he needs to grow into. He thrusts out his hand towards me.

'All right, mate,' he chirps, in an annoyingly cheery, cockney accent.

I reluctantly hold out my hand, and we shake. His grip is surprisingly strong for such a nipper. I notice him subtly look me up and down; probably thinks I'm just a bouncer.

'I'm Mr Mitchel, Lee Mitchel. But just call me Lee,' he says. 'It's just over here.'

He trots off towards the electronic glass doors of the showroom. I follow, trying to get an eyeful of his arse. Unfortunately, his suit jacket hangs down too low.

'How long you been doing this?' I ask, untrustingly.

'Since I was sixteen,' he proudly replies. 'I'm the test-drive boy.'

'Test-drive?' I enquire.

'Yeah, I know the Boss. Said he wants you to take it on a test-drive for him,' he says, grinning constantly.

Strange. Why can't the Boss go on his own test-drive? I know Sureforce have won a lot of new clients lately, but the girls in the office take care of all the paperwork. Surely the Boss can't be that busy. I would have thought he would be excited about checking out his new wheels.

'Here she is,' he announces. 'You'll never want to drive another car once you've driven this beauty.'

He hands me the keys. I'm probably not going to want to drive anything else after: it's just a shame I'm going to have to. He opens the driver's door for me. As I climb in, he gives me one of his cheeky grins. He's quite fuckable in a teenage sort of way.

He walks around the car and climbs into the passenger seat next to me. He takes off his suit jacket and throws it on the back seat. His crisp white shirt hangs off his lean young body. His eyes gleam at me from under his cute floppy fringe. I didn't realise car salesmen were so attentive.

I take off my puffer jacket to reveal my Sureforce T-shirt. The Boss only had small left, so it's really tight round my pecs. I throw my puffer in the back and catch a glimpse of him staring at my chest. Reckon it's a sizing up man thing. He can't be after a bit: looks a right little innocent.

I rest my feet on the pedals and press them down to get used to them. My thighs bulge in my tracky bottoms. Knowing he's checking them out, I continue to push down, making them look as muscly as I can. I stick the key in the engine and rev it up. Boy, that sounds smooth. I'm determined to get one of these one day.

'Come on then,' he says, egging me on. 'Take her through her paces.'

Half-nervous, half-exhilarated, I put her into gear, and we slowly move off the forecourt. I keep telling myself to take it easy and not get carried away. This is the Boss's car; you're not joyriding now, Matt.

She pulls out on to the road like a dream. I physically relax in the seat and put my head in the headrest. This feels good – almost better than sex.

We drive along a busy high street, having to stop and start for an assortment of women with push chairs, dogs and old grannies.

'Let's head out somewhere quieter,' he suggests, seeing I'm getting extremely frustrated by the traffic.

Wanting to really feel her speed capacity, I agree, and he directs me to a dual carriageway.

'Aren't these test-drives usually a drive round the block?' I enquire.

'Not this one,' he answers, grinning cheekily. 'Your boss is a good mate of my boss. Told him you'd probably need a little longer to familiarise yourself. Galaxy?'

'What?' I ask, not knowing what the hell he's talking about.

'The radio,' he replies. 'Shall I stick Galaxy on?'

I nod, not really knowing what Galaxy radio is. He presses a few buttons, and house music starts pumping loudly from the speakers. He starts nodding his head to the beat, his fringe flying from side to side.

'Tune!' he shouts excitedly. 'They played this one Saturday night at The Chair. Do you go clubbing, mate?'

'Not really,' I reply, his youthfulness really starting to grate.

The grey cityscape gradually begins to melt into lush, green fields. He holds up his right arm, indicating that I should drive down the narrow track that leads off the road we are on.

'Got a bird, then, mate?' he enquires.

'Um, no, not at the moment,' I reply, slightly taken aback by his sudden personal interrogation.

'So when did you have your last shag?' he asks boldly.

'A month ago,' I answer, dishonestly.

'Must be gagging for it, then?' he asks in his cocksure way.

'I'll live,' I reply, wanting to put an end to this conversation.

'Want me to suck your cock, mate?' he says, matter-of-factly.

I continue to stare at the road ahead, trying not to look surprised. What is going on here, I wonder? How does he know I could be up for a bit of arse? I'm pretty straight acting and looking and have done my best not to let him see I've been checking him out. Anyway, who cares how he knows? I'm not one to pass up the chance of a good blowy.

'How old are you?' I ask, not wanting to end up in Strangeways.

'Twenty-one,' he answers confidently. 'And I've been told I give the best head in Manchester.'

My cock starts to twitch with the thought of having his cute little lips round my meat. He's a cocky little fucker; I like a lad who knows what he wants.

'Prove it then!' I reply.

'There's a private road about a mile up on the right,' he instructs me. 'Pull in there, and I'll finish you off.'

'Finish me off?' I ask, puzzled. 'You'll have to get me started first.'

'I was about to,' he informs me, grinning cheekily.

With that, he undoes his seat belt and reaches over to my tracky bottoms. He starts groping my dick, staring at me as I start to grow hard. Shit, he's a randy little bugger. I grab hold of the wheel, trying to concentrate on the road ahead. He grabs my meat through the material and starts to wank me off. I haven't put any underpants on today, so my cock really looks huge against the material of my tracky bottoms. He pulls down the elasticated waist, and my rock-hard dick springs out. His eyes light up.

'Nice one, mate,' he remarks, obviously impressed with my size.

My cock starts to throb even harder as I realise that he really loves meat. I take my eyes off the road to get a glimpse of his young, wet mouth approaching my fat dick. He moves towards it, desperate for a taste. I grab hold of the steering wheel tightly, as I feel his warm, moist mouth sliding over my meat. His tongue begins to explore every vein bulging in my growing cock. He peels the foreskin right back so he can get his tongue right against my fat helmet. The dirty little bugger certainly knows what he is doing: must have started pretty young.

I try to concentrate on the road, reminding myself I'm driving the Boss's new car. I can't afford to have an accident in this. I look out for the turning, desperate to park and free my hands. I want to push his beautiful lips down further round my meat. Sod it, I can't wait.

I take one hand off the wheel and grab the back of his head. I shove him right down on me, making him gag in the process. He starts to gobble away at my cock like a hungry animal. I notice the sign up ahead. I reach over his strong back to the plastic gear-stick. He does not move and continues to lick and explore my fully erect cock. I concentrate on the road, not wanting to come in his mouth yet.

I pull into the narrow road, looking for somewhere to park. His head continues to bob up and down on my knob, his fringe covering his face. I spot a lay-by up ahead and pull into the deserted space. I reach under his chest and pull on the handbrake. He is in a world of his own and his mouth continues to familiarise itself with my cock. I watch him sucking and licking. I could be anyone: he obviously just loves cock. I reach down and move his fringe from his face, allowing me to get a glimpse of his youthful red lips sliding up and down my saliva-soaked, veiny weapon.

He suddenly looks up from my crotch. 'I want this up me,' he states, staring me in the eyes.

He quickly sits up and undoes his tie. He throws it in the back

and quickly rips off his shirt. As it falls off his body, I notice his
smooth, hairless torso. He sits back in his seat and begins to pull
down his trousers and underpants. He sits back up, and I get a
glimpse of his hard little dick. He kneels up on his chair facing me
and puts one knee over on to the edge of my chair.

'Get me ready for you,' he demands. 'Eat my tits, mate.'

I lean forward and start to lick his small nipples. Within seconds,
they grow into hard little fleshy lumps. He grabs my hand and
sticks it under his legs. He lays it against his twitching hole. It is
dilating so much, my fingers almost get sucked up inside. Boy, has
he been fucked before!

He grabs hold of the safety straps above the doors and positions
himself over the penis-shaped, plastic gear-stick. I part his cheeks
with my hand, and he slowly begins to lower his twitching hole
down until his entrance is resting on the actual knob of the gear-
stick. Surely he's not going to do what I think he is?

'Wank your cock, mate,' he insists. 'I'm getting it ready for
you.'

I grab hold of my knob and start beating it. I really want to slide
it up his tight, young arse; I haven't fucked anyone in ages. I begin
to chew his nipples, trying to get his arse even looser. He groans
in pleasure, and I feel his tits grow even harder. He pulls my head
off his chest and nods down at the gear-stick.

'This is where your cock'll be going in a minute, mate,' he
informs me.

I look down to see the top of the gear-stick slowly disappearing
between his pink arse lips. Jesus, he's a real dirty fucker this one.
He lowers his tight hole down further on to the gear-stick,
throwing his head back as the plastic stretches him apart. I start
wanking my cock harder, imaging what my cock is going to feel
like up there.

His dick is now fully erect and twitching. I wank it for him,
wanting to get him turned on so he'll lower his arse cheeks even
further. It works. He begins to slowly move his smooth arse up
and down on the gear-stick, grinding his teeth in pleasure and
pain.

I grab hold of his waist with one hand and touch his smooth

stomach with the other. He grabs the safety handles firmly and really starts to ride the gear-stick, not caring if he's doing himself any damage.

'You gonna fuck me like this, mate?' he shouts, obviously getting very turned on. 'You gonna get your fat gear-stick up me?'

I wank my dick, getting really excited by this dirty little fucker. He watches me milking my knob and pulls himself up and down even faster.

'Come on, mate, prove that northern lads can fuck better than southern lads.'

I grow even harder as he tempts me to screw him. I keep watching the plastic gear-stick disappearing up his arse. Boy, do I want to fuck this little cocktease. I look out of the car window: not a vehicle in sight. I jump out of the driver's seat with my throbbing cock still sticking out of my tracky bottoms.

I walk around to the passenger door and fling it open. I grab hold of his arm and pull him off the gear-stick. I drag him out of the car and throw him over the gleaming new bonnet. He groans in pleasure, obviously enjoying being treated roughly. I pull my tracky bottoms down to my knees and start wanking my meat again. I stare at his gaping hole, and my knob stiffens immediately. I stick a finger at his entrance, and I can feel it practically being sucked up inside of him. I cram a few more fingers in easily: that gear-stick has really opened him up.

I look around to check nobody is approaching. Apart from a few twittering birds, it is completely silent.

'Come on, northern lad, show us how hard you are.'

Not needing any more encouragement, I pull my fingers out of his hole. I reach into the pocket of my tracky bottoms and pull out a condom. I rip it open and spit into it. I quickly roll it down over my fat knob, desperate to stuff it up this little southerner's arse. I spit on my hand once more and rub my saliva over my rubber-covered meat. I position my bell-end against his pink hole and ram it home with one hard thrust. He throws his head back and pushes himself off the bonnet. I slam him back down on it with one hand and grab hold of his waist with the other.

I start to bang his hungry young hole with my rock-hard meat.

The car starts to rock back and forth as my cock plunges in and out of his tender pink lips.

'Go on, northern boy, fuck it,' he shouts, urging me to screw him harder. 'Fuck my southern cunt.'

I start to pump even harder, turned on by his egging on. I'll show him what us northerners are made of; I'll give him the fuck of his life. I grab hold of his hair and pull his head back. My hard tits dig into his back as I lean forward.

'Open up wider, you southern slag,' I whisper in his ear.

I feel his arse muscles relax even further, and I begin to really fuck him like a dog. I pull my hips back and start jabbing my meat deeper into his passage. I want to see his pretty face as I fuck him. I want to see his expression as he gets fucked harder than ever before.

I pull him up and drag him around to the back of the car. I open the boot and sit him down on the edge of it. I pull his legs in the air, and he is forced to lie back on the carpeted floor. He catches me staring at his pink hole.

'Go on, fill her up,' he yells.

I grab his ankles with both hands and pull his legs right apart. I move the tip of my dick against the entrance of his hole. He stares at me from beneath his ruffled fringe. Holding his ankles tightly, I thrust my meat home. He groans in pleasure and starts to wank his hard cock. I pump him with my rigid meat, my balls banging against his arse cheeks with every thrust.

Still holding his ankles, I lift his legs up higher, allowing my cock to get even further inside him. His face twitches in ecstasy, and he begins to really beat his meat.

I watch my slippery cock sliding in and out of his arse, stretching the sides to their limits. This little fucker is not going to be able to sit down for days.

He groans even louder. 'Fuck me with that big northern dick!'

I pump him with all my might, knowing the northern reputation relies on me. I lift his legs up and down as I prod him with my dick from all directions. I want him to feel exactly what us northern lads are made of. He certainly wouldn't get a dirty fuck like this down south.

I grab hold of the bottom of his thighs and push his legs over his head. I bang my cock right inside him, getting deeper than I ever have before. He starts to groan and his young cock suddenly begins to squirt his pure-white spunk over his smooth belly. His arse clamps around my cock as he releases spurt after spurt of steamy spunk.

Not being able to hold it in any more, I give his arse one final thrust and pull my steely cock out of his hole. I yank off the condom just in time. A huge load of spunk shoots out of my helmet and smacks him right in the face. Fuck, I'm really shooting it today. This dirty little fucker has really turned me on.

He looks at my cock and opens his mouth, hoping to catch the next load in it. I grab hold of my meat and wank it furiously, making sure my next squirt hits his face. I feel the rest of my spunk catapulting up through my dick. I aim my meat directly at him as if it were a machine gun. My piss slit opens once again, and I fire another huge round of spunk straight into the southerner's face. It hits him in the chin and splatters all over his face. He sticks out his tongue and licks the stray spunk off.

My cock suddenly releases another round of spunk, and it smacks him directly in his right nipple. He quickly rubs the spunk round his rock-hard tit, and then licks his fingers to taste me. I fire my last round, and it slaps down on to his cock and balls. He begins to rub it in like a spunk-crazed maniac. I stand over him, holding my dick, watching him writhe around in the boot of the BMW. He makes my spunk go as far as he can and rubs it all over his body.

Once he has rubbed it into his entire body, he licks his hands clean, wanting to taste every last drop. He looks at my dick and notices a few droplets of semen hanging off my tip. He quickly leans forward and licks it off, pushing his tongue into the slit to ensure every last bit has been swallowed.

Realising where we are, I pull up my tracky bottoms and stuff my semi-erect cock quickly down inside them.

'Congratulations, mate,' he says, grinning at me mischievously.

I frown at him, not knowing what the hell he is talking about. Congratulations for what? For being the best fuck? For having the fattest dick? He jumps out of the boot and walks round to the passenger door. He climbs into his trousers and puts on his shirt.

'Get in,' he orders me.

I climb into the driver's seat, wondering what he's playing at. He pulls open the glove compartment to reveal a bottle of champagne and two glasses. He carefully takes them out and hands me a glass. He points the bottle of champagne out of the window and opens it. The cork flies into the middle of the field next door, frightening a group of grazing sheep. He fills our glasses with champagne and puts the bottle on the floor. He raises his glass to me.

'Congratulations,' he shouts cheerily.

I stare at him, not knowing what the hell is going on. He laughs at me, obviously enjoying keeping me in suspense.

'Congratulations for what?' I ask, getting annoyed.

'You've been promoted,' he declares.

'Promoted?' I repeat, still not knowing exactly what is going on.

'Your boss has got plans for you,' he informs me, grinning like a Cheshire cat.

'Yeah, right,' I say, thinking he's winding me up. 'Look, I've got to get this car back to the Boss; bet he's wondering where I am.'

'No need, it's yours,' he says, still grinning. 'And he's given you the rest of the afternoon off.'

'It's mine?' I ask, gob-smacked.

'Yep. Your brand-new company car. You'll be able to take me out for a spin again sometime.'

I stare at the high-tech dashboard, trying to take all this in. I know the Boss likes me, and I know I've done a good job, but this! Lee looks at me, realising I still don't quite believe this is true.

'The Boss sends his apologies. Unfortunately he's too busy to celebrate with you,' he informs me. 'Sent me instead. I'm sort of your well-done present.'

If it weren't May, I would be waiting for him to say April fool. I look at him, still not completely believing this sexy piece of machinery is mine.

Needing to convince me he's telling the truth, he takes a letter out of the glove compartment and hands it to me. I unfold it. At the top of the letter is an insurance-company logo. I read the contents of the letter and soon realise that it is about car insurance – my car insurance. I fold the letter up and hand it back to him.

I grab hold of his head and plant a smacker on his spunky lips. 'It's my car. It really is my car.'

Six

___

'Company rep, Mr Matt Dalson,' I read proudly to myself.
      I stare at my name that is printed on the back of the
brand-new Sureforce Security brochure. I open my briefcase and
throw the glossy brochure into it.

So, it wasn't a wind-up. Not only did I get my very own
company car, I got five brand-new designer suits, a briefcase, and
a two-week course in Basic Presentation Skills. The Boss was so
impressed with my persuasive powers, he is sending me out to
meet potential clients. It's easy. I just tell them a bit about the
company, give them a brochure and hope that they sign up. If it
looks like they are going to need persuading, I demonstrate that
Sureforce can take care of more than just their security needs.
Well, the Boss doesn't need to know I'm mixing business with
pleasure. As long as he gets lots of new contracts, I don't suppose
he cares how I get the clients to sign.

I get to see more of the Boss as well, which is a major bonus. I
have to check into the office every morning to find out what
appointments I have that day. I'm seeing one of the leading events'
organisers in the Northwest today. Organises loads of festivals,
trade fairs and stuff like that. He is in Manchester for a few days.
The Boss says there is a massive bonus in it for me if I can pull this

one off. I am sat in the car park of his hotel now. I got here a lot quicker than I thought I would.

I look at my watch – ten to. May as well go in now. I pick up the piece of paper that is lying on the passenger seat. Above a roughly scribbled map is a name.

'Trevor Wheland,' I read aloud, trying to force the name into my memory.

I shove the piece of paper into my pocket, straighten my tie and climb out of the car.

I walk across the car park and up to the main doors of the hotel. As I'm about to push them open, someone opens them from inside. As the large door opens, I am greeted by a smiling, uniformed doorman. He wears a black suit with brass buckles. He looks about thirty-five and has dark, slicked-back hair. He cheekily winks at me as I walk into the reception.

'Morning, sir,' he says, in a deep Irish accent.

I nod at him and head towards the ornate reception desk, trying not to look too overawed by the splendour of the grand lobby.

I smile at the pretty, young male receptionist. 'I have a breakfast meeting in the restaurant.'

'Through there on the left, sir,' he says, smiling flirtatiously.

I make my way across the reception area and walk into the sumptuous hotel restaurant. An extremely smartly dressed waiter approaches me.

'Good morning, sir: table for one?' he asks in a snotty manner.

'I'm actually meeting someone here,' I reply, looking round the restaurant to see if anyone is sitting alone.

'Ah, you must be Mr Wheland's guest,' he says, obviously expecting me. 'Follow me.'

I walk through the busy restaurant behind the stuck-up waiter. The tables are mainly taken up with suited, middle-aged business-men. I imagine this place costs an arm and a leg. The Boss reckons my client will pay for breakfast, but he has given me a hundred pounds from petty cash just in case he doesn't. If that doesn't cover it, I'll be washing up.

We reach a table in the far corner. Sat at it is a man in his late forties. He has a shiny bald head and a moustache. He wears an immaculately pressed suit, with matching shirt and tie. As he stands to greet me, I see he is my height and is quite stocky, to the point of being chubby.

'Your guest, Mr Wheland,' announces the poncy waiter.

He holds out his hand, and I shake it as firmly as I can.

'Pleased to meet you, Mr Wheland,' I say politely, trying to tone down my Salford accent.

'Likewise,' he replies, checking me up and down. 'And please, call me Trevor.'

The waiter pulls out my chair, and I sit down. After faffing around with the contents of the table, the waiter eventually wanders off.

'So, it's Matt, isn't it?' he enquires, filling up my cup from his pot of coffee.

I nod, nervously taking a sip from the cup.

'I understand that you're going to demonstrate exactly how Sureforce operate,' he says. 'I've been hearing a lot of good reports about your company. Especially you.'

'Me!' I gasp, spilling some of my coffee.

'Yes, I believe you've worked your way up through the ranks,' he says, grinning. 'An old colleague of mine said he had the pleasure of meeting you when you were a security guard.'

Jesus, he seems to know a lot about me. His mate couldn't have been one of the office workers I have shagged or he wouldn't be here now.

'I understand that you're going to be giving me some sort of presentation,' he says.

'Well, it's just an informal chat and a video really,' I inform him, trying to play it down.

'It's quite noisy down here. Thought we could order and have it sent to my room,' he says eagerly.

Shit! I thought he'd have some sort of meeting room booked. I hope there is a video recorder in his room: my presentation will be really dull otherwise.

He calls the waiter over and points out a few things on the menu. The waiter scribbles on his notepad. Once he's finished, the waiter takes the menu off him and begins to walk away. Then he suddenly turns around, as if he has forgotten something.

'Will this be your usual room service, Mr Wheland?' the waiter enquires.

Trevor nods at him. The waiter grins knowingly and walks away. What does he mean by usual room service?

We walk out of the restaurant and into the grand hotel foyer. A group of uniformed male staff stand with the doorman near the lifts.

'Excuse me for one moment,' says Trevor.

He wanders over to the pretty receptionist and begins to chat quietly to him. They look in the direction of the group of uniformed staff. Trevor nods his head at a few of them, almost as if he's making a selection.

I stand next to Trevor in the lift, struggling for something to say. I can't help thinking he has been checking me out, but I'm sure it is just my paranoia. I'm still not used to doing these presentations. Sometimes I wish I was back patrolling building sites.

The lift doors open, and I follow him to his room. As we walk into the grand suite, I desperately try not to look impressed. I need to act as if I am in these kinds of surroundings every day. Along one side of the room are floor-to-ceiling windows with a panoramic view of Manchester. Incredibly enough, it actually looks quite like New York from this angle.

Two of the largest sofas I have ever seen in my life sit facing each other in the middle of the room. A door in the far wall leads to an adjoining bedroom and *en-suite* bathroom.

I suddenly remember why I am here and scan the room for a video recorder. I can't see a TV, let alone a video.

'Shit,' I whisper, not realising what I'm saying.

'Sorry?' says Trevor.

'Video – I can't see a video,' I exclaim, trying not to sound too panicked.

Trevor smiles and points a remote control at the large cupboard. The doors slowly slide open to reveal a massive TV and video.

'Will that do?' he asks, smiling smugly.

I nod and put my briefcase down on the coffee table. I click it open and take out my Sureforce presentation video and notes. I place the video into the machine and turn on the TV. I stand next to it holding my notes in my hand. Trevor takes a seat on the sofa, enjoying the fact that I'm quite nervous.

I clear my throat and take a deep breath. 'Right, before I start talking about the bonuses of employing Sureforce rather than employing and training your own security staff, I would like to show you this introductory video which demonstrates exactly why Sureforce are the most rapidly expanding security company in the Northwest.'

Just as I am about to start playing the video, there is a loud knock on the door.

'Come,' shouts Trevor.

The door bursts open, and a young black waiter walks into the room pushing a trolley full of covered silver platters. He is in his late twenties with short, cropped hair. He's about five foot ten and wears a fitted white shirt and a bow tie. His huge pecs press against the fabric of the shirt. He parks the trolley next to the window and stands by it, his arms behind his back.

Suddenly another waiter walks into the room carrying a silver tray. He places it down on the coffee table that stands in between the two large sofas. I reckon he is in his early twenties and he looks slightly oriental. He takes the lids off the platters to reveal scrambled eggs, smoked salmon, dishes of yoghurts and assorted pastries.

As he walks over to stand next to the other waiter, the door is pushed open again. Another waiter walks in, carrying a tray of cups and a pot of coffee. As he puts it down on the coffee table, I realise that it is the Irish doorman who opened the door for me earlier. He has now taken his jacket off and is wearing just a white shirt and bow tie like the other two. I can now see that he has a really muscly frame. He walks over and shuts the door before standing next to the other two waiters. He winks at me subtly, his eyes twinkling in the sunlight.

I stare at the assortment of food and then at the waiters. I hope

I haven't got to give my presentation with them standing there: I'd feel a right plonker.

'Would you make my guest a little more comfortable?' Trevor asks the young oriental waiter.

The cute waiter walks behind me and takes off my suit jacket. I stand rigid, hoping my client doesn't spot the sweat stains that have developed under my arms. He hangs it carefully on the coat rack.

'He still doesn't look very comfortable to me,' Trevor says to the black waiter.

The waiter walks over to me and starts to undo my belt. I stare at Trevor, wondering what is going on. He notices that I am a little apprehensive.

'Relax. Just think of it as part of your presentation,' he tells me. 'I'm eager to see what Sureforce have to offer me.'

The waiter finishes undoing my belt and begins to pull down my flies. I don't really understand what is happening here, but seeing as I never say no to a bit of cock action, I go with the flow.

I notice Trevor nodding at the other two waiters. They begin to undo their bow ties and take off their uniform shirts. Jesus, we're going to have an orgy. I start to realise that this must all have been planned. But how did he know that I was going to respond positively to getting my trousers ripped open? Well, I suppose as long as I get him to sign, I don't really mind what my business presentation involves.

The waiter moves his hand into my trousers and begins to wrestle with my boxer shorts. He stares at me in silence as his cold, firm hand starts rubbing my knob. Trevor watches him from the sofa. The other two waiters throw their shirts on to the floor. The oriental waiter has a beautiful, smooth little chest. The doorman with the slicked back hair has really muscly, pumped-up pecs. His red nipples stick out proudly from the mass of black hair that covers them. He catches me checking him out and grins at me cheekily.

The oriental waiter kneels down in front of Trevor and begins to undo his trousers. Once they are open, he pulls Trevor's hard knob out of his underpants. I'm quite surprised by just how big he is. Didn't look like he had it in him. The waiter pulls him forward and starts rubbing Trevor's cock around his hairless nipple.

The black waiter working on my knob suddenly yanks my trousers and boxers down around my ankles. My semi-erect cock springs up and down in front of me. He takes a silver bowl of yoghurt off the trolley and holds it underneath my dick. With his other hand, he presses my knob down into the cold yoghurt. I flinch at first, but then my cock begins to rush with blood. He makes sure my entire meat is covered with the thick, white substance, then places the bowl back on the trolley.

Staring at me continuously, he drops to his knees. Still making eye contact with me, he moves his mouth towards my hard cock. He stops when he reaches my yoghurt-covered bell-end. Still looking up at me, he opens his mouth wide and moves it slowly over my dripping dick. The warmness of his mouth, mixed with the coldness of the yoghurt, feels like nothing I have felt before. The creamy, white yoghurt drips down his beautiful, black chin: it looks as though a whole rugby team have just spunked in his mouth. I pull his head further on to my cock, watching more of the white substance cover his fat lips.

'Give him a hand,' Trevor says to the Irish waiter, nodding at the waiter on his knees in front of me.

The horny Irish waiter kneels down in front of me too. The black waiter already sucking me off moves his mouth around to the side of my dick, allowing room for the Irish waiter to start working on me as well.

Staring at me, the Irish waiter sticks out his tongue and begins licking my yoghurt-drenched cock. The waiters position them-selves on either side of my dick, and I push their lips hard against it. I start pumping my cock in between their lips. I close my eyes, and it almost feels like I'm fucking a man-cunt.

I open my eyes again and look down at the waiters' yoghurt-soaked lips. I look over to the sofa, where the oriental waiter has taken off Trevor's trousers and is busily sucking on his hairy balls. Trevor wanks his long knob as he watches me fucking the two waiters' lips.

The Irish waiter stands up next to me. I stare at his horny

pumped-up chest, wanting to stuff those firm nipples in my mouth. He pulls down his trousers and brings out his perfectly formed dick. He begins to wank it as he watches me fuck the black waiter's face. Once his dick is rock hard, he presses it next to mine. As the waiter in front of me continues to suck my meat, the Irish waiter slowly eases the tip of his cock into his mouth as well. The black waiter's mouth begins to engulf both of our cocks at the same time. The sensation of my cock lying next to another cock while fucking a mouth makes me even harder.

The Irish waiter puts his arm round my waist and pushes me further into the other waiter's mouth. His cheeks puff out with the thickness of our cocks. He gags slightly, still getting used to having two thrusting cocks in his mouth.

The Irish waiter next to me grabs hold of my arse cheek and starts to push me forward even faster. As our cocks plough into the black waiter's mouth, his lips are stretched to the limit.

Trevor pulls the oriental waiter's head off his balls and pulls him down on to his hard cock. The waiter's head moves up and down as he begins to unbutton Trevor's shirt at the same time.

The Irish waiter stares at me, slowly bringing his lips towards mine. As his lips are about to come into contact with mine, I grab the back of his head and force his lips down on my hard nipples instead. Well, I'm not bleeding snogging him. I only kiss when I make love. This is just a shag.

He starts gnawing on my rock-hard tits. My cock begins to really throb in the other waiter's mouth. The Irish waiter suddenly pulls his mouth off my nipple and his cock out of the other waiter's mouth. He quickly kneels down behind me. I suddenly feel his wet tongue slavering all over the backs of my chunky thighs. The waiter in front of me continues to eat my meat, eager to please.

The tongue on the back of my thigh begins to move nearer and nearer the crack of my arse. I reach behind and grab the back of his head. I shove his lips towards my arse, making it obvious I want him to lick me out. I throw my head back as I suddenly feel his fat tongue creeping in between the pink lips of my man-cunt. My body shudders in total ecstasy. The sensation of having both my erogenous zones licked at once is like nothing I have experienced before.

I push the black waiter in front of me down even further on to my cock. Trevor pulls the waiter sucking his dick to his feet. He starts sucking on his hard knob, obviously keen on the taste of meat himself. I'll have to make sure I give him a taste of my big chopper before the session is over. I might have more chance of him signing the contract once I have stretched his mouth with my wide girth.

While he sucks the young oriental waiter's cock, Trevor looks over at me being sucked and rimmed. He pulls the waiter's dick from his mouth.

'Why don't you show me the added benefits of signing with Sureforce?' he says temptingly.

This dirty bastard really wants my meat. Still, don't get too cocky; I want to make sure he signs the contract that is sitting in my briefcase. He is not going to get the presentation that I have rehearsed, but he is certainly going to want to hire Sureforce once he's tasted my credentials.

Trevor looks over at my thick, slippery meat sliding in and out of the black waiter's mouth. I pull my cock out of his mouth and push him out of the way. I pull Trevor from the oriental waiter's cock and push him down over the trolley load of food. Scrambled egg oozes out from underneath his chest. He looks half-shocked, half-turned on. I push the oriental waiter's head towards Trevor's hairy arse. They're obviously getting paid for this, so they can earn their fucking wages.

'Get him ready for me,' I shout at the oriental waiter.

I push his face right into Trevor's arse crack. Trevor gasps as the waiter's tongue disappears up his hole. I notice it start to dilate, obviously hungry for a piece of cock. I pick up the bowl of yoghurt and pour it over Trevor's arse cheeks. It drips down the crack of his arse and ends up in the waiter's mouth.

'Stick your cock in his mouth,' I shout over at the Irish waiter.

I'm getting a real turn-on from being in control. Judging by Trevor's groans, he's enjoying it too. The Irish waiter walks around to the front of the trolley and lifts up Trevor's chin. Trevor opens his mouth as wide as he can. The waiter stabs his long meat right down the back of his throat. Trevor gags and groans at the same time.

I stand over Trevor's arse and begin wanking my dick. I look over at the black waiter, who's busy wanking his fat meat while watching Trevor getting fucked in the face.

'Come over here,' I order him.

He walks over to me, still wanking.

'Get it ready,' I tell him, nodding down at his semi-erect dick.

He grabs hold of his black dick again and starts pumping it with his large hand. I look down at the waiter fucking Trevor's arse with his tongue. I grab the back of his head and shove his tongue even further up Trevor's arse.

'Get him nice and loose,' I shout at the oriental waiter.

His tongue moves in and out of his arse as he starts to really pump him with his tongue.

I turn to the black waiter who is pumping his dick next to me. 'Lie down on your back.'

He lies down on the carpet in the middle of the room, still wanking his meat. I pull Trevor off the Irish waiter's knob and to his feet. I push him down on top of the black waiter who is lying on the floor. He lands on top of him and their nipples touch.

The Irish waiter straddles the black waiter's face. Trevor looks up to see the Irish waiter's cock right in front of him again. He immediately begins to suck on it. The Irish waiter lowers his arse down on to the black waiter's mouth as Trevor eats his cock.

The black waiter begins to lick out the Irish waiter's arse. His cock grows harder in Trevor's mouth. Trevor sits on the black waiter's stomach, as he continues to have his face fucked by the Irish waiter. The black waiter's dick sticks up like a flagpole and knocks against Trevor's arse cheeks.

I click open my briefcase and pull out a condom. (Well, I never go anywhere without them.) I rip it open and roll it down over the black waiter's dick. I dip my hand in the dish of yoghurt and smear a handful over his rubber-covered dick.

I slap Trevor's arse cheeks and pull him back on to the hard cock. His hairy white arse begins to engulf the waiter's thick black cock. I wank my cock hard as I push him right the way down on it. Trevor groans in pleasure. The Irish waiter stands so that Trevor can still suck his cock while he's riding the black waiter's cock.

I pull the oriental waiter's mouth down on my hard tits as I roll another condom over my own throbbing meat. I pour a load of yoghurt over it and straddle the black waiter's thighs until my cock is touching Trevor's arse as well. Sensing I'm behind him, Trevor leans back to feel my hard tits on his back.

I wank my condom-covered dick as I watch Trevor move his arse up and down on the waiter's fat cock. He is a real dirty fucker who obviously loves cock. Let's see if he can handle two at the same time.

The Irish waiter realises what I am about to do and lifts Trevor up by holding him under his arms. Trevor's arse slides up over the black waiter's hard dick, until just the tip of it is still inside. I grab hold of my cock and place the tip of it next to his dilating hole. I gradually slide it up against the black waiter's cock, until the tip of it is inside Trevor's arse as well. He groans, still sucking on the Irish waiter's meat. The Irish waiter slowly lowers Trevor down on both of our hard cocks. His arse lips are stretched to their limit as both of our throbbing weapons disappear up Trevor's arse.

More blood pumps itself into my cock, I am so turned on by the tightness of this double fuck. Trevor throws his bald head back, as the pain of having two pieces of thick meat inside him turns to pleasure.

The oriental waiter continues to suck on my tits as he wanks himself off. They both stand out like corkscrews, enjoying the sensation of his hungry tongue. I begin to thrust my cock deeper into Trevor's arse. The waiter lying on the floor also begins to thrust himself up further, making Trevor groan in ecstasy. The Irish waiter starts fucking his face even faster, getting turned on by watching us pumping Trevor's arse.

I pull the waiter sucking my tits down on to my knob. He licks at it every time I pull it out of Trevor's arse. His saliva lubricates the condom, making it even easier to pummel the living daylights out of Trevor.

My cock is now throbbing continuously, as my balls begin to

tighten. I'm going to have to shoot this load in a minute. Well, I think this presentation has lasted long enough.

As I pull my cock out of Trevor's arse, the waiter's black cock slides out with it. I pull Trevor's head off the Irish waiter's dick and push him on to the floor. He lands on his back, his chest still covered in scrambled eggs. His large erect dick stands up vertically, pre-come oozing out of the tip.

I stand over him and really begin to tug on my cock. The other waiters join me, standing over Trevor in a circle. The Irish waiter stands next to me, pumping his massive erection. He reaches over and cups my balls with his free hand. I know he's been dying to do that from the moment he first clapped eyes on me. Certainly wouldn't turn down a session with just him. I'll have to make sure I book in here one night.

Trevor looks up at us all flogging our meat. He licks his lips, hungry for our spunk. The oriental waiter begins to groan, and a jet of cream leaves his cock and lands on Trevor's stomach. Trevor's body spasms as another few jets of his spunk land on his thighs.

'Fuck,' shouts the black waiter.

A huge stream of milky-white come fires out of his beautiful black cock and slaps down on top of Trevor's balls. Trevor begins to rub it in as another thick stream of spunk lands over his cock.

The Irish waiter grits his teeth and begins beating his dick like a wild animal. His face distorts. and jet after jet of dick juice flies all over Trevor's chest. Trevor stares at the exploding Irish cock in utter wonder. It even turns me on, and I feel my spunk being released from my balls.

I aim my weapon directly at Trevor's face, eager for him to see exactly what Sureforce are made of. He stares at my helmet, not wanting to miss the sight of me shooting my load. I give my foreskin a few last hard tugs, and my piss slit opens fully. My heavy, thick spunk lashes down on Trevor's face. He sticks his tongue out, wanting to taste my youthful load. I fire another few jets of creamy, hot spunk, and they hit him directly in the mouth.

He laps up my cock juice and rubs the other waiters' spunk all over his body. His cock suddenly releases a load of spunk without him even having to touch it. It slaps down on to his stomach, and he mixes it in with the rest of our semen.

I take a piece of toast off the trolley and drag it through the different shades of spunk on his face and chest. Once the bread is sodden with semen, I sit on his chest and feed it to him. He gulps it down like a hungry schoolboy, licking his lips in case he misses any.

Once he has finished, he stares at my flaccid cock that's lying on his chest. Shit, I hope he doesn't think I'm going again.

I quickly climb off him and begin to dress. The waiters follow suit. Once they are dressed, they begin to clear up the mess and pile it all on to the trolley. Trevor gets up off the floor and disappears into the adjoining bedroom.

The oriental waiter opens the door and pushes the trolley out of the room. The black waiter picks up the tray from the coffee table and follows him. The cocky Irish waiter strolls from the room, still doing up his bow tie. Before he shuts the door behind him, he turns back and winks at me with his twinkly eyes. My arse twitches with the thought of having him up me. He closes the door behind him.

Once I am dressed, I take my video out of the cassette player, not really knowing what to do next. I click open the case and throw the video inside. I take out a crisp, new Sureforce contract, hoping that Trevor's going to sign. I lay it open on the coffee table.

Trevor walks in from the bedroom wearing a dressing gown. He notices the contract open on the table. He sits down on one of the sofas.

'I think I'd like to read the small print before I actually sign,' he informs me.

I close my case, a bit pissed off that he's not going to sign today. He notices that I look slightly gutted.

'I was impressed with your presentation,' he says, trying to cheer me up. 'In fact, if you leave me a little reminder, I'll put this contract in the post tomorrow.'

I stare at him with a puzzled expression on my face. What does he mean when he says leave him a reminder? Realising that I haven't got a clue what he's talking about, he nods at my crotch and then at the open contract. Surely he doesn't want me to come all over the contract? Mind you, judging by how much he loved spunk, he probably does. Who said being a company rep was a piece of cake?

Desperate to impress the Boss by winning another contract, I put down my briefcase and slowly unzip my fly. Trevor sits rigid on the sofa, desperate for another glimpse of my meat. I pull it out of my boxers and start wanking it, not even bothering to lower my trousers. I walk up to the coffee table and stand directly over the open contract. I try and get my cock hard, but I haven't even got the horny Irish waiter here to get off on. Only one thing for it: I'll have to imagine I'm with the horniest man alive. The Boss.

I close my eyes and jerk on my meat, imagining the Boss is stood in front of me. I picture him unzipping his tracksuit top and exposing those huge, erect nipples. He smiles at me as he begins to put his hand down his tracky bottoms. I wank on my dick, waiting for him to bring out his huge stabber. I pull on my dick hurriedly, getting it harder and harder as I imagine its shape, size and smell.

As he pulls down the waist of his tracksuit bottoms with his other hand, I suddenly get my first glimpse of his huge meat. As his tracky bottoms drop to his knees, I have a bird's-eye view of him jerking his dick. Fuck, it's big. Bigger than I ever imagined. No wonder my eyes were watering when he bummed me in the pub stockroom.

I stare at the beautiful, long and fat shaft. It's beyond perfection. Underneath it hang two huge, shaved balls. They swing back and forth as he begins to jerk himself off. Imagining his meat in my mouth, I start to come.

I open my eyes and find myself back in the hotel room. Trevor sits on the sofa, watching me beat my knob. I suddenly release my hot load and squirt it all over the Sureforce contract in front of me. Trevor stares longingly at the puddles of spunk and sighs in pleasure.

★

I step into the lift, relieved to have got that over with. It has probably been my most demanding presentation yet. He had better sign that contract, or I will be well pissed off.

The lift reaches the ground floor, and the doors slide open. I notice two of the room-service waiters smiling over at me as I walk across the reception area. I expect shagging guests is all in a day's work to them. I expect they make a fortune in backhanders, especially being as horny as they are.

I continue to walk towards the grand main doors of the hotel. As I get nearer, I suddenly notice the Irish doorman stood back in his place. He wears his doorman's uniform once again. Now, he is one person I wouldn't mind having a private meeting with one day. As I get even closer to him, I suddenly have an idea.

I stop at one of the tables in the hotel foyer and sit my briefcase down on top of it. I click it open and start searching inside. I eventually find what I am looking for. I stare down at the VIP invite that I am holding in my hand.

The Boss is in the process of buying a new bar on Canal Street, thanks to all the extra business I am pulling in. He plans to completely gut it and renovate it over the next few months. He is organising a huge opening bash that will take place over the Mardi Gras weekend. He has even had the invites printed already. He gave me a handful of special VIP ones and said that I should give them to a few friends.

Well, I've been pretty intimate with this doorman, so I suppose that he could count as a friend. I would quite like to see him again, on a one-to-one. Doesn't look like anything is going to happen with the Boss, so I have got to keep my options open.

I close my briefcase and walk towards the hotel doorway. The cheeky Irish doorman beams at me as I approach. As I walk past him, I hold out the VIP invite towards him. He looks down at it, not knowing what to do.

'Take it,' I tell him.

Checking that none of his bosses are watching, he takes the ticket off me and stuffs it into his pocket. He obviously is not meant to take things from guests. Weird policy! Let the staff fuck your guests senseless behind closed doors, but sack them if they take a present off them in public.

As I carry on walking out of the hotel exit, I turn back and smile at him. 'It would be good to see you there.'

He grins at me cockily, knowing that I want him really bad. I continue walking along the pavement, knowing which part of my anatomy he is staring at. I put my hand in my jacket pocket and lift the back of my suit jacket slightly, giving him a better view of my rear. I continue walking along the pavement, wondering if he really will show up.

Seven

I throw a pile of mail down on the office desk. I roll over an office chair and sit down next to the desk. I begin to sort the mail into different piles. I suddenly come across a large, brown envelope addressed to me. I quickly tear it open and tip out its contents.

A crumpled Sureforce contract falls on to the desk in front of me. As I pull the pages apart, I realise that it is the one I spunked over last week. Trevor Wheland has signed his name on the dotted line. Great, another contract. The Boss will be really made up with me. Don't know how I'm going to explain the state of it, though. Still, as long as the client has signed it, that is all that counts.

I walk over to a box of Sureforce brochures and stuff a few of them into my briefcase. I look at my watch impatiently. Come on, Twinny. I can't do anything till he gets here. He is in charge of appointments. He tells me where I'm going and who I've got an appointment with every morning. Don't think he's too happy about me being promoted to company rep. He hates me being around the office and doesn't hide the fact. May find out what his problem is one day: that's if we don't murder each other first.

I hear someone clomping up the staircase that leads to the office. That'll be Twinny: I'd recognise his footsteps anywhere.

The office door opens, and Twinny swaggers in. He raises his eyebrows at me as he passes. That's his way of saying, 'Morning, Matt, how are you this fine day?' He pulls out a copy of the *Sun* from his back pocket and sits on his chair. He throws his legs on to the desk and starts reading his paper. Just what exactly does he do? I had thought I would be able to suss that out now I have started working at the office on a regular basis. But, apart from setting up my appointments, he doesn't seem to do anything.

'So, where am I today?' I enquire.

A sigh drifts from behind the paper. Twinny slowly lowers it and looks at the diary that is open in front of him.

'Mr Scott. Cheshire Golf Club, at one,' he snaps, pissed off with being disturbed. 'It's a biggy. He owns most of the bingo halls in the Northwest. So, don't blow it.'

Well, it is safe to say that Twinny hasn't been on a staff motivation course. I close my briefcase and look at the office clock: nine forty-five.

'Just got a few things to do in town before I go,' I inform him, as I begin to walk out of the door.

'Hang on!' he yells. 'Got someone else I want you to see this morning.'

I stop in the doorway and turn around to face him. We stare at each other, our facial expressions saying more than words ever could. I'm just so lucky the Boss likes me. If it were up to Twinny, I'm sure I'd be sacked from Sureforce by now.

I walk back into the office and put my briefcase on Twinny's desk. He picks up the phone and dials a number.

'Mr David Hill, please,' he asks, trying to disguise his thick Mancunian accent. 'Hello, Mr Hill; this is Mr Adams from Sureforce Security. I've been able to arrange for our company rep to come out and give you a presentation this morning. Ten thirty it is, then. Bye.'

He slams down the phone and smiles over at me.

'Better get your skates on,' he says smugly, as he scribbles an address down on a piece of paper. 'You've only got three-quarters of an hour to get there.'

He hands me the sheet of paper, enjoying the fact that he is putting me under pressure. I snatch it from his hand, wanting to shove it down his throat. Cocky little bastard is going to get his comeuppance one day. Just what is his problem with me?

The Boss suddenly marches into the office, wearing another brand-new tracksuit.

'Morning, lads,' he growls in his deepest Salford tones.

'Morning,' I reply, trying not to let him see just how pleased I am to see him.

'So, how's my star company rep doing?' he asks, grinning.

Before I get to answer, Twinny jumps up and interrupts.

'He was just going actually,' he snaps.

I glare at Twinny behind the Boss's back, wanting to smack him in the mouth. I grab my briefcase, annoyed that I couldn't spend longer in the Boss's presence. I hardly ever get to see him: Twinny manages to keep us well apart.

'I'll see you soon, Boss,' I say, smiling forlornly.

'Yeah, later,' he replies, more interested in flicking through Twinny's copy of the *Sun*.

I start to walk across the office. Twinny completely ignores me, pretending to be busy with some paperwork. I reckon he feels well threatened by me. He knows the Boss likes me. He's seen him checking out my arse when his bird's not around. He just wants to get over it. It's not as if he's got anything going with the Boss.

I throw on my suit jacket and head towards the door.

'Make sure you get a few more signatures for me today,' the Boss says, winking over at me.

I smile at him and disappear out of the office. I walk along the dirty landing, thinking about the Boss. I'll never forget our first meeting; I still wank about it now. Whenever I'm in a bar with pounding music, I imagine I'm back in that stockroom with his cock between my legs. It was as if he was thrusting his meat up me in time to the house music playing out in the bar. He felt like nothing I've had up there before. I just wish I had had a chance to actually get a glimpse of his weapon. I wonder if I'll ever get to see it again. I reckon he just shags the bouncers he fancies on their first night and that's it. Seems like his chick services him the rest of the time.

As I carry on walking along the landing, I suddenly remember I haven't put any extra Sureforce contracts into my briefcase. I've got two to cover my meetings today, but I always like to carry a few extra. Well, you never know. I was taught on my Basic Skills Course to always be prepared.

I turn around and head towards the office door, which is slightly ajar. As I get nearer, I suddenly hear my name being mentioned. I freeze, wanting to hear exactly what is being said. I listen intently as Twinny and the Boss's voices drift down the corridor.

'Yeah, well, he's only got all of his clients to sign so far because they've been on the List,' Twinny says to the Boss.

The List? What the hell does he mean?

'What do we do when we've run out of names on the List?' Twinny continues. 'There's only so many board directors who like the occasional bit of cock!'

So that's it. They've been setting up meetings with clients who want more than their security needs taken care of. I thought it was surprising that they all wanted a bit of cock. I'm as good as acting as a prostitute for them. And there's me scared that the Boss was going to eventually find out that I've shagged half of his clients. Bastards! Just where did they get that list of names from? I continue to listen in on the conversation, furious about what I've just discovered.

'There's fucking pages and pages of names on that list we bought from Luke,' the Boss reminds Twinny.

'Yeah, but what happens when the names run out, and he has to go repping in the real world?' Twinny snaps. 'When he has to start using his brain instead of his dick, how many contracts is he going to win then?'

Luckily, I'm managing to control my temper these days. If this had been happening three years ago, I would have stormed in that office and kicked the little shit's head in by now.

'He's a horny little fucker,' the Boss tells Twinny. 'He'll be able to win anyone over.'

'Well, we're about to find out,' Twinny announces.

'What do you mean?' the Boss asks.

'I've sent him to meet David Hill,' Twinny sheepishly admits.

'Hill! He's not on the List,' the Boss angrily yells. 'I told you I was going to send Linda to that presentation. He'll fucking brain Matt if he tries anything on.'

'It's make-or-break time then, isn't it?' Twinny says smugly. 'Anyway, things were better before that cocky little shit was around.'

'What do you mean?' the Boss snaps. 'He's made us a fucking fortune in contracts.'

'No, I mean between us,' Twinny replies. 'I could easily have fucked my way down the List like him.'

'No, you couldn't. He's versatile: he can appeal to all sorts.'

'Have you forgotten why you chose me as your right-hand man?' Twinny asks him.

'Shit, I've got to pick up Trish,' the Boss says, ignoring his question. He picks up his keys off the desk.

'Meet me here at seven, and I'll remind you,' Twinny tells him.

The Boss nods at him and heads towards the door. I quickly race along the corridor and down the dusty staircase, not wanting to be caught. I dive out on to the pavement into the bright sunlight, my head swimming with all the information it has just taken in. What the fuck is going on? Just what is the List, and why has Twinny got such a hold over the Boss?

I sit in my stationary car, convinced that the red light is never going to change to green. It always seems a lot longer when you are late for something. Listening to Twinny and the Boss's conversation has made me well late for my first appointment. Still, I'm glad I did hear it. The Boss has got some talking to do when I get back to the office tonight. I'll have to make sure I get back at seven. I want to try and find out what else Twinny has to say to him.

I start thinking about the List again. How could they possibly have got hold of a list of high-fliers who swing both ways? Anyway, wherever they got it from, it's clear that this next prospective client is not on it. I didn't realise just how much Twinny has got it in for me. I'm going to have to get this contract signed: I don't want to give him any reason to get rid of me. I know the Boss likes me, but the more ammunition that Twinny can gather, the more chance he has of getting me out. It's obvious that Twinny has a real hold over the Boss.

The man behind me starts beeping his horn. I pull off through the green light, making an impolite gesture to the impatient driver behind.

I pick up the piece of paper that is on the passenger seat to see exactly where I am heading. I read Twinny's scribbled handwriting: David Hill, Hill Clothing Manufacturers, Oldham Rd.

'David Hill,' I whisper to myself.

The name seems very familiar to me. I keep repeating it over and over in my head. In the distance, I spot a factory with the words HILL CLOTHING MANUFACTURERS printed on a large sign outside. I indicate and pull into the car park.

'Shit, Hill!' I shout, suddenly remembering why I recognise the name.

If it's the bloke I think it is, then he was one of the sergeants at our barracks where I was based with the army. I quickly open my briefcase and take out my mobile. I dial a number and await a reply.

'Gazza, it's Matt. Yeah, fine . . . I know, we'll have to go for a beer next week. Listen, do you remember Sergeant David Hill? That's him, you got anything on him?'

I begin to grin from ear to ear as Gazza begins to tell me all about Sergeant Hill's past.

I walk across the gloomy reception area of Hill Clothing Manufacturers. I press an old brass bell that stands on the reception desk. A doddery old woman walks out of the back office.

'Morning,' she croaks, looking like she could have a heart attack at any minute.

'Mr Dalson. I've got an appointment with Mr Hill at ten thirty,' I inform her.

She looks over at the huge clock that hangs on the wall opposite. The time is ten forty-five.

She shakes her head as she picks up the phone. 'You're rather late, young man,' she says disapprovingly. 'Someone to see you, Mr Hill,' she shouts down the phone, obviously deaf in one ear.

She places down the phone and points over at a set of double doors. 'Through there, second door on your right,' she snaps.

I head towards the double doors, eager to see if it's the same Sergeant Hill Gazza has just been filling me in on.

'He can't abide people who turn up late,' the grumpy receptionist shouts after me.

I walk up to the solid wood door and adjust my tie. I knock on it firmly.

'Enter!' a sergeant-major type voice booms from the other side of the door.

So far, so good. I open the door and walk into the sparse office. Sat behind the old-fashioned desk is a large man in his mid-fifties, wearing a suit and tie. He is balding, with grey hair and a large, grey moustache. It's him: I'd recognise that moustache anywhere. He has a stack of paperwork in front of him.

'You're late,' he says grumpily, not even looking up from his calculator.

'Sorry, traffic,' I apologise feebly.

He throws down his pen and takes off his glasses. He looks over at me.

'So, you're Sureforce Security,' he says.

'Well, me and about two hundred others,' I reply.

Excellent: he obviously doesn't recognise me in a suit. I wasn't in his regiment anyway. Gazza was, though. Just been hearing some very interesting stories. He stands up and walks around the desk. He towers over me.

'I've got a problem with some of the scum I've had the bad fortune to employ,' he informs me. 'There is more stock going out of this factory in their handbags than in my lorries. Got to put a stop to it.'

'We're exactly what you need, sir,' I respond confidently.

'Are you sure you've got enough experience?' he asks sarcastically. 'Looks like you're only just out of nappies.'

'We've plenty of experience,' I reassure him. 'Some of the

largest companies in the Northwest use Sureforce to protect their property.'

'OK, OK, spare me the waffle,' he says arrogantly. 'I'll show you the factory.'

I follow him briskly out of the office and along a corridor. We reach a large pair of double doors. As he pushes one of the doors open, the deafening sound of industrial sewing machines fills the air. I step into the huge factory. Hundreds of sewing machines are lined up on the factory floor. Women of different ages sit at them, sewing various garments. A few of them nudge each other and look over at me. Two of them are obviously talking about my crotch. The Sureforce guards are going to have a field day manning this place. Looks like there are a bunch of nymphomaniacs working here.

'Show's over ladies,' snaps Mr Hill, as he leads me through the factory. 'Think the world owes them a living, you see. Think nothing of walking out of here with a garment stuffed in every possible orifice.'

I could see why most of the women were giving him the V-sign behind his back. He sounds a right pompous old git. He leads me to the back of the factory. A woman wolf-whistles me as we disappear from view.

We pass a few industrial steam presses and head towards a small door right at the back of the factory. Mr Hill takes out a large bunch of keys from his pocket.

'This is the place your security guards will have to watch like a hawk,' he explains. 'The stockroom.'

He puts a key into the padlock that secures the chain around the door handles. The padlock clicks open, and he pulls the chain off the handle. He pushes the door open and switches on the fluorescent lights. They flicker on and eventually fully illuminate the stockroom. Wall-mounted clothes rails hang all around the room. Various coloured garments covered in polythene covers hang off them. A huge box of wire coat hangers stands next to a pattern-cutting table in the middle of the room.

Mr Hill walks into the centre of the room and places the

padlock on the pattern-cutting table. I notice that his bunch of keys remain in the lock. Good: that will help me with my little scheme.

'So, come on then, sell your company to me,' he says abruptly. 'Why should I use Sureforce rather than any other security company?'

I take a deep breath, knowing these next five minutes are going to be the toughest. Once I'm through that, I know I'll have proved Twinny wrong. I'll have won a new client who isn't on this famous List. Let's just hope Gazza got his facts straight. Here goes.

'And tell me why Sureforce should look after your factory rather than someone else's,' I reply, cockily.

'I beg your pardon!' he shouts, outraged by my tone. 'It's me who's interviewing you here, young man. I need to look at a contract. Have you got one with you?'

I place my briefcase on the pattern-cutting table and click it open. I take out a standard Sureforce contract and lay it open on the table. I take out a pen and place it next to the dotted line at the end of the contract. Mr Hill notices this.

'Hold your horses, I'm not signing today. I need to read the small print. Want to see how much all of this is going to cost me.'

'I don't think you understand, Mr Hill: this is a one day only offer,' I inform him. 'If you don't sign today, you'll miss out on the chance of having Sureforce protecting your property.'

He turns around to face me, looking extremely red-faced.

'Who do you think you are?' he shouts angrily. 'I'll sign when I'm good and ready. I don't even know if I'm going to use your company yet, anyway.'

His booming voice brings back memories of the army. I can't believe I'm talking to an ex-sergeant like this, but I have to carry on. It's the only way I'll get this contract signed.

'Mr Hill, I really don't think you understand your position here,' I reply confidently. 'You have to ask me if I'll let Sureforce protect your factory.'

'I think it would be a good idea if you left,' he growls, getting redder by the minute.

'Not until you ask me to look after your factory,' I say firmly.

'Get out, come on, get out!' he orders.

Come on, Matt, you're going to have to get tougher, I tell myself.

'Beg me to look after your fucking factory!' I shout aggressively.

Mr Hill suddenly looks down at the floor. Yes, I've got the dirty old fucker. Thank Christ for that. I owe Gazza a few pints. He was right all along: he does love to be dominated. Got chucked out of the army for it. His senior found him tied up to one of his squaddies' bunk beds while he got the lad to whip him.

I look over at Hill; it's as if a button has been pushed in his brain. He's a completely different person. Right, let's get stuck in. I can't stand the guy, so it should be easy.

'Didn't quite hear you,' I shout. 'Now are you going to beg me to look after your factory, or am I just going to walk out of here?'

His huge, manly frame starts to hunch down, like a small boy being told off. He continues to stare at the floor.

'Haven't you got a tongue?' I yell at him. 'Looks like I really am going to have to make you beg. Take your fucking clothes off!'

He remains still, staring at the floor. I wave my hand in his face, loving every minute.

'Hello? I said, take your fucking clothes off – now!'

He slowly starts to take his jacket off, unable to look me in the face. He's like a little puppy dog that knows it's done wrong, but just wants to please its master. It's so easy when they're into being dominated: you can do anything to them. And that's my speciality, being sexually aggressive to people.

I suddenly remember my appointment at the golf club and look at my watch. Shit, I've got to be there in an hour and a half. Better hurry this up.

'Come on, fucking get them off!'

Mr Hill quickly kicks off his trousers. He stands in front of me naked, still looking at the floor. His body is covered in grey hair, and his small, shrivelled penis is semi-erect.

I'm now quite glad Twinny has really pissed me off, because I can take all my anger out on this one. It's not the sort of business presentation that I was taught on my course, but if it gets him to sign, and the Boss is happy, then I'm happy.

'Get over there,' I order him, shoving him in the direction of one of the wall-mounted clothes rails.

He stands next to the clothes rail. I pull the hangers of clothes to one side, revealing the bare chrome bar.

'You should have more respect,' I yell. 'You should beg me to look after your factory.'

I summon up enough strength to forcefully push him down on to his knees.

'Come on, beg me, you worthless piece of shit!' I continue.

He begins to quietly mutter something.

'I can't hear you, speak up,' I shout in his ear.

He mutters something indecipherable again.

'Right, get up,' I shout angrily.

He climbs to his feet and stands under the clothes rail, still not being able to look me in the eye. I grab hold of his hands and pull them above his head until he is holding on to the clothes rail above. I grab a thin, wire coat hanger from the cardboard box. I slowly begin to unwind it in front of him until it is one long strip of wire. I reach up and start to wrap it around his wrist and the clothes rail, binding them together. He tries to pull his hand away, but I grab hold of it.

'Keep still,' I spit, coating his face with phlegm.

I continue wrapping the wire tightly around. I grab another hanger and begin wrapping that around his ankles. I then attach it to the bottom bar of the clothes rail. Once I've finished, I stand back to admire my handiwork. Hill stands spread-eagled to the rails, with one arm free. I pull a small table out from the corner of the room and stand it in front of him. I take the Sureforce contract off the pattern-cutting table and place it open on the table.

'So, if you want to taste some cock, you're going to have to be a good boy and sign that contract,' I inform him.

I notice his cock beginning to twitch and grow slightly larger. He obviously wants this to go on for as long as I let it. He's soon forgotten about the troop of women next door. Can you imagine if they were to find him like this?

'I know you want some cock,' I say teasingly.

I've got to get this over with soon. I can't be late for my next appointment. I'll have to show him what's on offer.

I slowly begin to unbuckle my belt and lower my trousers. I notice his head lift slightly to get a glimpse of my firm thighs. I shove my hand down my underpants and start playing with myself. He lifts his head even higher to get an eyeful. His cock begins to grow even larger. I pull down the elasticated waist of my underpants with my other hand. His eyes widen as he waits to catch a glimpse of my meat.

I slowly pull my flaccid knob out of my pants. He lets out a groan as his eyes feast on my fat manhood. I begin to wank it slowly.

'So, want some of this?' I ask temptingly.

He eagerly nods his head.

'What do you say?' I command.

'Yes, please,' he mutters.

'I didn't fucking hear you!' I yell dramatically. 'What do you say?'

'Yes, please,' he shouts desperately.

I take a pen out of my jacket pocket and click it open. I lay it on top of the Sureforce contract.

'Sign it, and I may let you have a taste,' I tell him.

He stares at me wanking my dick, his hard cock informing me that he's enjoying every minute. He is not going to budge yet, though. I look at my watch. Shit, I've got to get off to my next appointment. I'm going to have to finish him off later.

I pull down my trousers and underpants and kick them off. I pick up my spunk-stained pants and pull them down over his head. I had a wank this morning and just stuffed my spunky dick inside them because I was late. Bet they are smelling nice by now.

I arrange them so that the groin area is directly over his mouth and nose. He quietly begins to sniff my dried spunk like a dog.

'Yeah, go on, have a good sniff,' I taunt. 'There'll be plenty more where that came from if you sign like a good boy.'

I pull on my trousers and close my briefcase, leaving the contract open in front of him. I pick up the chain and padlock. He begins to grunt through my pants when he hears it clink. Realising he's going to get locked in, he tries to pull his wrist free of the wires. No chance. I was a boy scout.

'Don't go away!' I call sarcastically, as I head towards the door.

I walk out of the stockroom and slam the door behind me. I wrap the chain around the handles and padlock it.

I walk back across the factory floor to dirty gestures and deafening wolf whistles. Now I know how the Chippendales feel.

Eight

I speed along the motorway, pushing my BMW to the limit. I just can't be late for my golfing appointment; I know what a huge account it could be. In the distance I hear a police siren. Shit, no. Please God, don't let me be stopped now. I haven't even got my first contract signed today. I can't blow another.

In the rear-view mirror, I spot a flashing blue light in the distance. I feel myself sweating. Memories of my joyriding days come flooding back. Matt, get a grip. You're above board now. You're fully insured, fully taxed: what's the problem?

I indicate and pull over into the middle lane. I watch the police van in the outside lane getting closer and closer. My heart starts to pound like it did when I was eighteen and always on the run in some nicked vehicle. Me and my mate Andy used to always go out riding together. I turn and picture him sat in the passenger seat next to me.

'Put your foot down, Matty,' shouts Andy, getting excited.

I press my foot down further on the accelerator, getting a real buzz from the speed.

'Let's see those pigs catch us now,' I yell.

'Go, boy.'

I swerve right out into the outside lane. Andy looks out of the passenger window and gives the V-sign to cars we speed past in the inside lane. I feel the hairs on the back of my neck stand on end. No matter what anyone says, the buzz you get when you go joyriding cannot possibly be beaten. Me and Andy have been doing it for about six months, and we haven't got caught yet. We have been involved in some mad car chases, though. The pigs just have not been able to keep up with us.

Andy turns around and looks out of the back window. 'Shit, they're catching us!'

I push down the accelerator until it will not go any further. The car speeds along the dual carriageway, shuddering from the speed I am making it do. People in the cars we pass look at us, shaking their heads in disgust. I suppose we are what they would call juvenile delinquents. Fact is, we are two healthy, intelligent lads who have got nothing to do where we live. Every sports centre has been closed down. So it is either joyriding or shagging. The shagging usually comes after the joyriding, as you get such an adrenalin rush, you are dying to shoot.

Andy keeps looking out of the back window. He watches the police van getting nearer and nearer. 'Bastards!'

Up ahead I suddenly notice a police car parked on the side of the road. As we get nearer, we make out two coppers stood on either side of the road, holding something that is stretched across the road.

'They've got a fucking stinger!' shouts Andy.

Sweat starts to pour down my forehead with the realisation that we are going to be caught. A stinger is a device the cops use to puncture joyriders' tyres to bring them to a standstill. There is absolutely no getting away now.

The tyres of the car bang as we drive over the metallic spikes of the stinger. As the car slows down, I steer it towards the side of the road, resigned to the fact that we have been caught. It will probably only mean a caution, so we both feel pretty chilled.

I pull on the handbrake, and the car grinds to a halt. The police van that has been chasing us pulls up in front of our car. Two coppers get out and walk to the front of our car. They open the front doors and aggressively pull us out. The taller copper throws me over the bonnet of the car and begins to frisk me. The other does exactly the same to Andy.

'So, have you taken anything, Sterling Moss?' the tall copper asks me.

I shake my head. He pulls me up and keeps a firm grip on my jacket.

The tall copper turns to face the shorter one. 'So, do you want to caution them?'

The other copper looks me and Andy up and down. 'Yeah, I wouldn't mind.'

Grabbing hold of our T-shirts, the coppers drag us towards the back of the police van. One of them opens the door and pushes us into the back. The shorter copper jumps in the back with us.

'I'll keep an eye out,' says the taller copper, before slamming the doors shut.

The back of the van is plunged into darkness, the only light coming from the small window in the back door. The copper reaches up and turns on a light that is fixed to the ceiling. He motions to us to sit down on the hard wooden bench that is fitted to the side of the van. He sits down on the bench opposite.

The van rocks back and forth every time a heavy goods vehicle thunders along the dual carriageway. The copper picks up a clipboard and begins writing on the form that is attached to it. He asks us all the usual questions: name, address, next of kin, etc., etc. I stare at him as he jots all of the information down on the form. He looks as though he is in his late thirties. He has a sensible, side-parted haircut and a trimmed beard and moustache.

Once the copper has collected all the information that he needs, he places the clipboard underneath his seat. He takes his uniform jacket off and hangs it on one of the hooks that are attached to the ceiling of the van.

He looks over at us both. 'Right, lads, I'll ignore this little incident, so long as you don't make any complaints.'

I look at Andy, not understanding what he is talking about. Andy looks none the wiser.

'If you open your mouths, these incident reports will be filed, and you could face a prison sentence,' he informs us.

We look at each other, still not knowing what he is implying.

'So, another few minutes in this van is better than a few years in prison, isn't it?'

Certain that we don't want to get banged up, we both nod in agreement.

'Get your tops off, then, lads,' he orders.

I look over at Andy, thinking this is a bit of a strange request. With the thought of prison hanging over our heads, we both obediently take off our T-shirts. The copper looks over at our smooth, compact chests. He reaches to his belt and unclips his handcuffs. He grabs hold of Andy's hands and clicks the handcuffs closed around his wrists. Andy looks over at me, wondering what the fuck is going on. I shrug my shoulders, pretending I don't know, but suddenly realising that we've got a bent copper – in more ways than one. Andy is going to freak when he realises we've landed up with DC Pervy.

The copper leans over to a wooden box built in the side of the van and takes out another pair of handcuffs. He grabs hold of my hands and snaps them shut around my wrists as well.

'Put your arms up, lads,' he says.

We both slowly raise our arms. He leans over and takes hold of the two chains linking the metallic wrist locks together. He pulls both of the chains over the hooks that hang from the ceiling. Andy and I sit on the wooden bench with our arms in the air hanging off the hook. We subtly look at each other, wondering what this is all about.

The copper kneels down in between us. 'Right, lads, just relax. You can be on your way in ten minutes.'

He reaches for the waistband of Andy's tracksuit bottoms and begins to pull them down. Andy wriggles his arms, trying to pull the handcuffs over the hook.

'What the fuck are you doing?' Andy spits.

The copper glares up at him. 'Shut it, lad, or those reports will get filed.'

Andy stops moving his arms and stares at the copper angrily. He hates the fact that the copper is in total control. The copper continues to pull Andy's tracksuit bottoms down until they are around his knees. He stares at Andy's Y-fronts. They look like the type that your mother would buy you for Christmas. The copper is transfixed by the bulge in Andy's pants.

The copper reaches for Andy's Y-fronts and puts his hand inside them. Andy turns away, not being able to look the copper in the eye. If his hands weren't handcuffed above him, he would probably have smacked him in the mouth.

I look down at Andy's Y-fronts as the copper moves his hand around inside of them. I don't know what he thinks he is doing: Andy is as straight as they come. That old bastard is never going to get him hard.

Still massaging Andy's cock, the copper starts to pull Andy's underpants down with his other hand. As the material moves past his fair pubic hair, his erect cock suddenly bursts out. Fuck, he's hard! I look down at Andy's long, thin piece of meat. I have seen his cock before in the showers when we have been playing football, but I have never seen it fully erect.

Now that Andy's cock is completely exposed, the copper slowly starts to wank it back and forth. He stares at it in a trance, obviously being a dick worshipper.

He moves his head forward and begins to lick Andy's smooth chest. He slowly moves his tongue up towards Andy's armpits, which are fully exposed due to his arms being hooked above his head. The copper maniacally licks his wispy underarm hair, wanking Andy's cock at the same time. Andy turns away, embarrassed that he has produced a magnificent erection without even having a girl present. My knob starts to grow hard just from watching the scene in front of me.

The copper moves off Andy and turns to face me. 'Your turn, pretty boy.'

He grabs for the button on my jeans and quickly undoes it. He unzips my fly and pulls my jeans down to around my knees. He stares at my rock-hard cock pressing against the material of my boxer shorts. His eyes widen. Dying to get a glimpse of the real thing, he pulls down the waistband of my boxers over my hard cock. My throbbing young knob springs out and bounces up and down in front of him. He pulls down my boxers further, until he can see my tight, hairless balls. He suddenly lunges towards them and starts licking them. With my arms handcuffed above my head, he knows that I am not going to be able to do anything to stop him.

His huge, wet tongue begins to soak my young balls with its saliva. Andy slowly turns his head to get a glimpse of what is going on. He looks down at the greedy copper eating my nuts. I notice Andy's cock twitch, filling up with even more blood. Shit, he is actually getting turned on. He must be enjoying this experience after all.

The copper moves his warm tongue off my balls and wraps it around my hard cock. As he begins to suck me off, he reaches over and takes Andy's dick in his hand. The van continues to rock back and forth every time a large vehicle speeds past. Muffled voices from the police radio in the front of the van drift through the metallic partition.

I feel my nipples harden as the copper continues to suck me off. Despite being old enough to be my father, he does give a pretty good blow job. He moves his tongue to the base of my cock and starts to wet my pubic hair. His tongue travels up my stomach, licking out my navel as it passes. My nipples begin to get even harder as I feel his tongue getting nearer. It suddenly comes into contact with my nipples, and I let out a loud groan. Fuck, that feels good. None of the girls I have been out with so far have bothered to go anywhere near them.

My nipples immediately turn the hardest that they have ever been. The copper starts nibbling on them with his teeth. He reaches down and takes my cock in his hand, and begins to wank me and Andy off at the same time.

The copper suddenly pulls his mouth off my nipples and straddles Andy, hunching down so as not to knock his head on the roof of the van. He unzips his fly and pulls out his hard cock. It is about six inches long, with quite a thick girth. He lets it hang directly in front of Andy's mouth.

Andy looks up at him angrily. 'Put that in my mouth, and I'll bite the fucking thing off!'

The copper stands in front of him, laughing. 'Oh, so you would rather go to prison than give me a little suck, would you?' He starts to put his cock back into his uniform trousers. 'You should be getting used to sucking cock: you'll be having to do it every night in prison. A good-looking lad like you will be the prison bike.'

Andy looks up at the copper, horrified. The copper continues to stuff his cock back into his jeans.

'Wait!' shouts Andy.

Grinning smugly, the copper pulls his semi-erect knob back out of his uniform trousers. Andy closes his eyes and slowly opens his mouth. The copper grabs hold of his dick and guides it into Andy's mouth. As he slides it right the way in, I can actually see it growing in Andy's mouth. The copper's fat bell-end knocks into the side of Andy's cheek.

The copper reaches down and pushes Andy's chin up, closing his mouth tightly around his cock. 'There, that's not too bad, is it?'

The copper starts moving his pelvis, sliding his meat in and out of Andy's mouth. Andy keeps his eyes tightly closed, clearly not enjoying the experience any more. The copper reaches up and grabs on to the hooks that our handcuffs are attached to. Holding on to them tightly, he starts thrusting his cock deep into Andy's open mouth. Andy's head begins banging against the side of the van, knocked back by the force of the copper's thrusts.

The copper looks down to check that Andy is fully erect. He stares at Andy's throbbing young weapon. He pulls his cock out of Andy's mouth and kneels down in between his legs. He leans forward and takes Andy's meat in his mouth. I stare over at Andy; he still has his eyes tightly closed. Even if he is enjoying this, I can imagine he is feeling guilty about it. I had a mate suck me off years ago, so I'm not going to be too hung up about this little encounter.

The copper really starts to pump his mouth round Andy's cock, trying to get him to come. Andy rolls his head around, beginning to enjoy the experience. The copper pulls his head off Andy's dick and starts wanking him quickly. He leans forward and starts licking his young nipples, desperate for him to come. Andy cannot contain his pleasure and begins to groan loudly. I look over at Andy's rigid, young meat as the copper tugs on it. He cups his other hand under his purple helmet.

The chain from Andy's handcuffs starts to rattle as his whole body spasms, and his cock fires out a long stream of healthy come. It lands in the palm of the copper's cupped hand. The copper continues wanking Andy and another few streams of healthy young fuck juice squirt into his hand.

Andy opens his eyes and looks down at his creamy, white spunk that has collected in the copper's hand. The copper moves over next to me and grabs hold of my cock and balls with his spunk-filled hand. I feel him rubbing Andy's warm cream all over my privates. He then takes my shaft in his hand and starts wanking my meat, using Andy's spunk as lube.

Andy looks over at the copper wanking me off. The copper leans forward and sticks his tongue under the end of my cock. The warm moistness of his tongue against my sensitive young helmet makes me come instantly. I fire a thick trail of semen right into his mouth. All of a sudden, another few spurts fly out and land on his waiting tongue. He gulps all of my fuck juice down instantly.

Once he is sure my cock has finished shooting, he cleans the end of it with his tongue. He stands up, grinning at us both.

'That was painless enough, wasn't it, boys?' he says smugly.

He stuffs his cock back into his trousers, content with just watching us two come. I expect he will finish himself off in the police station loos, dirty old bastard.

He takes out his keys and unlocks the handcuffs. Our arms fall free of the metal. I shake my arms, trying to renew the circulation. Andy and I both quickly pull our trousers up and put our T-shirts on.

The copper opens the back doors of the van. 'Now, if that car isn't back where you nicked it from in the next hour, I'll be filing those reports.'

We jump out and rush to the car. We get in, avoiding eye

contact with each other. I start the car and quickly drive away, knowing that this incident is never going to be mentioned again.

I skid to a halt in a haze of dust. All that reminiscing about my joyriding days has got me to the golf club in no time. As the dust settles on the outrageously expensive cars lined up in the car park, I realise that all eyes are fixed on me. Embarrassed, I jump out of the car and leg it towards the clubhouse, my cock still hard from thinking about Andy and the copper.

I rush into the clubhouse bar. It is completely empty apart from a man sat on his own, clutching a pint of lager in front of him. That must be my Mr Scott. He looks in his mid-forties and has slicked-back brown hair. I reckon he's about my height, but he's sitting down so I cannot be sure. He is dressed in the obligatory golfer's uniform: check trousers, tank top and short-sleeved shirt. His smooth, chunky forearms stick out of his shirtsleeves, giving an indication of the rest of his frame. I straighten my tie and head towards him, praying that I can get him to sign a contract.

'Fore!' shouts Jason Scott, as he powerfully knocks his golf ball high into the blue, spring sky. In the distance, we see it landing gracefully in the middle of the green. We are on the sixteenth hole, and I'm frigging knackered. He's a very experienced player, and I've only ever had a knockaround in my local park when I was a kid.

This is hard work. I've run out of things to say about Sureforce already. Good job he has got plenty to say for himself. He has told me that he is married with two kids, owns forty bingo halls in the Northwest, and was brought up on a council estate in Rochdale. What does he want, a bloody pat on the back? Bet he hasn't got where he is from hard graft. Probably got someone to break a few kneecaps along the way. He may have his posh golf kit on now, but that borstal tattoo on his forearm says it all. Bet this poncy golf lot cursed the person who signed him in. Oh well, just two more holes to go, and I'm out of here.

I press my bright-yellow tee into the ground, and place my golf ball on top of it. I grip hold of my golf club tightly and stand over the ball, hoping that this shot will be a little better than the rest. I've got the power; it's the aim I'm lacking.

I pull my arms back and give the ball an almighty swipe. The ball shoots into the air like a bullet. Wow! It's certainly going further than the rest of my shots. It's just a shame it's not going anywhere near the green. Shielding our eyes from the sun, we both watch it slowly begin to land. It falls into a tree, sending leaves flying as it ricochets against all of the branches. It eventually falls out of the bottom of the tree, and lands in the long grass and bushes that lie to the right of the green.

'She's in the rough,' Jason Scott kindly informs me.

I smile falsely, wanting to wrap my golf club around his neck. We place our clubs into the golf bags and set off towards the jungle that my golf ball has decided to call home. I think I prefer being sat behind reception desks.

I can't believe the rules of golf. We've been thrashing our clubs around in this undergrowth looking for my golf ball for the past half an hour. Why the hell can't I just take a new ball out of my golf bag and start again. Apparently that is very unprofessional – his words, not mine.

I suddenly remember that I have left the factory boss in a compromising position. I've been gone ages. Let's hope the old receptionist hasn't gone looking for him. She'll blow her pacemaker if she finds him.

I continue to thrash through the undergrowth. We're at least three hundred yards from the green. The people behind us couldn't wait any longer and have carried on. Are we ever going to find this bleeding ball?

'Found something!' Jason suddenly calls from behind a large oak.

Hooray! We'll be able to get back to the clubhouse for a few pints at long last.

I head towards the tree and walk around its thick trunk. Jason stands leaning against the tree holding something in his hand. As I look down, I realise it isn't my golf ball he is holding. His chequered golfing trousers are unzipped, and his raging hard cock sits in his hand. As he slowly rubs it, it grows thicker by the second. Shit! Aren't any of these company directors getting it at home?

He looks down admiringly at his thick cock. He continues to slowly rub it. He suddenly looks over at me and grins cockily. What is going on here? Is this geezer on this famous List? Just how does he know I may be interested in giving him a quick suck? The Boss has got a lot of talking to do later.

'So, I hear you're not just an expert in the field of security,' he says.

Jesus, word certainly travels fast in the business world.

'People tell me that Sureforce have been looking after their cocks as well as their property,' he informs me, grinning down at his dick. 'You going to show me how well you can take care of my property?'

The Boss has really got some talking to do. I thought I was the company rep, not the company bike. I'll make sure I get this contract, then I want questions answered.

Right, let's give him a Sureforce presentation. Actually, his cock looks really suckable, so it should be quite an easy task. It's not too long, but it certainly has the thickest girth I've ever seen. I've never tasted one as fat as that before. He looks a right dirty bugger as well, so I reckon he'll know what to do with it.

I drop my golf club and reach over for his meat. He lets go of it, and it springs up and down in front of him. I grab hold of it tightly. Fuck, it's hard. This guy must have had a stiffy all the way round the course. Bet he's got two full balls of spunk as well.

In the distance, the sound of swiping golf clubs can be heard. I peer around the tree to see if any golfers are near. Three men stand putting on the green, totally unaware of the action going on in the rough.

Jason nods down at his dick, indicating that he wants it sucked. I slowly kneel down in front of him. I stare at the tip of his fat, purple bell-end that hovers in front of my nose. The smell of his knob takes over from the smell of freshly cut grass.

He grabs his cock and shoves it forward against my lips,

desperate for a warm mouth around it. I slowly peel his foreskin back to reveal the rest of his throbbing helmet. These are the perks of the job that make it all worthwhile.

I move my tongue forward and start to lick around the thick ridge of his bell-end. I feel even more blood being pumped into his meat as my tongue works its way right the way around. I pull his trousers and boxer shorts right down to his knees. I lift up his steely cock to catch a glimpse of his balls. Two huge, hairy sacks hang before my very eyes. My mouth begins to water in anticipation. I get really turned on by older men's balls.

My cock starts to twitch and grow. My underpants are still wrapped around the factory owner's head, so the bulge in my trousers is very noticeable. He looks down at it and smirks, enjoying the fact that he's turning me on. I cup my hands around his balls and draw them towards me. I eagerly stretch out my tongue to get my first taste of his sweaty testicles. As my tongue makes contact with his sack, he lets out an ecstatic groan. I look up at him, and our eyes make contact. He watches my tongue explore his heavy balls. He starts to wank his cock as I continue to lick his manly bollocks.

I open my mouth and stuff one of his balls inside. I begin sucking on it as if it were a giant gobstopper. He wanks his cock even faster, the warmth of my mouth obviously turning him on. I move my head right under his crotch, just to see if I can get both testicles in at the same time. I open my mouth as wide as I possibly can, imagining I'm sat in the dentist's chair. I slowly ease my mouth up over his juicy sack and manage to get both balls in at the same time. Once they are completely in, I slightly close my mouth around them. They're certainly not going anywhere now.

I begin to really suck on the fleshy sacks. He jerks himself off even faster. My rock-hard cock tries to burst through the thin material of my trousers. As it begins to grow even harder, it feels as if it is going to rip through the material at any minute.

His balls begin to move around in my mouth as his hand pumps the skin of his meat back and forth. Wanting to make sure I get a taste of pre-come before he shoots, I release his balls from my mouth. I stare at his cock as he wanks it in front of my face.

His shiny, fat bell-end begins to noticeably throb, and milky, white pre-come dribbles out of his piss slit. I reach down and rip open my fly, desperate to start wanking my weapon. My fully erect cock bursts out and bobs up and down in the long grass. I grab hold of it tightly and begin to milk it.

His strong hand suddenly grabs the back of my head and pulls me forward, forcing my mouth around his knob. 'Come on boy,' he taunts, 'I thought you were here to show just what Sureforce can do for me.'

He lets his cock go and uses his free hand to hold the other side of my head. Holding it completely still, he starts to thrust his fat cock in and out of my mouth. His huge balls bang against my chin with every thrust.

I move my free hand under his golfing shirt and move it up his torso, parting the thick expanse of hair as I go. My hand reaches his chest, and I start searching for his nipples. I soon find one of his huge, rigid tits. It is already rock hard. He throws his head back and groans as I start to pull on it. My cock grows harder just thinking about what they actually look like.

As I pull and twist his hard tit, he begins to jab my mouth with his cock even faster. He tries to grab a handful of my short hair, but it's too cropped. Instead, he grabs hold of my ears and pulls my head down on to his cock every time he thrusts forward. I lap up his salty pre-come that oozes out of his tool. I pull on his tits harder, wanting him to release even more pre-come into my mouth. My balls tighten as I taste more of his salty juice. I'm so horned up I could probably come without having to even touch my dick. Even so, I start wanking my cock even harder. It stiffens even more when I imagine some prudy old golf pro catching us at it.

I pull my mouth off his knob, needing some air. I take a deep breath as my spunk rises and my body begins to shudder. Realising I'm about to come, he lets go of my head and cups one of his hands at the tip of my pulsating cock. His other hand burrows under my T-shirt and grabs hold of one of my erect nipples. As soon as he starts yanking on it, my balls release my juice. White-hot spunk shoots out of my helmet and lands in his cupped hand.

'Come on, lad, let's have some more,' he shouts, egging me on.

With that, stream after stream of semen squirts out of my veiny dick, filling the palm of his hand. When he is sure every last drop is out, he brings his hand to his stiff cock and rubs my spunk all around it. My dick starts to harden again; I'm getting really turned on by what the dirty bastard is doing. He continues to smear my juice around his helmet and all over the shaft. Then he moves his hand to his tight balls and rubs the rest of my creamy spunk round them. Once they are dripping in come, he rapidly starts jerking himself off. His dick squelches as he wanks, my spunk foaming all over his shaft.

He suddenly grabs hold of my head with his spare hand and forces my mouth on to his spunk-coated meat. My lips slide easily over his naturally lubricated knob. I taste my own salty semen as he starts fucking my face vigorously. My cock grows fully stiff again, turned on by the fact that he is in control. I look up at him. I can tell that he's just using my mouth: I could be anyone.

He grits his teeth and grabs the back of my head. He pulls my mouth right down over his meat, making sure my lips go right up to the hilt. I feel his fat helmet digging in to the roof of my mouth, and I start to gag. He pulls it out slightly, letting me recover. Within seconds he bangs it back in, making me gag even more.

He starts pumping my face furiously, obviously reaching climax. Then, he suddenly pulls it out completely and wraps his big hand around it. He pulls his foreskin right back and pumps out his cock juice. I stick out my tongue, really wanting to taste him. His face reddens, and he blows through his clenched teeth. A jet of hot spunk unexpectedly smacks me in the cheek. I move my tongue right under his bell-end, not wanting to miss the next squirt. I catch it just in time and roll the thick mixture round my mouth. I drink it down quickly and stick out my tongue again for the next load. Three more streams of spunk shoot on to it and begin to slide down the back of my throat. I coat the inside of my mouth with it, wanting the taste to linger.

As soon as he's sure he has emptied every last bit of spunk inside me, he shakes his hard knob and stuffs it back into his trousers. I'm so hard again, I really want to come, but I know I should save it for later. I stand up and ram my dick into my trousers. I struggle to pull up my zip because it's still so hard.

Once he's adjusted his trousers, he picks up his golf club.

'I'm pretty impressed with what Sureforce can do for me,' he informs me. 'Let's get back to the bar, and you can talk me through your contract over a pint.'

I try not to show just how pleased I am. I feel more able to confront the Boss about the List now I've got a signed contract under my belt. Let's hope I can get Sergeant Hill to come up with the goods as well.

I screech past the HILL CLOTHING MANUFACTURERS sign and grind to a halt in the car park. I jump out of the car, eager to get the next twenty minutes over with. Hill has been tied up in there for six hours; I should think he's signed the contract by now. I hope he has, for his sake: I'm in no mood for messing around with that fat bastard.

I barge through the main doors, startling the old woman still sat behind reception. I march straight across the foyer and head for the double doors that lead to the factory. The old woman stands up and rushes around the reception desk.

'Excuse me, young man,' she shouts. 'Mr Hill is no longer on the premises.'

'I think you'll find he is,' I smugly reply, as I barge into the factory.

'But his afternoon tea has gone cold,' she yells.

Her voice fades as the doors swing closed behind me. I walk across the now empty factory floor, my footsteps echoing eerily around the giant space.

I reach the stockroom and click open the padlock. I slide the chain through the door handles and kick open the door. As the lights flicker on, I see that Sergeant Hill remains wired to the clothes rail. He is completely naked and still has my underpants over his head.

I put my briefcase down and walk over to the table that the contract sits on. I look down at the dotted line at the end of the contract. It is still unsigned. Shit! I can do without this. He obviously wants me to force him to sign it, the masochistic old git. Right, he's asked for it.

I walk over to the large box of coat hangers. 'I think there's something you forgot to do, isn't there?' I yell at the top of my voice.

I grab a wire coat hanger from the box. I storm over to where he is bound and place the cold wire against his hairy arse. He flinches slightly, not prepared for the cold metal.

'Now, you know you're not getting a taste until you've been a good boy and signed,' I tell him aggressively.

It's beyond me how they get off on this, but, seeing as I've got a natural sadistic streak, it suits me fine. I pull the hanger back and slap it hard against his arse. His body quivers in pleasure.

'Do you hear what I'm saying?' I shout in his ear.

He nods pathetically. I slam the coat hanger hard against his arse once more. He lets out a quiet groan.

'Didn't hear you,' I spit.

'Yes,' he murmurs.

I whack him across the arse once more for the hell of it. The wire hanger leaves a red imprint on his white, flabby buttock.

'Now, if you sign it, I may give you a lick of my meat,' I say, teasingly. 'Wanna feel it?'

He nods his underwear-covered head vigorously. I unzip my trousers and pull out my meat. I grab hold of his free hand and direct it towards my flaccid dick. I let the tips of his fingers briefly touch it, before yanking his hand away again. He tries to reach back, wanting more. I grip his hand firmly, not letting him get anywhere near it. I pick up the pen next to the contract and stick it in his hand. He clasps hold of it tightly.

'That could be my meat you're grabbing if you sign the contract,' I say, sliding the coat hanger against his hairy buttocks. 'Are you ready to sign?'

He nods his head, eager to get a taste of my knob. I suddenly snatch the pen from his hand. He stretches out his hand, reaching for the pen.

'Are you going to beg me to look after your factory?' I ask him. 'Come on, beg me to let you sign the contract.'

He murmurs something, but my underpants wrapped round his head prevent me from hearing what he is saying. I reach up to the clothes rail and unwind the wire coat hanger that's wrapped around his wrist. As soon as his hand is free, he drops to his knees in front of my cock. I pull my pants from over his head; his eyes widen as he gets a glimpse of my fat, flaccid cock. Crusty, dried spunk sits all around the head of it from my golf-course wank. He stares at it in wonder.

I unbutton my shirt and pull it open to let him get a glimpse of my muscly chest and six-pack. He stares up at me longingly. He begins to move his mouth towards my dick, but I pull away quickly. He looks up at me like a little boy who's just had his sweets taken from him.

'Not until you beg me to let you sign the contract,' I inform him.

My cock starts to grow slightly. I'm getting turned on by the fact that this dirty old git wants me bad. I grab hold of it and slowly begin to tug on it. I stroke my chest with my other hand. He stares at my knob as I pull my foreskin back and forth. He licks his lips every time he gets a glimpse of my purple bell-end.

I grab the base of my semi-erect meat and start to slap it around his face.

'Come on, are you going to beg me to let you sign?' I shout, repeatedly slapping him with my dick.

He sticks out his tongue and tries to get a taste of me. I pull it away from him every time he gets near.

'If you wanna taste this, then fucking beg me,' I yell at the top of my voice.

'Can I sign it?' he feebly whispers.

'Did you say something?' I ask aggressively. 'I didn't hear you.'

'Will you let me sign it?' he says, slightly louder.

I continue to slap my cock around his face. 'What did you say?'

He looks up at me, desperate for a piece of meat. 'Please let me sign it.'

I start to slap my cock hard across his face, getting rid of all my pent-up anger. I lean forward slightly and slap the wire coat hanger hard across his arse.

'Beg me,' I shout at him. 'Go on, beg me, you worthless little piece of shit.'

'I beg you to let me sign,' he says desperately.

I beat his arse even harder with the coat hanger. 'Speak up, you fucking waste of space.'

'Please give me the pen,' he shouts.

I slowly hand him the pen, grinning cockily to myself. He snatches it off me, not taking his eyes off my cock as I continue wanking it. He maniacally scribbles his signature across the dotted line at the end of the contract. He drops the pen and opens his mouth, waiting for me to shove my cock in.

'You want to lick it?' I ask him.

He nods his head vigorously. 'Please let me lick it, please let me lick it.'

'Sir to you,' I inform him.

'Sorry, sir, please let me lick it, sir,' he babbles.

I let go of my cock and let it hover in front of his face.

He thrusts his head forward and starts to lick every inch of my knob like a lizard. As he drenches my meat in saliva, he looks up at my flat stomach and hard chest. I stand up even straighter and stick my chest out, loving every minute of him worshipping my physique.

He begins to wrap his lips round the fat head of my cock. I pull it away and start slapping it across his face again.

'My cock's too good for your mouth; just lick it,' I shout.

I keep a firm hold of the base of my cock as he starts to lick all round my shaft, greedy for meat.

'Want some spunk?' I ask him.

He nods his head as he continues to lick my veiny contours. I start wanking it slowly. He licks my helmet frantically, desperate for a taste of spunk.

'Come on, you dirty fucker, let's hear you beg for some spunk,' I yell, wanking my cock faster.

'Please let me taste it, please,' he says desperately, as if his life depended on it.

I wank my dick even faster and thrust out my chest further. My tits are now rock hard and stand out like buttons. He starts panting as he looks up at me and licks around the rim of my meat. I reckon this one could come by just looking at my youthful body. I start to really tug on my meat.

'Ready for this spunk then, are you?' I shout fiercely.

He nods his head excitedly, desperate for a taste of my creamy, young juice. I suddenly stop wanking my dick and pull it away from his mouth. He looks up, desperate for me to let him taste my semen.

I look down at him, grinning cockily. 'Maybe next time.'

I pick up my underpants from the floor and wipe my pre-come off with them. I throw them down at his face.

'These should keep you going for a while.'

I stuff my rock-hard dick back into my trousers and zip them up. He begins to panic, realising he's not going to taste me after all. Boy, this one is sure desperate for a lick of spunk.

I button up my shirt and throw the signed contract into my briefcase. He stares at the bulge in my pants, wanting me to release it again. Dirty old bastard can dream on. I head towards the door, leaving him with his ankles still wired to the rail at the bottom. He stares after me, not quite believing I'm actually going. I grin to myself, knowing the signed contract is safely in my briefcase. Twinny is in for a real surprise.

I walk across the reception area and disturb the old receptionist, who is still sitting there reading a book. She obviously isn't going anywhere until Mr Hill gives her permission.

'Mr Hill says could you take him some tea,' I inform the woman. 'He's doing a stocktake in the storeroom.'

The woman jumps off her chair and walks into the back office. I walk through the main doors, wishing I could be there to watch her drop the tea tray when she sees the state of her boss.

I jump into the car and take my diary out of my briefcase. I scribble a note to remind myself to take Gazza out for a drink. Thanks to the information he gave me, I have just won Sureforce another contract.

Nine

I push open the office door and stride confidently across the room. The Boss and Twinny look up from what they are doing. I throw my jacket down on a chair and click open my case. I pull out the two signed Sureforce contracts and hand them proudly to the Boss. Twinny stares at the signatures in disbelief.

'Looks like another bonus is heading your way,' the Boss says, leafing through the contracts.

Twinny looks over at me and scowls, wondering how I managed to get David Hill to sign. He is the client who was not on the List. I've just got to find out exactly what this List is.

'Boss, can I have a word?' I ask cautiously.

'Sure. Fire away,' he replies.

'In private?' I ask, staring over at Twinny.

'Whatever you've got to say, you can say it in front of me,' Twinny snaps.

Not wanting to confront the Boss in front of Twinny, I close my briefcase and head for the door.

'Another time,' I say to the Boss as I pass him.

'You OK?' asks the Boss, realising I'm pissed off about something.

I nod and walk out of the office. I storm down the corridor, annoyed that Twinny wouldn't leave us in peace. I just don't understand why he's got such a hold over the Boss.

I climb into my car and look at my watch. I suddenly remember Twinny and the Boss were having a meeting at seven. I really just want to have it out with the Boss, but if I can never get him alone I'm going to have it out with them both. If they are having a meeting anyway, it may be a good time to confront them. I realise that I have left my jacket in there anyway, so that makes up my mind for me. I climb back out of the car.

As I walk along the corridor towards the open office door, I hear Twinny speaking my name in a derogatory manner. I freeze, suddenly feeling a sense of *déjà vu*. Wanting to hear where this conversation is going, I silently edge nearer the open door.

'He's trouble,' shouts Twinny.

'He's winning us contracts,' the Boss reminds him.

'But we don't need him around,' insists Twinny. 'I'm your right-hand man.'

The Boss ignores him and gathers together a few invoices from his desk.

'You haven't forgotten why you chose me to be your right-hand man, have you?' asks Twinny.

The Boss shakes his head.

'You haven't been round to see us for a while,' Twinny reminds him.

'I've had to concentrate on the bird twenty-four seven,' answers the Boss.

Twinny stands up and walks over to the Boss's desk. He takes out his mobile and dials a number.

'We're ready for the meeting,' he says to the person on the other end of the phone.

He puts his phone back into his pocket.

'I think you need a little reminder of exactly why I am your right-hand man,' Twinny says to the Boss.

'Look, Twin, I've got to get off,' the Boss tells Twinny. 'I'm supposed to be taking Trish out tonight.'

Twinny suddenly begins to unzip his Sureforce bomber jacket. As he slowly pulls the zip down, it opens to reveal his bare chest. He takes the jacket off completely and throws it on the desk. He stands in front of the Boss, bare chested. His torso is very muscly and compact, and he has an extremely well-defined six-pack. Just what the fuck is going on here? Don't tell me the Boss is shagging Twinny.

Twinny begins to undo his trousers. They fall to the floor, revealing a crisp, white jockstrap. It contrasts with Twinny's dark skin. The Boss stops what he's doing and stares longingly at Twinny. He kicks off his trousers and stands right in front of the Boss. He takes hold of the Boss's massive hand and places it on his smooth, black arse. He starts rubbing the Boss's cock through his tracksuit bottoms. It starts to grow, stretching the shiny fabric of his bottoms. I stand, frozen, in the hallway, not believing what I am seeing. How could I have been so stupid? It was obvious all along.

'Come on, Boss, just whack it up me,' Twinny says temptingly.

The Boss quickly reaches into his tracksuit pants and pulls out his weapon. I stare at his beautiful, erect meat. I cannot believe I'm actually getting to see it after all this time. It is just a shame it is not me who is touching it. Twinny starts to wank it back and forth. It begins to grow even bigger. I stare at it in wonder. Lucky bastard has got the body and the cock.

Twinny frantically pulls open one of the desk drawers. He takes out a condom and begins to roll it down over the Boss's dick. The rubber of the condom is stretched to its limits as it is forced down over the Boss's thick knob.

The Boss passionately turns Twinny around and pushes him over the desk. He grabs hold of his waist firmly with both of his hands. He kneels down and gobs into Twinny's arse crack. White saliva trickles down Twinny's black arse. The Boss stands back up again and directs his huge cock towards Twinny's hole.

'Yeah, ram it home, Boss,' Twinny says, egging him on.

My cock begins to twitch; I'm getting turned on by the scene in front of me. But I feel completely jealous of Twinny. I wish it was my waist that the Boss was holding.

The Boss slides his huge helmet into Twinny's hole. Twinny pushes his arse back on to the Boss's dick, eager for it to go in up to the hilt. The Boss starts to pound his arse like a real fuck machine. I rub my cock through my trousers, watching these two big men fucking.

I stare at the Boss's fat, veiny cock sliding in and out of Twinny's black arse. My arse lips begin to contract, thinking about the first time I met the Boss. I reminisce about him stabbing my tight arse, praying it will happen again soon.

Getting really turned on, I start to pull my erect cock out of my trousers. As I'm about to flop it out, the main door downstairs suddenly clicks open. Someone enters the building, and their footsteps grow louder as they begin to climb the wooden stairway. Shit, who's this? Must be the person that Twinny rang.

I quickly zip up my fly and dive into the empty office next door. I keep the door slightly open so I can see who the visitor is. The person marches along the corridor. As he sails past the door, I get a quick glimpse of him. Shit, it looks like Twinny! But it can't be, he is already in the office.

I sneak out of the disused office and slowly peer in through the door, which has been left ajar. The Twinny lookalike stands in the middle of the room, watching the Boss fucking Twinny. As I get a better look at the newcomer, I realise that he really is the spit of Twinny. The penny drops. Of course, it must be Dave, his twin brother. That's how Twinny got his nickname.

Dave rips off his jacket and kneels down behind the Boss. He starts licking his arse as the Boss continues to ram himself up Twinny. Jesus, I wish I had a video camera. I could flog this little session for a fortune.

I forget all about my jealousy and whip out my cock, eager to beat it. I watch Dave's tongue disappearing up between the Boss's muscly butt cheeks.

The Boss turns and looks over his shoulder at Dave. 'I want to fill your brother's arse. Make me come.'

Dave stands up and pulls his jeans down around his ankles. His rock-hard, black cock springs out, and he grabs hold of it. He takes a condom out of the drawer and slides it over his meat. He knows where they're kept, so he must have done this before.

He guides his big cock into the Boss's shaved hole. Once his helmet is safely inside, he grabs the Boss's waist and bangs his black cock right the way up his pink hole.

The Boss stops fucking Twinny while he lets the walls of his arse get used to Dave's dick. Dave reaches round and pulls on the Boss's hard tits. The Boss immediately starts to pump Twinny again, as if Dave had just turned him on by his switch.

'Fuck it, Boss, fuck it,' yells Twinny.

The Boss really starts laying into him, slapping his arse as he fucks him. Dave pumps his cock up the Boss's arse each time he thrusts himself back out of Twinny's hole. I wank my cock harder as I watch Dave's knob disappearing up the Boss.

'Yeah, shove that big, black knob up there, boy,' shouts the Boss at the top of his voice.

Dave grabs the Boss's waist and really begins to fuck him. I wank my cock, imagining I am the one being fucked. The Boss kicks Twinny's legs wider apart, allowing him to get even deeper up inside him. Reaching climax, Dave stabs the Boss's arse really hard. His muscly, black butt cheeks wobble as he thrusts. The Boss lifts a leg slightly, allowing him to get further up. Although he's being fucked, he's still in control. He just wants to shoot his load up Twinny's man-cunt. He knows he'll shoot his load further with a cock inside him teasing the roots of his own knob.

I wank my cock harder, wanting to walk into the room and be gangbanged by the three rough bastards. My arse twitches with the thought of Dave's thick cock ploughing into me. I imagine him pulling his dick out of me and ripping off the condom. I then feel him slide his juicy black meat up my arse, grabbing my waist firmly with his huge hands. I relax my arse muscles as he starts to stab me with his weapon. I feel it throb inside me as he begins to squirt load after load of hot cream up me.

The Boss tugs on his dick, wanting to get inside me next. Dave pulls his still raging hard knob out of me. The Boss pushes him out of the way, obviously on the verge of coming. He stands directly behind me, watching Dave's thick fuck juice dribbling out of my arse and down the inside of my thighs. I feel his helmet enter my spunky cavern. Once it's safely inside, the Boss rams it all the way in, smacking his huge balls against my arse. He starts to bang me, using Dave's spunk as lube. He leans forward and puts his arm around my neck, allowing himself to pull his dick further up me. As his chest presses on my back, I feel his hard tits digging into my skin. I feel his huge body spasm as he is about to come. His cock slides back and forth up my arse, swimming in Dave's spunk. His cock throbs inside me as he begins to fire his cream right up my man-cunt. I feel it shoot inside me, mixing itself with Dave's cream that is already there.

'Fuck it, Boss,' Twinny yells, bringing me back to reality with a bump.

I carry on pumping my knob, watching the scene in the office. The Boss continues to pump Twinny's arse, sweat pouring from his forehead as he fucks him like a dog. I stick my free hand down the back of my trousers and feed a finger up my moistened hole. I begin fucking my arse with it, wishing it was the Boss's cock.

The Boss's face suddenly distorts, and he pulls his meat out of Twinny's arse. He yanks the condom off his cock. He aims the head at Twinny's smooth black arse and pumps it fiercely with his hand. Dave continues to ram the Boss's muscly arse.

'Come on, boy, poke that meat up my man-cunt,' the Boss shouts fiercely. 'Make me come over your brother's arse.'

Turned on even more by the Boss's orders, Dave whacks his meat further up his arse. Not being able to hold it in any longer, the Boss releases his stream of hot come all over Twinny's arse. As he continues to pump his knob, the Boss releases even more thick, white semen. It slaps down on top of Twinny's buttocks and begins to slide down the crack of his arse. The Boss slaps his huge hand down on Twinny's cheeks and begins to rub his cream all over them.

Watching him, Dave begins to groan, ready to empty his contents as well. He slides his meat out of the Boss's arse and rips off the condom. He stands next to the Boss and aims his rigid cock at his brother's spunked-up arse.

'Come on, broth!' yells Twinny, pounding his meat in his fist.

Dave looks up at the ceiling and groans. I wank my cock, wanting to come at the same time. A continuous spurt of liquid streams out of Dave's meat. It lands on Twinny's right buttock, and the Boss begins to rub it in with his huge hand. Dave shoots another few loads over his brother's arse, some of the spunk hitting the Boss's hand.

I beat my dick quickly, wanting to spunk as fast as I can. My knees weaken as I feel my cream shoot up through my shaft. I pull my finger out of my arse and clamp my hand over my mouth to muffle my groans. A thick load of semen flies out of my helmet and lands on the door that I'm peering through. I watch the Boss continue to rub his and Dave's spunk all around Twinny's crack. More spunk flies out of my cock, I'm so turned on by the sight in front of me.

As soon as my dick has emptied my balls, I stuff it back inside my trousers. I have to get out of here before I'm spotted. I'll have to call back for my jacket when I am sure they have gone. As I zip myself up, I look to see what is going on in the office. Twinny pulls his trousers up over his spunk-drenched arse, while Dave sticks his hard, wet dick back inside his trousers. The Boss is pulling his tracky bottoms up with one hand, and holding his mobile phone to his ear with the other.

'Trish, it's me,' says the Boss, talking into his mobile phone. 'Meeting went on longer than planned. See you in five.'

He clicks his mobile closed and grins over at Twinny. If she only knew.

I quickly climb into my car before any of them spot me. I lean on the steering wheel thinking about the scene I have just witnessed. Twinny and the Boss must have had something going for ages. I know for a fact that they met each other in borstal when they were young lads. Gazza told me that they shared a cell together. That is where male bonds are really cemented. The person who helps you survive that regime remains a friend for life.

I feel gutted knowing just how close Twinny and the Boss really are. I bet the Boss used to take good care of Twinny in borstal. Everyone would have been shit scared of someone the Boss's size. I bet Twinny paid him back in kind for keeping him in one piece.

I know exactly how borstal works. I will never forget my six months at Oakwood before I joined the army. I shared a cell (although the screws liked to call it a room) with Gary Donoly, the youngest brother of the roughest family in the Northwest. He was actually a really nice kid. Just had a really quick temper. He's dead now: killed in a hit-and-run. The Boss has told me that he was involved with one of the Moss Side gangs.

Next to the Boss, I reckon Gary is the hardest man I have ever met. But if you were in his good books (which I luckily was) he would do absolutely anything for you. He said I used to make him laugh. This was good for me, as he made my time in borstal just about bearable. No one laid a finger on me because they knew I was Gary's boy.

Although I knew he was just using me as his sex partner, he always treated me really well. He was the first guy ever to fuck me. He knew I was a virgin and didn't want to at first – had a real hang-up about doing virgins, for some reason. But I used to get so turned on when I was giving him blow jobs, I asked him to break me in one night. Fuck, I was in pain for days.

I was really glad that he was the first. He used to do me regularly after that. I think that's where I got my love of being screwed from. I knew that there was nothing in our relationship and that he would go back to his bird as soon as he was released, but I didn't care. While we were in borstal, I was his. Especially on visiting days.

Visiting day was the day I used to look forward to the most. Gary's girlfriend always came in to visit him. The dirty cow used to wank him off under the table in the visitors' room. So he was always really horned up when he came back to the cell.

I used to get myself ready for him. I would strip off and lie face down on the hard bed, the light from the corridor shining in on my arse. I would wait for the screw to turn his keys in the metal door at the end of the corridor. My hole used to dilate when I eventually heard that key sliding into the lock. I would lie rigid, waiting for Gary to rush into the cell.

The door would open, and he would be stood there, already half out of his borstal uniform shirt. He would stride over to the bed and quickly pull his trousers down. His erect, condom-covered dick would bounce up and down in front of me. His girlfriend used to put the condom on his knob in the waiting room. It was some perverse ritual they had. She was fine about him shagging me, just so long as she always put the condom on.

I would then feel his hands around my ankles, as he pulled me to the end of the bed and began buggering me senseless.

I was to Gary what Twinny is to the Boss. If Gary were still alive today, I know he would still want to see me for a session now and then. Even if he did not class himself as being gay, he loved to fuck me. I was his boy, and I would have gone on being his boy for the rest of his life. It looks like Twinny is the Boss's boy, and there doesn't seem to be anything I can do about that. Guess I am just going to have to live with it.

Ten

'Well, I'm glad you chose Sureforce as your security company, Mr Kirk,' I shout into my mobile, trying to make myself heard over the building works. 'I look forward to receiving your contract. Bye.'

I click my mobile closed and slip it into the pocket of my Sureforce bomber. It's a nice change not having to wear a suit today. No appointments until tomorrow.

Shit, I just realised my client said that they were sending their contract over to me now. That means I've got to wait for the courier to turn up. Still, it's another signed contract; suppose I can't complain.

The noise of drilling grows even louder. I'm spending the afternoon checking over the Boss's new venture. He's decided to plough some of the fortune he is making from the security company into a theme bar. Its theme at the moment seems to be bare breeze blocks and exposed wires. The builders have got a long way to go, and it's supposed to be opening in a month. Still, when it is up and running, I'm sure he'll be raking it in. We'll get all the wealthy southern students in, blowing their grants on tequila. I've asked him if I can do a night on the door. It's an easy way of getting a hot shag. There is always some pissed-up student willing to give you head in the loo.

I'm stood in what is going to be our new office. It's more like a plasterboard hut at the moment. The painters have knocked off for the day, surprise, surprise. They've left two pairs of stepladders with a waist-high plank across them. I think it's supposed to be an indication of how hard they've been working. Yeah, right! Oh well, at least I can use it as a substitute desk. The only other thing that's in the bare office is a minifridge for the Boss's bottled beers. He certainly gets his priorities right.

I put my briefcase down on the plank of paint-stained wood. I click it open and look inside for something that I could be doing to kill time. A loud pneumatic drill sounds from below and the whole building begins to shake. I close my case, resigning myself to the fact that I'm not going to get anything done. Oh well, the courier will be here in a bit. I'll be able to get off and have a few pints then. I've arranged to take Gazza out on expenses. He's the mate I used to be in the army with. It's my way of thanking him for introducing me to the Boss, and also giving me the inside information about the factory boss. I'm looking forward to it – haven't seen him in ages.

I walk over to the paint-stained window and stare out at the busy street below. It's only a Thursday afternoon, but it's still full up with people sat drinking at the pavement tables. The Boss was right to invest in a place along Canal Street. It seems to be getting busier and busier. During the peak summer months the whole street is filled with an army of partygoers clutching bottles of designer beer.

The Boss's car suddenly screeches to a halt outside the building. I wonder what he is doing here. All of the people sat drinking turn to see who this flash car belongs to. He must be coming to check things over. The last time I saw him he had his cock shoved up Twinny's arse. I still get really aroused when I think about their little floor show. Still, I'm upset that the Boss and Twinny have something going. That must have been the reason why Twinny has been such a bastard to me. I know he feels threatened. I also know the Boss really wants my hot little buns in his hand again. And that's not just me being cocky.

I suddenly realise that this could be the perfect opportunity to confront the Boss about this so-called client list that him and Twinny were talking about. Let's just hope he's alone. I can't quite see into the passenger seat from here.

I watch him get out of the car, praying nobody is with him. He climbs out, wearing tracky bottoms, T-shirt and shades. A few queens sat outside the next-door bar nudge each other, staring open-mouthed at this perfect specimen of manhood.

He slams the car door and points his key fob at it. The doors bleep and click closed. Great, he's alone.

I sit on the plank that stretches across the pair of stepladders, waiting for the Boss to make his way up to the makeshift office. I hear him having a banter with the workmen on the floor below. They are all related to him in some shape or form. I think it's the first time half of them have been out of Salford. They've been a bit freaked by some of the sights they have seen walking along Canal Street. They all went for a drink next door after work last Friday. One of them copped off with a real leggy stunner. It's just a shame he didn't realise it was a bloke until he got her home.

I take a deep breath as I hear the Boss's footsteps climbing the concrete steps. I feel like a nervous sixteen year old out on his first date. The Boss always has this effect on me. I suppose it's because I fancy and admire him more than anyone I've ever met. He's from a really rough, working-class background like me, yet he's made something of himself – big time. He's exactly where I want to be when I am his age.

He suddenly breezes in through the half-finished doorway, wearing his extra-large Sureforce bomber jacket. He notices me and beams over. His gold fillings sparkle in the sunlight.

'Matty!' he shouts, surprised to see me. 'So what do you think?'

'Good space,' I answer pathetically, lost for words.

'Good space!' he repeats. 'Can't you do better than that? It's going to be the hottest bar in Manchester, matey.'

His mobile phone starts to ring, and he pulls it out of his back pocket. He stands in front of the window, staring down on to the street. I stare at his huge shoulders and muscly arse. He laughs and jokes with the person on the other end, obviously in a really good mood.

I want to confront him about the List, but I don't want to risk anything coming between us. I think that he secretly does really like me, physically as well as mentally. I know I'm not going to get him alone like this again for a while. Twinny is never far away, and now I know why. Still, I've got a gut feeling that the Boss would sooner have me around than Twinny. I just think he feels a certain loyalty to him as they go back so far.

The Boss clicks his mobile phone closed and turns around to face me. He frowns at me, sensing that something is wrong. 'Come on, Matty, out with it.'

Knowing this is the perfect opportunity, I stare him directly in the eye.

'What is the List?' I ask confidently.

The Boss turns his back to me and stares out of the window. This is a moment he has obviously been dreading. He suddenly walks over to the minifridge in the corner of the room. He takes out two bottled beers and opens them with his teeth. He walks over to the plank I am sitting on, sits down next to me and hands me a beer.

'Matty, before I say anything, I just want you to know that you're the best thing that has happened to Sureforce,' he says sincerely. 'The List is just a way of finding suitable clients. I never intended to use you.'

'But where did you get this list from?' I ask.

The Boss smiles over at me. 'You got a spare half an hour?'

The Boss chucks his empty beer bottle into the half-full black bag that sits in the corridor. He has fully explained what exactly the List is and where it came from. It turns out a mate of Twinny's bought it from an Internet company. Apparently, when all of these high-powered businessmen sit in their offices surfing the net, their e-mail addresses are relinquished when they visit certain sites, without them knowing. So when those company directors who are into an occasional bit of cock click on to a gay porn Internet site, their name and address are monitored. Their personal address can then be legally passed on by the website company without their knowledge. And then it can fall into the hands of dodgy geezers like Twinny's mate.

Apparently they bought the List ages ago. The Boss was just waiting to find the right person to send to some of these clients to see if it would work. He said that as soon as he first clapped eyes on me, he knew I was just what he was looking for. The day of my interview, he knew he had found the face (and body) of Sureforce. After testing me out sexually, he didn't think I would mind if these blokes came on to me. He didn't want to tell me about the List because he thought I wouldn't be up for it. He wanted me to see just how much I'd enjoy being company rep for myself.

He said he nearly sacked Twinny the day he found he had sent me to a client who wasn't on the List. He had a feeling I could take care of myself, though. I believe him. I really don't think he would use me. I think he respects me nearly as much as I respect him. He told me that I remind him of how he was when he was my age.

The Boss stares at me as I mull all this information over. 'Am I forgiven?'

He holds out his firm hand. I stare into his eyes through his shades. He knows I'll forgive him. He knows how much I want him. I slowly stretch out my hand towards him. He grabs hold of it tightly, and we shake hands. As I attempt to let go of his hand, he tightens his grip. I look at him, wondering what he's doing. He stares at me longingly. Shit, he wants me. He really wants me.

He slowly moves his head towards mine. I suddenly realise that he is going to kiss me. I stare at his fat lips, perched in the middle of his goatee beard. I cannot believe the moment I've waited so long for has finally arrived. His eyes pierce through the tinted glass in his shades as his lips move closer. He lets go of my hand and grabs hold of my shoulder. He starts to pull me closer to him. As our lips are about to meet, there is a sudden loud knock on the wooden doorframe.

The Boss quickly pulls his head away from me and lets go of my shoulder. We both turn around to see who it is. Stood in the doorway is a young bicycle courier. He has a large courier bag over his shoulder, and is still wearing his cycle helmet. The letters CCT cover the side of his courier bag. He stares at us both, realising that he has interrupted an intimate moment.

The Boss glares at him furiously. 'Who the fuck let you in?'

The young courier stares at the Boss with a petrified expression on his face. He is unable to speak. The Boss is red with rage, angry that his homosexual tendencies have been witnessed. I notice the Boss clenching his fists tightly. I shake my head at him, not wanting to see this innocent bystander get hurt.

The Boss angrily jumps off the plank. 'Later!'

He barges past the courier and disappears down the stairs. His heavy footsteps fade into the deafening sound of drilling. Fuck! That's blown it.

The cycle courier looks at me, not quite knowing what to say. Poor guy, bet he wondered what he had walked in on.

'He's had a bad day,' I say, trying to make him feel better. I don't know why I'm worried about the courier, though. He just lost me the shag I've been waiting a year for.

'Mr Dalson?' he asks tentatively.

I nod. He walks over to where I'm sitting and places his courier bag down on the plank. He notices the raging hard on that the Boss has given me. He quickly opens his bag, realising I've caught him staring. He begins to search inside for the package I am expecting. As he leans over and really begins to delve into his bag, I study his face. I suddenly realise that he is the courier who used to deliver packages to the advertising agency I used to work at. Jesus, that was back in the days when I was just a Sureforce security guard. I look down at his pert arse cheeks in his tight cycling shorts. Yep, he's definitely the one. I'd recognise those peaches anywhere.

I start to check him up and down. I reckon he is in his early twenties. I remember him being quite well-spoken. Probably a student studying here – along with the other ten million. Bet he is doing this job for the pose, not the money. I imagine he gets lots of attention with a nice pair of tanned, muscly legs like that.

I suddenly remember that I used to wank about fucking him

when I was sat behind the reception desk of the advertising agency. A cleaner caught me at it once.

My cock is still hard from my encounter with the Boss. I think he's the only person who has given me a stiffy by just putting their hand on my shoulder.

I'm feeling really horned up now. I reckon this one could be on for it: I saw him staring at my packet. He seems pretty inexperienced, though. I don't reckon any cock has been near that Lycra-clad arse. Still, there's a first time for everything. I think I should just go for it. We'll just change courier companies if I screw up.

He finishes delving into his bag and pulls out a large, brown hard-backed envelope. He looks up and catches me checking him out. He flushes slightly, embarrassed by my interest.

He hands me the envelope. I take it off him, allowing my hand to linger on his longer than necessary. He looks away, not knowing how to deal with the situation. He pulls a clipboard and pen from his courier bag.

He holds them out to me. 'Would you sign?'

I take the pen off him and scribble my name next to the cross indicated, staring at him constantly. I hand him back the clipboard, and he quickly shoves it into his bag. He nods at me and walks towards the door. Shit! I've blown that one. I'm going to have to go and have a wank in the loo.

He suddenly stops in the doorway and turns to face me.

'So when does it open?' he enquires.

Got him. He's fucking stalling. There's a huge sign on the door he must have walked through saying OPENS SEPTEMBER. I reckon student boy is up for a bit.

'September,' I reply, grinning from ear to ear. 'Want an invite to the VIP party?'

'Wouldn't mind,' he says eagerly.

'They're like gold dust,' I inform him. 'Everyone's trying to get their hands on them.'

'I know – reckon it's going to be pumping,' he says excitedly. 'I hear The Unabombers are going to be on the decks. I'd do anything to see them.'

I put one of my feet up on the plank of wood, giving him a bird's-eye view of my bulging packet. 'Anything?'

'Anything,' he repeats.

'Give us a blowy, then,' I say brazenly.

'What?' he says, trying to sound disgusted.

'I'll give you a free membership to the Basement Club as well,' I say, trying to tempt him into loaning me his mouth. 'Go on, student boy, I know you want to.'

He stands in the doorway, too embarrassed to admit that he wants to. However, by the bulge in the front of his Lycra cycling shorts, I can tell that he's gagging for a mouthful of Salford spunk. He's just playing one hundred per cent hetero boy at the moment. Come on, I think to myself, I haven't got all night. I've got to meet Gazza in a bit.

Sod it, he is not going to make the first move. I'm going to have to get in there. Well, after all, he fucked up my shag with the Boss, so he can let me fuck him up.

I reach down and unzip my jeans. He stands in the doorway, not knowing where to look. Once my zip is completely lowered, I begin to unbuckle my belt. He grabs hold of his courier bag, using it as a security blanket. He looks as if he is going to run out of the doorway at any moment. I'll have to carry on and see just how desperate he is to taste his first bit of cock. I just want a quick suck and a fuck. I don't want to go anywhere near his packet. I just want him to service me.

Once my belt is unbuckled, I slowly lower my trousers to my knees. I catch him glancing over at my bulging white Calvins and brown meaty thighs. Got him. He's definitely a part-time cock lover.

I start to temptingly rub my semi-erect cock through the white fabric of my briefs. He watches my every move, his Lycra-covered packet growing larger by the minute.

Suddenly, a huge crash sounds from downstairs. He quickly turns his head towards the corridor, remembering where he is. He begins to look nervous again, concerned about being discovered while sucking my cock.

'Chill. They don't come up here, mate,' I reassure him.

Convinced, he looks back over at me rubbing my meat. Is he ever going to get his fucking arse over here or not? Looks like I am going to have to tempt him a little bit more.

I slowly start to lower the waistband of my Calvins. His eyes widen, eager to see what I've got to offer. I grin, knowing that he is not going to be disappointed.

As I pull the white fabric of my briefs lower, he gets his first glimpse of the thick base of my meat. He stares at it intensely, probably having waited for a moment like this all of his teenage years.

I continue to lower my briefs until I am displaying the whole of my shaft to him. He keeps staring at it, trying to restrain himself from rushing over and stuffing it straight into his mouth.

One last pull, and my bell-end pops out. My semi-erect dick flops proudly up and down in front of me. I put my hands on my hips, displaying my fat piece of meat to him in all its glory.

He stares open-mouthed at my knob, not believing it could be all his if he wanted it. I sense that he is still a bit apprehensive about the whole situation. What am I going to have to do, ram it down his face by force?

I grab hold of my dick and start slowly wanking it.

'Don't be shy,' I tell him. 'Come over here and have a sniff.'

He stands frozen on the spot, obviously riddled with guilt. He is probably a good little Catholic boy. Thinks he'll get struck down by a bolt of lightning if he so much as touches it.

Well, he's had his chance. Doesn't look like I am going to get a lick. I begin to stuff my knob back into my Calvins. His expression turns to horror as he watches it disappear.

'Wait!' he shouts.

I stop what I am doing. Looks like he wants a bit after all. Little fucking pricktease.

He nervously begins to walk over towards me. He stops a good distance away. He stares straight at me for the first time, not knowing what to expect. I bet he thinks I'm a right scally gangster. Still, some of these innocent little student boys love that. They think they are really living on the edge if they get screwed in some council flat in Salford.

I yank my dick back out again. I notice his hard knob growing down the inside leg of his cycling shorts. Seems like he is really turned on already. I expect he'll shoot as soon as I touch him. These virgin cock suckers always have a bad case of premature ejaculation.

He looks down at my semi-erect dick as I slowly wank myself off.

'It won't bite,' I say, nodding down at my meat.

He lets go of the courier bag he has been clutching for the past ten minutes and slowly reaches his clammy hand over towards me. I let go of my cock, letting it stand out fully erect. His hand moves nearer to it, and he nervously touches my bell-end with his fingers. He acts like an alien who has just landed on earth, discovering things for the first time.

He begins to lightly run his fingers over my shaft, not really knowing what to do next. Sod this for a laugh. I grab hold of his hand and wrap it around the thick girth of my meat. I pull his hand back and forth, indicating that I want him to wank me off.

Once he is doing it of his own accord, I take my hand off his. He looks down at my piece in his hand, still wearing his cycle helmet. He is totally engrossed in the size and shape of it. I start to realise that this is probably the first one he has ever touched, apart from his own, of course. I expect he's touched that a lot, wanking over porno magazines in his bedroom when his mum and dad think he's studying.

I stare him in the eyes as he continues to wank me off. He can only just bring himself to look at me, still embarrassed to admit to being a dick lover.

As he continues to awkwardly wank my dick, I reach over and grab hold of his Lycra-clad arse. He has certainly got a pert pair of cheeks. I really want to butt fuck those.

I pull him nearer to me and slap my hand down on his other cheek. I start to rub all around his arse and up and down his crack. I soon realise that the dirty little fucker has not got anything on under those cycling shorts.

As I sit down on the plank behind me, I feel the splinters digging into my exposed arse. I pull him down on to his knees and yank his courier bag over his head. He continues to wank me off, not wanting to let go of his precious new toy.

Kneeling right in front of me, he closely inspects every inch of my dick.

'Suck it,' I order him.

He slowly begins to bring his head towards my hard, veiny cock. He stops inches away, wanting it in his mouth, but still feeling incredibly nervous. He begins to sniff at it, acclimatising himself to the smell. He sticks his tongue out and stretches it forward. The tip of it comes into contact with my purple helmet. He nervously moves it away again, not sure if he wants to go through with it. Fuck this.

I grab hold of his cycling helmet and pull him down on to my fat meat. He gags as my throbbing tip slams into the back of his throat. Keeping hold of his cycling helmet, I move his mouth up and down the length of my shaft. He grabs hold of my firm thighs as he starts to move his head up and down himself.

I let go of his cycling helmet and watch him lick my length. I grin to myself, pleased that I am the first person he has ever sucked off.

He is certainly a quick learner. He pumps his head up and down like there's no tomorrow. I notice his cock bulging down the inside of his cycling shorts. It's so long, his purple tip sticks out of the leg hole of the shorts.

He continues to eat me, getting more and more turned on. I bet he has wanked about doing this for years. He is probably going to wank about it for years to come as well. I mean, he isn't going to find another piece of meat like mine in a long while.

I grab hold of his hands and move them up under my Sureforce bomber jacket. I rest his fingers on my rock-hard nipples, and he groans in delight. He starts to pull on them as he moves his head around my cock in a sucking frenzy.

I lean forward and put my hand between his legs. I start rubbing his tight crack through his Lycra shorts. He groans in ecstasy, probably never having had anyone's hand anywhere near it before.

His clammy hands move all over my chest, obviously getting

pleasure from my muscly pecs. My cock gets even harder as his mouth begins to maintain a steady rhythm.

I suddenly think about the Boss's lips moving nearer to me. I imagine him fucking me here over this plank of wood.

My cock throbs even more. I want to see it disappearing up this student's virgin arse.

I pull his head off my dick and stand up in front of him. I pull him to his feet and turn him around so that he has his back to me. I lift his leg over the plank of wood that is supported by the two ladders. Then I kick off my jeans and lift my leg over as well. We both stand in the middle of the room, straddling the plank of wood.

I stare down at his pert arse in his cycling shorts. He nervously looks over his shoulder, wondering what I am about to do next. I unzip my bomber jacket and take out my wallet. I pull a twenty pound-note out of it and stuff it down the front of his cycling top.

He turns the top half of his body around to face me. 'What's that for?'

'A new pair of cycling shorts,' I answer.

'But I don't need a new pair,' he replies, frowning at me.

I suddenly reach for the seat of his Lycra shorts and grab the material in both hands. I muster all my strength before tearing the fabric apart. The Lycra splits right down the seam, exposing the perfect crack of his arse.

'You do now!' I say, grinning to myself mischievously.

He starts to lift his leg back over the plank, shocked by what I have just done. I grab hold of his waist tightly and pull his leg back over until he is straddling the plank once more.

'It's OK,' I reassure him. 'You're gonna enjoy it!'

He stops struggling and stands still. I stare down at the crack of his gorgeous, smooth arse that is poking out of his torn cycling shorts. More blood begins to pump into my cock as I imagine fucking his tight virgin hole.

I reach down and grab hold of his bare cheeks. I use one hand to pull them apart, and the other to touch his beautiful pink lips. He flinches, not used to having fingers so near his rim. He had better start getting used to it; I'm about to give him an internal examination. He's going to need loosening before I can get my meat up inside him.

I push him forward, and he leans over the plank of wood, still looking over his shoulder. He really doesn't trust me. Probably thinks I am going to pull a knife out on him or something. I sit down on the plank and stare at his arse hovering in the air in front of me.

I rip open his shorts a bit further, wanting to see more of his ripe cheeks. I slap my hands down on each buttock and slowly pull them apart. His crack begins to open, revealing his beautiful, pink, virgin hole. Fuck, it looks tight. I don't know how I am going to get my fat cock up that. I'm definitely going to have to loosen him up.

I pull my head back and gob at the rim of his arse. He jerks forward as my cold saliva smacks him right in the centre of his hole.

With both hands firmly on his arse, I start to lick his butt cheeks. I notice him grab on to the plank as my tongue moves nearer to his hole. I eventually reach his rim, and his whole body starts to tremble in pleasure. I get a firmer grip on his cheeks and pull them as far apart as they will go. I stare at his beautiful, untouched man-cunt as I move my tongue slowly towards it.

Stretching my tongue out as rigidly as I can, I move the tip of it into his anus. He throws his head back and groans loudly as I start to fuck his virgin arse with my moist tongue. I grab hold of his waist and pull his arse right back into my face, feeling my tongue venturing further up his hole. I lick right inside him, wanting to taste what no man has tasted before.

My cock begins to throb. I get really turned on by licking virgins out. I love hearing them groan as they experience one of the ultimate sexual pleasures. I love feeling their whole body go limp as I inject them with my sharp tongue. It's as if I have given them a sexual anaesthetic.

I continue to lick and fuck him with my tongue. Judging from his loud groans, his embarrassment and fear have now completely disappeared. He grabs hold of the plank and thrusts his arse right back into my face. Jesus, this one is greedy for tongue already.

I slide my hard tongue further up his arse, tasting his sweet man-cunt juices. He is definitely nearly ready for me. I can feel him getting looser and looser by the minute. I'll hopefully be able to fit all of my meat up there when I break him in. You can't beat doing a virgin from time to time. Their tight passages make you want to come in seconds.

I grab hold of my dick and start tugging on it, getting it nice and hard for his arse. I pull my tongue out of his crack and stand over him, looking down at his newly opened hole. He reaches behind, wanting to feel my hard cock as I wank it back and forth. He starts to wank it for me, not realising what I am about to do with it.

I reach down into my jacket that is lying on the floor. I take out a condom and rip it open with my teeth. He looks over his shoulder and suddenly realises what I am about to do. He begins to pull his leg over the plank of wood. I grab hold of his waist and pull him back down.

'It's OK,' I whisper in his ear. 'It's not gonna hurt.'

'But I never –' he begins.

I slap my hand over his mouth. 'Just relax. Matty'll do all the work.'

Needing to get his arse muscles relaxed, I start nibbling at his smooth neck. I push his helmet-covered head to one side to get better access to his neck. I start to lick and gnaw at it, reaching down to get my cock ready. I move my head away from his neck and gob in my hand. As I continue to bite his neck, I start rubbing my phlegm around the tight rim of his passage. I slowly begin to edge one of my fingers inside. He tightens his arse muscles, not used to having someone entering him.

'Relax,' I whisper in his ear.

I start really ripping into his neck with my teeth. (I'd like to be there when he explains these marks to his girlfriend later.)

His arse muscles slowly begin to relax again, and I move my finger further up inside him. This boy is really tight. I don't know if I am going to get my fat dick up him after all.

I edge the tip of another of my fingers slowly up inside him. He groans as both of my fingers begin to stretch him open. I bite into his neck, trying to get him even more relaxed. I feel him open wider, and I quickly slip another finger inside.

I begin to move my three fingers up and down inside his hole. He throws his head back, obviously starting to enjoy the experience. Pain has at last turned to pleasure.

I look over his shoulder and watch him take his dick out of his cycling shorts. As he starts to wank his long, thin meat, his arse relaxes more, and I move my fingers further up inside him.

Knowing he is just about ready, I slowly pull my fingers out of his arse, and it snaps shut. Standing over him wanking my meat, I look down at his smooth arse sticking out of his ripped shorts.

My cock throbs continuously and I move the tip of it against his entrance. I gob down on my rubber-covered meat and rub the warm saliva all over my helmet. I slowly begin to ease it into his tight ring. My massive head stretches it open like it's never been stretched before.

He groans in pain and pleasure as my meat starts splitting him in two. More blood pumps into my shaft as it slides into the tightest orifice it has ever entered.

Once I am sure my tip is securely in, I grab hold of his waist and pull him right back on to me, spearing him with my weapon. As it slides further up his virgin arse, I pull his head back and start biting the front of his neck. I feel like a lion mating with his lioness.

As I continue to rip his neck apart, I slide myself further inside him. I pull my head back, wanting to get a glimpse of my fat shaft stretching his rim to its limits.

Once I am right inside of him, I give his passage a minute to acclimatise before I start to pump back and forth. I begin to slide it in and out of his hole, the torn fabric of his cycling shorts rubbing against my shaft. All I can see is my slippery shaft disappearing through the hole in his shorts.

I push him forward and really begin to aggressively bang him. I want to get him nice and loose, ready for the next bloke who's going to fuck him one day.

He grabs hold of the plank of wood with one hand, and jerks himself off with the other.

The drilling coming from downstairs suddenly stops, and the

building falls into silence. All that can be heard is his squelching virgin cunt and his quiet whimpers of pleasure.

I start to slap his arse, and the loud whack of flesh on flesh echoes through the building. I'm sure the builders will have a fair idea of what is going on up here now.

I start to pump him even faster, wanting to shoot my load right up inside him. Judging by the speed with which he's using his arm, I reckon he's about to come as well.

I reach forward and tear his shorts right open, wanting to see my bright-red hand marks on his pink buttocks. I rub my hand all over them as I feel my balls tighten.

He suddenly groans loudly, and his arse clamps tightly around my knob. I look over his shoulder as he suddenly spills his young come all over the plank in front of him. As I start pumping him harder, desperate to fill him up, a few more streams of fuck juice fly out of his knob. I keep pumping him, not wanting to come over his arse but up it. I want him to remember my throbbing cock as it releases its mess right up inside him.

I grab his waist tightly and thrust it into him, my balls banging on his smooth arse.

'Fuck,' I yell, my voice echoing throughout the building.

I feel my spunk flowing through my dick and flying right up into his arse. I continue pumping as my cock shoots more and more thick, hot come inside his virgin hole. He groans, enjoying the feeling of having a cock throbbing inside him for the first (and probably not last) time.

Once my balls are completely drained, I slowly pull my still rock-hard meat out of him. He groans as his tight young ring snaps back closed.

He quickly pulls the front of his cycling shorts up, covering his dick. I carefully pull the condom off my dick, making sure I do not spill any of my precious spunk from it. Once it is completely off, I tie a knot in the end of it like a balloon. I hold the tied condom in my hand, feeling the warmth of my spunk through the rubber.

I hold the used condom out to him. 'A souvenir.'

He stares at the full rubber bag that has just been up his arse. He reaches over and takes it from my hand, then opens his courier bag and carefully drops it in. He reaches around the back of his arse and pulls the fabric together, trying to cover his exposed arse. I pull my leg over the plank and pull my trousers up, pleased that I can add another virgin to my list.

He hooks his courier bag over his shoulder and pulls it across his arse to cover his ripped shorts. He suddenly moves his head towards mine and puckers his lips. I pull my head away, not wanting to kiss him. Oh shit, I hope he doesn't think that meant anything.

He looks at me, deflated. I hold out my hand towards him. He grips it tightly, and we shake.

I grin at him. 'I'll have to make sure I use your company again.'

He smiles, trying to hide his disappointment. He probably thought that we were going to ride off into the sunset on his courier bike. Dream on.

He walks out of the room, making sure his courier bag is covering his exposed arse.

I move over to the window as I hear the door downstairs bang closed. I look down on to the street. I notice his bike chained to a tree near the pavement tables, which are filled with laughing people.

The young courier walks into view, still holding his courier bag over his split shorts. He unlocks his chain and wraps it around his waist.

As he mounts his bike, his bag slips, and I catch a glimpse of his winking pink hole. My cock begins to stir again. He quickly adjusts his bag until it is covering his arse. Sensing I am watching his every move, he suddenly looks up at the window. I grin at him cockily. The fact that he has just been bum fucked suddenly hits home, and he quickly cycles away, red-faced.

I rub at my cock, imagining him getting home to his shared student household and locking himself in the bathroom. I picture him stripping off and taking the condom full of my spunk out of his bag. My cock grows hard again as I imagine him rubbing my spunk all over his body, concentrating on his newly stretched arse. I pull my meat out again and start wanking.

Eleven

Gazza swills down what is left of his lager and slams the pint glass down on the table next to the other empties.

I nod at the glass. 'Looks like I've got some catching up to do.'

He holds out one of the empty glasses towards me, indicating that it needs filling. 'Better hurry up, then.'

After three hours of catching up on what's new and reminiscing about our old army days, the table is littered with empty pint pots. The landlady has a particular policy: she will only collect glasses when she has run out. Seeing as there are only about ten people in the place, she has not run out yet.

I do not get to see Gazza as often as I would like these days. We used to hang around together all the time as teenagers, but since we've left the army we have gone our separate ways.

He has now got his own garage down under the arches in Salford. Apparently he is doing really well for himself. Seems like repairing all those army tanks gave him a skill to set up some sort of business when he left. He ended up marrying Julie, his child-hood sweetheart. They have got two kids already. Knowing how often Gazza needs a shag, I am surprised they haven't got more.

I've been meaning to take him out for a booze-up on expenses for ages. It is my way of thanking him for giving me the dirt on

Sergeant Hill, the factory boss who liked to be dominated. I won Sureforce a crucial contract because of that tip-off. The Boss said the least Sureforce can do for Gazza is to get him pissed.

We were going to go out for some sort of meal, but it looks like we are going to do our usual fourteen-pint starter, followed by a kebab main course.

I really miss seeing Gazza: we used to have such a laugh in the army together. He is totally on my level. Always sort of treated me like his younger brother. I have always fancied the pants off him, though. He looks particularly horny tonight in his greasy overalls and freshly shaved hair. He apologised for not being able to get home and change, but I am too embarrassed to tell him that I'm glad he didn't. He knows about my cock habit, of course. He really plays up to it; but that is another story.

'So, you've done really well for yourself at Sureforce,' he says, slightly slurring his words.

'Yeah, thanks to you,' I reply.

'Me?' he asks.

'Well, you introduced me to the Boss,' I say.

'But you made the big impression on him,' he answers, raising his eyebrows at me suggestively.

'Did I?' I say, pumping him for more information.

Gazza swills his lager down. 'You know you did. He raves about you every time I see him. I knew he was going to like you.'

I grin to myself, happy that the Boss talks highly of me. I down the contents of my glass. 'So, how long are you allowed out?'

'All night. She's staying at her mum's in Oldham. Taken the kids with her,' he says with a grin, obviously happy to be free for a night.

Thank God I haven't got any appointments tomorrow morning. I reckon this is going to be quite a session.

The peroxide landlady starts to ring her brass bell. 'Time, gentlemen, please.'

'Hungry?' I ask.

'Fucking starving,' he answers.

'Kebab!' we both shout at once.

★

144

We lean against the grimy glass of the kebab shop, faces covered in chilli sauce.

'Got beers in the fridge,' Gazza drunkenly announces.

I look over at him in a drunken haze. 'Well, they won't be there tomorrow.'

Gazza grins at me. 'Got something else to show you as well.'

I look at him curiously, wondering what he means. We begin to stagger along the pavement, ricocheting off each other every few steps.

Gazza slides back the UPVC patio doors of his council house, and practically falls out on to the patio. He puts the cans of beer he is holding on to the white plastic patio table, and slumps into the chair next to it. I fall out on to the patio after him, dropping my can of beer in the process.

We look over at each other and put our fingers on our lips. 'Ssssssh.'

We both start laughing hysterically. Through my blurred vision, I notice an empty child's paddling pool lying on the grass. I walk over to it and lie in it, using the side as a head rest. I look up at the sky. For once the stars are visible on the Manchester skyline. The moon is full and looks a lot like the one from ET. It's a very hot summer's evening. I could just nod off here in this paddling pool, it is so comfortable.

Gazza throws me another can of lager and holds his can up to me. 'To old times.'

'Old times,' I repeat, as I open the can and also hold it up in the air.

'Fuck, it's hot,' he says.

He zips down his overall to reveal his smooth muscly chest and obligatory gold chain. I stare at it, thinking back to when I used to let him shag me as if I was his bird. I so clearly remember that huge chest leaning over me as he pumped away. Well, that's what mates were for in the army, helping each other out in their hour of need.

Gazza looks over at me. 'So, how's your love life then?

I turn to face him. 'Nonexistent. I'm too busy with Sureforce to have one of them.'

'So you ain't got a bird?'

I shake my head in reply.

'A bloke?'

I shake it again.

Gazza shakes his head in disbelief. 'What a waste. A looker like you going spare.'

He scrunches up his empty beer can and throws it into the bushes at the end of the garden. 'You know me and Jules are happy, and I'm not that way inclined . . . but I'd be with you if I wasn't straight, matey.'

I smile over at him, knowing it's his roundabout way of telling me I'm really shaggable. He picks up another can and opens it. He puts his head back on the chair and looks up at the stars.

I stare over at him. He looks even hornier in blurred vision than he does normally. He still has an oil mark on his chest from where he has been rolling under some car at the garage.

I suddenly realise that I really want him again. I know this is probably the last time that we are going to be together like this in a long while. Jules and the kids are always around when I visit him usually. We haven't had a shag in two years. I know I could tempt him for a session before he got married (he even fucked me in the loos of a strip bar on his stag night), but now he is actually married, it is probably a different story. I continue to stare longingly at his bronzed chest. I should just go for it. He's too fucking pissed to remember that I tried something on if it all goes horribly wrong.

He suddenly puts down his can of lager and pulls himself up from the chair. 'I need to go up for a slash.'

I stare at him, thinking this could be my opportunity. 'Do it down here.'

'What, here in the garden?' he says, wondering why I've suggested that.

'No, over me,' I say brazenly, not wanting to miss out on the chance of having my Gazza near me again.

He looks down at me lying in the paddling pool, and laughs loudly. 'What are you fucking on, Matty?'

'Nothing,' I say. 'It's just something that I've always wanted someone to do to me.'

Gazza realises that I am not joking around. 'You fucking perv!' He thinks to himself, swaying back and forth. 'Well, you used to help me out in the army, so I suppose I owe you one.'

Knowing that Gazza is up for it, my cock starts to stir in my trousers. I quickly pull my T-shirt over my head before he changes his mind. I unzip my jeans and pull them off along with my underpants. The hot summer air next to my skin makes me feel really horny. I rub my hands over my smooth chest, looking up at Gazza from the paddling pool.

He looks down at me. 'Are you sure you're not joking?'

I shake my head. 'Come on, Gaz, you must be bursting by now. You've practically drunk Manchester dry.'

He turns around and looks up at the neighbours' bedroom windows, checking that nobody is watching.

'It's half one,' I remind him, trying to reassure him that nobody will be awake.

He slowly begins to zip his open overalls right the way down. As the material parts completely, I get a glimpse of his forest of dark pubic hair.

He looks at me, sobering slightly. 'You sure about this?'

'Just piss,' I shout, desperate to feel his hot, steaming urine on my naked body.

He moves his hands inside his overalls and brings out his cock, the cock that I have had endless wanks over since leaving the army. It's even bigger than I remember, and that's totally flaccid. He grabs his tool in his hand and aims it at me. I cannot believe that he is actually going to do it. I've always had wanks about someone pissing over me, but my fantasy has never become reality – until now.

Gazza's grin slowly disappears as he stares down at my naked body. I notice his dick growing slightly. Shit, he is actually getting turned on. Nice one!

Before I can prepare myself, a stream of his bright-yellow piss begins to shower down on me. I groan as the warm liquid hits my cock and balls. My meat begins to grow larger as I smell the aroma of his lager-filled urine.

Gazza steps nearer the paddling pool, a stream of piss still pouring out of his pipe. He starts moving his cock all around, making sure he has soaked all of my body. His bright-yellow piss continues to pour out of his dick as he stands there using me as a urinal.

As he continues to pump out the gallons of lager he has drunk, his urine starts to fill the bottom of the paddling pool. My cock grows to its fully erect size, turned on by the thought of just bathing in his piss.

He eventually finishes pissing and shakes his cock all over me. I lean forward and start to lick the droplets of piss from his bell-end. His urine-sodden meat begins to grow in my mouth.

He suddenly pulls it out and looks down at me. 'Upstairs. I've got something to show you.'

Gazza flings open the bedroom door, his overalls still unzipped to the crotch. I walk into the room wearing just a towel around my waist. The curtains are wide open, and moonlight streams in, acting as a subtle lighting. Gazza turns on the main light, and the whole room is illuminated. As I inspect the walls of the room, I soon realise that it is his kids' bedroom. Brightly painted pictures cover the walls, and boxes of games and books fill the shelves. Gazza nods over at the bunk beds in the corner of the room. I look over at the brightly painted wooden structure, not sure of exactly what he wants me to look at.

He walks over to the bunk beds and strokes the wood caringly. 'Recognise them?'

I inspect the bunks more closely. 'Shit! They're not! They can't be the ones from the barracks, can they?'

Gazza nods his head. 'Yep, the very ones. They were knocking the old dormitories down. Sergeant Whatto gave me a ring to see if I wanted them for the kids.'

I touch the bunks, not quite believing that they are the same ones.

'I've put new mattresses on them. Wouldn't want my kids to

have as uncomfortable a night's sleep as we used to,' he says. 'Still, we used to have some fun on them, didn't we?'

I nod, my cock stirring under the towel from just thinking about what we used to get up to. Gazza suddenly jumps up on to the top bunk. The whole structure bags against the wall as it wobbles under his weight.

'Lights out, soldier,' he shouts, imitating our old sergeant major.

I turn off the main light, and the whole room darkens, the full moon acting as subtle lighting once again. I notice the whites of Gazza's eyes as he looks down at me. He confidently sits on the edge of the top bunk with his legs dangling over the side. His overalls hang open, and I can make out one of his erect nipples in the moonlight. It has been so long since I've felt that strong chest on top of me. I want him so much. I just hope he's capable of performing after all of that lager.

'You going to be my bird tonight, soldier?' he asks, slurring his words.

I walk over to the bunk beds and stand in front of him, my head directly in line with his crotch. He looks down at me from his position on the top bunk. He slowly reaches into his overalls and yanks out his flaccid knob. He holds it in his hand, wanting me to give it some attention.

I lean forward and take the tip of his long, soft flesh in my mouth. He lets go of it and leans back on the top bunk. His overalls open further to expose his incredibly well-developed pecs. The moonlight casts shadows from his nipples over his huge chest. Ex-squaddies always seem to keep themselves in shape. Must be the discipline you have drummed into you when you are in the army. Still, I'm not complaining. I'd lick a squaddie's hard chest any day of the week.

I move my mouth down further over his cock and feel it rapidly expand in my mouth. The towel that is wrapped around my waist begins to rise as my growing cock pushes it up.

Gazza looks down at the fat base of his cock that is sticking out of my mouth. I begin to move my head up and down over his shaft, wanting to get him even harder. I feel more blood being pumped into his meat. I suddenly remember that you can always rely on Gazza getting a hard on, even when he has been on one of his three-day drinking binges.

As I continue to slide my wet tongue around his helmet, he reaches down and pulls off the towel that hangs around my waist. He looks over my shoulder to get an eyeful of my smooth arse. I clench my buttocks tightly together, wanting to make it look as pert as it possibly can. I imagine what it must look like in the moonlight. It must look pretty hot, judging by the way his cock is now rock hard in my mouth.

He leans forward and grabs my head with his strong hands. He rubs them all over my cropped hair. His wife's is long and fine, so it must be a refreshing change touching mine. A change that he is obviously enjoying.

He runs his hands down my neck and back until he reaches the tops of my buttocks. He leans forward even more to allow himself to get a good grip of each cheek. I feel my cock swell even more as I lick and suck his knob frenziedly. I reach for his nipples and start to pull on the bulletlike lumps. He groans and rubs my arse even harder.

He suddenly jumps down from the top bunk; the structure bangs against the wall as it wobbles under his weight. He stands next to me with his hard nipples and cock proudly sticking out of his overalls. I yank the overalls over his shoulders, and they fall to the floor, revealing his huge, muscly biceps and firm thighs.

He grabs me by the waist and, with his great strength, throws me over the top bunk. I land across the width of the mattress, face down in the brightly coloured duvet. My arse sticks up in the air, and my legs hang down over the side.

I suddenly feel his warm tongue come in contact with the back of my smooth thigh. It starts to wander towards my winking hole. I grab hold of the duvet as I feel his tongue making its way nearer my crack. Fuck! He certainly knows what to do with it. I bet he makes his missis come without even having to put his dick anywhere near her.

His hard tongue eventually reaches my crack, and his strong hands part my buttocks. I flinch as I feel the tip of his wet flesh circle my hole. I grab the duvet tighter as my arse starts twitching for more.

Realising he is really getting me worked up, he starts to lick my hole repeatedly. He digs his erect tongue into my passage, parting my juicy, pink lips.

I hear him groan as he deliriously starts to eat his Matty. It could be his wife's cunt for all he knows, he is so pissed. He just needs an orifice. Any orifice.

My arse begins to relax even more, and he moves further up inside me. My cock hardens, sandwiched between my stomach and the duvet. Who would have thought I'd end up lying on our old bunk beds getting licked out by my best mate. I thought that had all stopped. I'm not going to be able to look his wife in the face for a while.

His tongue suddenly leaves my arse and the bunks shake as I feel him sit on the lower bed. He grabs hold of my ankles and starts to pull me forward. I grab hold of the edge of the mattress to make sure I do not fall.

He continues to pull my legs downward, until they are either side of his body. My face reaches the edge of the top bunk, and I grab hold of the wooden frame. My biceps flex as they support the whole of my weight.

I suddenly feel his mouth clamp around my cock. He moves his head up and down on it, hungry for some meat after not tasting any for a while. His wrist bangs into the bottom of my arse as he starts to wank his knob behind me.

He releases my cock from his mouth and pulls my arse down further, until my ring is hovering over his helmet. He reaches into his overalls on the floor and pulls out a condom. Dirty bastard must have known I was going to be up for a shag. He quickly pulls the condom out of the packet and gobs into it.

He begins to roll it down over his rock-hard cock. 'Sit on it!'

I place my feet on the bottom mattress, either side of his stocky body. Grabbing hold of the top bunk tightly, I start to lower my ring down over his dick.

I grit my teeth as his fat tool stretches my arse cheeks apart. He lets go of his knob and grabs hold of my firm, flat waist. As he pulls me down even further over his dick, my face moves past the top mattress, and our eyes meet. He stares at me longingly.

'My Matty,' he says softly.

My arse engulfs his knob until I am practically sat on his lap. We stare at each other in silence, his knob throbbing violently inside me.

He leans forward and starts chewing on my nipples. My hard cock presses against his firm stomach. His tongue works on my hard lumps of flesh, saliva dribbling out of his mouth and on to my pecs. I clamp my arse around his swollen meat, wanting to get him even harder.

Once I have felt more blood being pumped into his dick, I grab hold of the top bunk and start to pull myself off his meat. My juiced-up arse starts to slide up over his cock. He puts his hand under my arse and feels my rim as it slides off his length.

I pull my arse up until I've just got his big bell-end inside me. He grabs hold of my waist and tries to pull me back down over his meat. I grab the top bunk tighter, not letting him have my arse again yet. Frustrated, he continues to try and pull my waist down, but I arsetease him by keeping it hovering in the air.

Once I am sure I've really got him going, I thrust my whole body down over his cock. He helps to force me down, wanting his cock back inside me.

I begin pulling myself up and down on him, really riding his fat meat. He grabs my waist, throwing his head back in ecstasy. The bunk beds begin to bang loudly against the bedroom wall.

'Oh yeah! Ride it, Matty,' he yells.

I close my eyes and continue to lever myself down on to him, the splinters from the rough wood digging into my hands. I begin to smell the strong smell of bleach that used to waft through our army dormitories. I suddenly hear an army of marching soldiers coming from the parade ground outside the window. The soldiers' footsteps quicken to the loud instructions of the sergeant major. I open my eyes as I continue to plunge down on Gazza's dick. The dormitory is empty and silent apart from the sound of our creaking bunk bed.

Gazza's combat pants hang round his ankles, and his army shirt hangs off his shoulders. His shiny dog tags hang down between his sweaty, brown pecs.

My combat pants still hang off one ankle as I sit astride him. My green army vest is rolled up, and the chain from my dog tag is caught around one of my hard tits.

I lever myself up and down on Gazza's fat dick as if I were doing pull-ups in the exercise yard outside.

As he continues to pummel me, the bunk bed rocks back and forth. The mops that had been leaning against them fall to the floor with a bang. We are supposed to be on cleaning duty, but Gazza wanted me to read him the letter he had got from Julie that morning. He spent his school days bunking off, so he never got to read and write. He hasn't even told Julie. Anyway, the contents of her letter turned out to be extremely explicit, and he got really turned on. He asked if he could use my arse again, pretending it was Julie's cunt. Being his best mate, of course, I had to oblige. Well, what are best mates for?

The sergeant major in the parade ground shouts even louder, as if he was instructing Gazza to pump me harder. He starts to groan louder, his voice filling the empty dormitory. I let go of the top bunk with one hand and pull on his hard tits.

His cock starts to really throb inside me as I feel him empty his huge load.

'Oh, Julie, Julie,' he yells loudly.

At that point the parade ground falls silent, and Gazza's voice flows out of the open windows and echoes all around the parade ground.

Spunk suddenly starts to shoot out of my hard cock and spray all over his chest. Stream after stream of my youthful come pumps out and hangs off his shiny dog tags. My arse clamps around his cock. I close my eyes as I continue to shoot.

Imagining the army of soldiers running into the dormitory to see what is going on, I quickly snap open my eyes. I realise that I am back in the kids' bedroom, holding on to the same bunk. I look down to see Gazza beneath me, still thrusting his cock up into me.

He grabs hold of my knob and starts wanking it as I continue to slide up and down on his pole. He stares at my smooth six-pack and touches it with his other hand. The bunk bed creaks and bangs loudly against the wall, as I really start to pull my arse up and down on his dick.

He suddenly pulls me off his tool and stands up. He pulls my feet from the mattress and down on to the ground. He stands behind me and pushes my head and arms over the top bunk. Grabbing hold of his fully erect dick, he shoves it straight back up my arse.

As he thrusts it right the way up, he leans over me. I feel his rock-hard nipples digging into my back, and he groans loudly in my ear.

As he starts to bang it in and out of my arse, I stick my head in the duvet, muffling my loud groans. The bunk bed bangs loudly against the wall with every thrust. He'll be waking up the neighbours if he's not careful.

He grabs my waist tightly and starts pumping me faster. As he leans over me even further, I can smell the stench of lager on his breath. I grab hold of my dick and start wanking it, nearly ready to come.

Gazza's hands move up past my waist and grab on to my erect nipples. As soon as he starts to pull on them, I feel my balls tighten.

With one of my tits in each of his hands, Gazza really starts to screw me. The bunk beds hit the wall even louder. Someone starts banging the wall from next door, obviously trying to get some sleep.

Gazza ignores them and keeps slamming into me. I give my cock a few last tugs before my come shoots out and flies all over the duvet covering the bottom bed. As Gazza continues to ride me, more and more of my fuck juice flies out on to the bed. He looks over my shoulder at my young spunk flying through the air.

Once my cock has finished squirting, he pulls his hard cock out of me and throws me down on to the bottom bunk, eager to get back in me. My back lands on the spunk-covered duvet, and I feel my hot semen slide all over my muscly back.

He lifts my legs into the air and jams my feet into the ladders that are either end of the wooden frame. He looks down at my pink hole, my arse cheeks stretched apart. I stare at Gazza in the moonlight. Fuck, he's horny. He wanks his cock, getting it ready for my hole again. The muscles in his right arm flex to maximum size as he tugs on his veiny meat.

He kneels on the edge of the bottom bunk and pulls my arse towards him. He slides his cock right back up my hungry hole. My cock starts to grow again as his helmet rubs against the root of it inside.

He grabs hold of my firm thighs and begins to pump me again. His head and shoulders are above the top bunk, so all I can see of him is his hard chest and muscly, thrusting six-pack. He shoves his pelvis back and forth, his hairy nuts banging against my arse.

I suddenly hear a bang coming from downstairs. Gazza doesn't notice and continues to fuck me in a drunken stupor. I hear someone climbing up the stairs. Shit, it better not be Julie. There is a knock on the bedroom door, and it is slowly pushed open.

'Gaz, can you keep the noise down, mate,' says a deep male voice.

In the light of the moon, I make out a bloke wearing a white dressing gown. He stands in the doorway, trying to work out what is going on as his eyes acclimatise to the dim light.

'Gaz, is that you?' asks the man.

'Yeah, come over here, Pete,' he says, snapping out of his drunken state.

'Your front door was open, mate,' says the man as he walks across the room. 'Wondered what you were up to.'

As the bloke reaches the bunk beds, he peers over Gazza's shoulder. He watches Gazza's cock sliding in and out of my arse.

'So that's what you're doing,' he exclaims. 'You randy little fucker.'

Gazza bangs into me even harder, getting even more turned on by the fact that he is being watched. The neighbour starts to undo the belt of his towelling dressing gown. It falls open to reveal a completely hairy stomach and chest. From my position on the bottom bunk, I cannot see the neighbour's head and shoulders because of the top bunk.

The neighbour reaches for his rapidly growing cock and starts to wank it quickly. He slaps his other hand on to Gazza's arse and pushes him further into me.

'Go on, Gaz, fill the little fucker up!' he shouts, encouraging Gazza to pump me harder.

The neighbour's meat is now rock hard, and he walks around to the side of the bunk beds. He sticks his cock between the two end supports, hoping that I'm going to give him a suck.

As I take his long knob into my mouth, my dick starts to grow hard again. He starts to pump my mouth in time with Gazza pumping my arse. My tongue moves up and down over his hairy shaft.

I watch both of their headless and shoulderless bodies as they bang their cocks into both of my fuck holes. My cock grows solid, imagining them egging each other on over the top bunk.

Gazza groans loudly.

'Go on, boy,' the neighbour yells.

Gazza pushes my legs as far apart as they will go as he pumps me the fastest he has ever pumped me.

'Yeah, give it to him, Gaz,' the neighbour shouts, apparently trying to wake the whole street.

With that, Gazza pulls his dick out of my man–cunt and yanks the condom off it. He pumps it violently with his fist.

The neighbour pulls his rigid cock out of my mouth and starts tugging on his as well. He aims it directly over me. With synchronised moans, Gazza and the neighbour's cocks start to spurt their come all over me. Thick, white semen flies from all directions and slaps down on my smooth, firm body.

I start to wipe it into my chest, cock and balls. Another few streams squirt out of the neighbour's tool and smack me in the mouth. I stick my tongue out and lick his salty come off my lips and chin. I watch all of the muscles in their bodies flex as their moonlit cocks continue to fire out even more fuck juice.

Gazza eventually finishes shooting and leans over the top bunk, knackered and pissed. The neighbour pulls his dressing gown over his spunk-covered cock and ties it back up.

He walks towards the door. 'Later.'

I listen to his footsteps fading into the distance as I fall into a drunken slumber, still covered in thick come.

Loud birdsong vibrates around my head. I quickly snap open my eyes, then just as quickly close them again, protecting them from the intense brightness. Slowly, I begin to open them up once again. Sun streams in through the large window. Birds tweet happily (and annoyingly) outside.

My head bangs, and my mouth tastes like a sewer. Where the hell am I? I look above me and see the bottom of a mattress. I suddenly have a vague flashback from the night before.

I slowly lift my head and look down at my naked body. I stare at the patches of dry spunk that have set all over my body. I notice the brightly coloured duvet under me and realise that I am in a child's bedroom.

I look up at the springs above me. I suddenly notice a hand hanging over the side of the top bunk. A chunky gold wedding ring sits on the person's ring finger. Having been Gazza's best man, I'd recognise his wedding ring anywhere. I hear him quietly snoring above me. I look down at the floor and notice his oily overalls. That means he must be lying above me naked.

Forgetting all about my hangover, I slowly lift myself up off the bed and start to climb the wooden ladder that leads to the top bunk. Well, it's the last time I'm going to have an opportunity like this in a long while.

Twelve

Three revolving searchlights shine high into the night sky. The beams are so strong, they can be seen for miles. They are positioned on the roof of the Boss's new bar. They seem to be attracting a huge crowd of partygoers. It's just a shame none of them are going to get in. It is the grand opening tonight, VIP invites only. The lord mayor is even going to be there.

As I walk along Canal Street towards the new bar, the pounding music grows louder and louder. In the distance I spot a sea of Sureforce bomber jackets. The Boss has got every available Sureforce security guard working tonight. He wants to make sure it goes as smoothly as possible. He doesn't want the Moss Side gangs trying to muscle their way in.

I reach the large doorway. A sign made up of huge neon letters spelling out the word TOKYO sits above the door.

One of the bouncers suddenly notices me. 'Hey, Matty. How are you doing? The Boss has been looking for you.'

The Boss has actually noticed I'm not there yet. Excellent. I nod over at the group of bouncers as I walk through the doorway. I quite miss the camaraderie of working the doors. It can be quite lonely being company rep.

I walk into the huge, packed bar. Wow, it is really buzzing. Up until now, I've only seen it in the day with builders and painters in it. With subtle lighting and glamorous partygoers, it looks a completely different place.

High on a platform above the thronging crowd is an outrageously dressed DJ. He is throwing his arms in the air to the records he is playing.

The Boss has laid on free booze all night, so there are going to be some alcohol casualties later. Some pissed guests have already started to dance, turning a corner of the bar into their very own dance floor.

I make my way to the bar through the crowds of Mancunian liggers. It is full of the same old faces who would turn up to the opening of a fucking envelope. I eventually reach the bar and get served by what must be the cutest barman in Manchester. The Boss certainly knows how to pick his staff.

As I take a sip of my bottled beer, I sense that someone is watching me. I turn to face the figure. Stood surrounded by his bunch of cronies is the Boss, staring directly at me. Judging by his huge grin, it looks like he has had a few to drink already.

He bursts through his entourage and walks over to me. He puts his arm around my shoulders and pulls me close to him.

'So, what do you think?' he shouts, slightly slurring his words.

'You were right: it's the hottest bar in Manchester,' I reply.

I suddenly notice Twinny stood on the balcony above the bar. His twin brother Dave stands next to him. Twinny stares daggers at me, obviously noticing the Boss's arm around me. I smile a sarcastic smile, wanting to piss him off as much as I possibly can.

The Boss's dollybird girlfriend suddenly bursts through the crowd and walks up to us. She stands in front of us dancing on the spot, wearing next to nothing.

'Top, innit!' she squeals in her thickest Mancunian accent.

She grabs hold of the Boss's hand and starts to drag him off. 'Come and meet some of me mates.'

The Boss smiles back at me as he is dragged away. 'Have a good one, Matty.'

Why the fuck did his bird have to be here? I reckon he would have been well up for a piece of my arse tonight. I notice Twinny looking down at me with a smug expression on his face. I lean back against the bar to get out of his view.

I begin to entertain myself by checking out the barman's cute arse. I get a perfect view every time he bends over to get a bottle of beer out of the fridge.

The crowd let out a huge appreciative yell as the DJ starts to play one of the latest dance records. Virtually everybody in the bar begins to dance. People stand on tables and chairs, throwing their arms in the air to the beat of the rhythm.

I suddenly notice one person who isn't moving to the music. It looks like he is too busy watching me. He leans against the far wall, watching my every move. It is pretty dark in the bar, so I can't quite see his face. I can just about make out that he looks quite tall and has dark, slicked-back hair. Our eyes suddenly meet, and I quickly look away. I don't want to go getting into a fight with a straight lad on the Boss's opening night. That is the last thing he wants when he is trying to create the coolest bar in town.

From the corner of my eye I can see the guy still staring over at me. He suddenly puts down his glass and starts to walk over towards me. Shit, here we go. I put my bottle of beer down on the bar and clench my fists in preparation. He is probably well pissed up on free booze and is looking for a scrap.

Still peering from the corner of my eye, I can see him getting nearer and nearer. He eventually reaches me and stands about a foot away.

'You don't recognise me, do you?' he shouts over the music.

I suddenly recognise that Irish accent and slowly turn to face him. I stare into his twinkly green eyes. I look at his handsome face, racking my brains trying to remember where I have met him before.

'The Oakwood Hotel,' he reminds me. 'I'm the doorman.'

Shit, that's it. I had given him a VIP ticket for tonight when I left the hotel. I had forgotten all about that. I can't believe he has turned up. I feel slightly embarrassed that I did not recognise him. He looks so different out of his uniform. His Fred Perry top and jeans make him look even hornier.

He nods at the bottle stood on the bar in front of me. 'Fancy another?'

I nod. He leans over the bar next to me. I check out his firm, muscly little arse. The cute barman serves him, flirting his arse off. I realise just how horny this guy is. His Irish accent certainly helps as well.

He turns around and hands me the bottle of beer. 'We weren't properly introduced before, were we?' He holds his hand out towards me. 'Mick.'

I grab his hand tightly and shake it firmly. 'Matt.'

'I don't make a habit of doing that with all the guests staying at the hotel,' he says.

'Doing what?'

'Shagging them. Mr Wheland has been coming to the hotel for years. Flopping your dick out for him is an easy way of making fifty quid. Everyone wants to work the shifts when he is staying. Even the completely straight lads.'

As he talks to me, I begin to remember that meeting in the hotel. I remember the size of his dick as he fucked my client's face. Wouldn't mind having a bit of it to myself.

I look around at the bar that seems to be getting even more packed out with clubbers. The cute barman stocks up the fridges to try and keep up with the demand. He looks over at me and Mick getting acquainted. I smile at him; he looks away, embarrassed.

I turn to Mick, who is knocking back his beer. 'It's a bit loud and hot in here. Fancy some fresh air?'

Mick nods approvingly. We make our way through the pissed crowd. I reach a door with a fire-exit sign above it. A huge bouncer stands in front of it, wearing his thick Sureforce bomber jacket. Sweat drips down his forehead.

'All right, Matty,' he says, suddenly noticing me.

'We need some air, Kev,' I inform him.

He pushes down the bar on the door, and it swings open. 'Just give us a knock when you want to get back in.'

As I walk past the bouncer, he gives me a knowing wink. Mick follows me through the doorway, and the bouncer slams the door behind us. The loud music turns into a quiet thud.

I walk along the dirty yard of the bar. It leads to a huge wooden door. On the other side of this door is Canal Street. We can hear a stream of partygoers laughing and shouting from the other side of the door. Rolls of barbed wire are fixed above it to prevent anyone getting on to the premises.

We reach two large, industrial waste bins on metallic castors. To the side of the bins is a door marked KEEP CLEAR. I lean against one of the bins and take a swig from my bottle. Mick leans against the wall next to me. Shouts and laughter continue to drift over the top of the doorway as people leave and arrive at the bar.

Mick stares at me. 'So, you glad I came?'

'Yeah, it's good to see you.'

'Would you like to see a bit more of me?'

'Sorry?' I ask, not sure what he means.

He nods down at his crotch. 'Would you like to see a bit more?'

Thank God he means his dick. For a moment there I thought he was asking me if I wanted a relationship with him. I nod my head to his question. He knocks back the contents of his bottle and throws it in the industrial bin. It smashes on the bottles that are already piled up in there.

He leans against the wall and thrusts his crotch forward. 'Help yourself.'

I down the contents of my own bottle and chuck it in the bin. I reach over and start to undo his button-fly jeans. I love a good wanking session out in the open air. My cock starts to twitch just thinking about it. He stares at me, grinning every time I pull a button through one of his buttonholes.

Once they are all undone, I pull open his jeans. I untuck his Fred Perry top and notice that he isn't wearing any underwear. I stare at his forest of jet-black pubic hair. I reach into his jeans and pull out his flaccid cock. Fuck, it's even bigger than I had remembered.

I start to slowly wank it, feeling his meat rapidly growing in my hand. He grabs hold of my head and runs his hands all over my cropped hair. He tries to force me down on his cock, but I keep my head firmly where it is. I'm not letting him think I will suck him just like that.

As I continue to wank him, I start to unzip my trousers. I flop my hard dick out and wank us both off at the same time. I let go of his cock and grab hold of his head. I try and push him down on me, but he isn't having any of it. So, we both want to be in control. I think we've a bit of a stalemate on our hands. Oh well, at least we can just have a wank together.

He grabs hold of his now fully erect meat and starts to pump it with his fist. I open my jeans fully and pull out my balls. I start to wank myself off slowly. We stare at each other as we both tug on our juicy, thick cocks.

I move my spare hand up under his Fred Perry top. I feel my way through his thick chest hair, and eventually reach one of his rock-hard nipples. I flick it with my fingers. He lets go of his cock for a minute and pulls the front of his top over his head. His arms and shoulders remain inside the shirt, but his huge pecs stand out bare and proud. His nipples stick out like football studs. Not being able to resist them, I lean forward and take one of the hard lumps in my mouth. I start to chew on the fleshy tit, still wanking my rigid cock.

The door marked KEEP CLEAR next to the waste bins suddenly opens. We both freeze, cocks in hand. Over the top of the bins I see the cute barman who served us earlier. He is carrying a pile of empty boxes. He throws them in the industrial bins and turns to go back inside. As he is about to pull the door back closed, he suddenly notices the top of my head. He stops what he is doing and stares over at me. He slowly walks back into the alley, closing the door behind him.

As he begins to make his way around the rubbish bins, he realises that I am holding my dick in my hand. He looks down at my rigid length, obviously impressed. As he moves closer, he suddenly spots Mick leaning against the wall. He stares at his huge, exposed chest and pre-come-covered cock. He looks back and forth at us, suddenly realising that he has interrupted something. He turns around and heads back towards the door.

'Wait!' I shout.

He turns to face me. I nod down at my dick. He is perfect. He is just what we both need. I reckon he'd be a good little cocksucker. He begins to walk back towards me. He crouches down in front of me and takes my hard cock in his cute mouth. Feeling the warmth of his mouth around it, my cock starts to have more blood pumped into it.

Mick starts wanking his cock even harder, getting turned on from watching the barman sucking me off. The barman reaches over to Mick's dick as he continues to lick my fat bell-end. He takes it in his hand and begins to wank it furiously. He moves his mouth from around my meat and begins to wank mine as well.

He stares at both of our dicks in his hands as he continues to try and wank our come out of them. I sort of guessed that he would be a bit of a cock worshipper.

Mick grabs the barman's head and forces his mouth down further over his cock. I reach over and pull on Mick's tits as the barman really begins to eat his big Irish cock. His hand pumps my foreskin back and forth as he slurps greedily on Mick.

I move over closer to Mick, our cocks almost touching. The barman moves his mouth off Mick's dick and on to mine. Mick reaches under my T-shirt and begins to pull on my tits. They quickly become erect as I watch my cock sliding in and out of the barman's mouth, stretching it to its limit.

Mick reaches down and pulls the barman's arse into the air as I keep his mouth down around my knob. He reaches under the barman's white apron and undoes his trousers. With one tug, he pulls them down around his knees, his white apron staying tied around his waist. The apron parts slightly at the back, revealing the beautiful, dark crack of the barman's young arse.

Mick starts rubbing the barman's arse as he continues to wank himself off. Getting turned on by having his arse played with, the barman begins to suck me even harder. He reaches up under my T-shirt and grabs hold of my firm nipples, the cool night air making them the hardest they have ever felt. I thrust my pelvis back and forth, slowly fucking his face.

Mick reaches into the top pocket of his Fred Perry and pulls out a condom. I reckon that originally had my name written on it.

The cocky sod. He tears it open and slides it over his knob, wanting to get the job over with as quickly as he can.

He gobs down on his covered knob and rubs his phlegm all around it. He pulls the barman's arse cheeks apart with one hand and thrusts his cock straight up him with the other. The barman makes a muffled groan, still sucking on my cock. He didn't expect to have a dick shoved straight up there like that. Must be used to it though: it certainly went up without much difficulty.

Mick grabs hold of the barman's waist and starts pumping his cock. It disappears through the gap in the barman's apron and straight up his hairless man-cunt. The barman starts sucking on me even more, loving getting fucked up the arse. I look over at Mick's huge chest, his tits protruding from the hairy forest on his chest. His nipples seem to grow harder and harder as he continues to bum the barman. I reach over and grab Mick's nipples in both hands. I feel his rigid lumps of flesh in between my fingers.

Mick starts to pump the barman even harder, just wanting to shoot his load. The barman's head gets pushed further into my groin as Mick stabs him harder with every thrust. I grab on to the barman's head and hold it still as my dick slides in and out of his mouth.

Mick suddenly rams forward extremely hard, and the barman bangs into me. I fall against the fire-exit door behind me with a crash. Mick carries on fucking the lad, completely oblivious to what is happening. The bar on the other side of the fire-exit door is pushed down and the door swings open.

The rough-looking bouncer sticks his head out of the door. 'You ready to come in, Matty?'

He suddenly freezes on the spot as he clocks the scene in front of him. Shit, we've been caught. He had better not say anything to the Boss, or I'll be in big trouble. I stare at Kev the bouncer, not sure what he is going to do. He steps into the alleyway and closes the door behind him, keeping it slightly ajar so that he can get back in.

'Mind if I join you?' he asks, unzipping his jeans.

He quickly flops his cock out and stands next to me. I stare down at his chunky little dick. He pulls the barman's head off my meat and forces him down on his. The barman starts sucking his cock, wanting to get it to grow as quickly as possible.

Realising the bouncer is up for a bit as well, I start to wank my dick again. Mick pulls the barman's arse back towards him and begins pumping his cunt. I look down at the bouncer's knob. It is now fully erect, and the barman is gobbling the chunky length in his mouth.

I pull the barman's head off the bouncer's cock and force him back down on to mine. As the barman begins to eat me, I grab hold of the bouncer's cock and begin to wank him.

Mick starts groaning loudly, obviously nearly coming. I feel my balls tighten and my spunk begin to rise. I shove the barman's head back over the bouncer's dick, wanting him to come at the same time as us. The barman sucks hungrily on the bouncer's meat, wanting to taste his manly fuck juice.

As Mick continues to poke his cock up the barman's arse, I reach over and pull on his huge tits again. He starts pummelling the barman even harder, lifting his apron up to get a good look at his smooth cheeks. He raises his hand and slaps him hard across the arse. A red hand print is left on the lad's right buttock.

I wank my cock off aggressively, watching the barman sucking on the big bouncer. Mick watches me wanking my meat, sliding further up him with every thrust. The bouncer grabs the barman's small head with his huge hands. He begins to pump his cock into him ruthlessly.

The bouncer begins to groan loudly. Mick pulls his cock out of the barman's arse and pushes him against the plastic industrial waste bins. The barman stands facing the bins, his pert arse cheeks poking out of the parting apron at the back. Mick kicks his legs apart and pulls the apron over his arse cheeks so we can all get a good view. We all stand around the barman's arse in a semicircle, wanking our cocks furiously. The bouncer grabs hold of one of Mick's nipples, giving him a helping hand. We all look at each other wanking our pieces of meat, racing to see who can cover the lad's cheeks first. The barman looks over his shoulder at us all wanking away.

The bouncer puts one hand on the fire-exit door to prevent anyone from coming out. Mick grabs hold of my arse as his body starts to tense. With a huge groan, he suddenly releases a great spurt of hot cream over the barman's cute arse. As he continues to pump more of his come out with his fist, the bouncer starts to groan. A huge, long stream of white come shoots quickly out of his meat as well. The first huge spurt lands on the back of the barman's shirt, and the following few squirts slap down into his crack.

As I watch both sets of spunk dribbling down the lad's arse, I feel my semen ripping through my shaft. I point my knob at his arse as a long trail of thick, white cream flies out and lands on top of the barman's already spunk-covered arse. As I shoot more and more, the collection of spunk starts dribbling down the lad's inner thigh. He opens his legs wider to let it dribble down even more.

Not being able to stop himself, the bouncer grabs hold of the barman's arse with his huge hand and wipes the assorted shades of fuck juice all over his cheeks. He runs his hand right under the lad's crack, covering his balls with spunk. Once he has had his grope, he wipes his hand on the barman's apron and shoves his cock back into his pants. Mick shoves his still hard dick in his jeans and tucks in his Fred Perry. I wipe the end of my dick on the barman's apron and stuff it back inside my jeans.

Not wanting to wipe our fuck juice off, the barman pulls his trousers up over his spunk-covered arse. He grins cheekily at us all and walks back through the kitchen door that he came out of. That little cutey is going to be breaking some hearts in years to come.

The bouncer opens the fire-exit door. We all walk back into the stuffy, packed bar. The crowd seem a lot more drunk than ten minutes ago. The bouncer pulls the fire-exit door closed, looking around to check that nobody has seen us.

Mick holds out his hand towards me. 'Thanks for the invite, mate. See you again.'

I nod and shake his hand, more interested in trying to see where the Boss has gone. Realising I'm not really that interested in him, Mick disappears into the crowd. I look up at the balcony to see if Twinny is still around. There is no sign of him anywhere.

I begin to climb the metallic staircase towards the office. I notice the barman is now back behind the bar. He gives me a flirtatious smile as he pours a customer a pint of lager. I imagine our spunk sticking his trousers to his arse. I expect the Boss has already had him at his interview.

I reach the top of the stairs and push open the office door, hoping to see the Boss. Instead, sat in the office chair behind the desk is Twinny. He smiles at me smugly. I frown at him, not knowing why he is looking so pleased with himself.

He swivels around in his chair and presses a button on the security surveillance equipment. A video slowly slides out of a slot. Twinny reaches over and pulls it out completely.

He holds it up in the air. 'At last, all the evidence I need.'

I stare at the video and then over at the surveillance monitors. Twinny presses another button, and the monitors flicker on. Each screen displays a picture of the alleyway that we have all just had a wank in. Shit, he has got us all on tape. I can't believe I've been caught on security cameras again. And to think I'm in security. I should know that big brother is watching everything we do these days.

Twinny throws the tape in a drawer and locks it. 'I think the Boss may like to see that. I think he should know just what his Sureforce rep has been getting up to on the opening night of his bar.'

Just as I am about to dive on top of Twinny, the office door suddenly opens. We both turn around. Stood at the door is a very drunk-looking Boss.

He smiles at us both. 'What's happening, boys?'

Thirteen

Well, Twinny got just what he wanted. The Boss, all to himself. The sneaky little bastard showed him the video tape. The Boss wasn't very happy with me. He doesn't mind what I get up to off Sureforce premises, but he thought shagging a punter on the opening night was taking the piss. Especially when the lord mayor was literally feet away. I like to think that the Boss was a bit jealous really. I have kidded myself into thinking that he hates seeing other men touching me.

Anyway, Twinny blew it all out of proportion, surprise, surprise. I reckon the Boss would have just given me a telling-off and carried on as normal. But not Twinny. He had to go one step further. If it had been up to him, I would have been sacked. However, the Boss told him that I deserved a second chance, because of all the work I had put into making Sureforce what it is today. So, he gave me another option.

Since Sureforce now lead the market in security in the North-west, the Boss wants to see if he can establish his company further afield. He thought the Northeast would be as good a place to start as any. So, here I am, sat on the Intercity to Newcastle.

He wants me to get the ball rolling. I have got to set up an office and start making some appointments from a list of Northeast clients. It is a list that Twinny has managed to get his hands on. Probably got it from his dodgy Internet-provider friend.

I am picking up another car at the station. Twinny got his hands on my old one. He's decided he wants to be company rep in the Northwest now that all the hard work is done.

I am really going to miss seeing the Boss. I've got a sneaking feeling that he's going to miss me as well. I just wish Twinny was the one going to Newcastle. The Boss is clearly not interested in him any more. I am hoping he wants me as his boy.

I gaze out of the window at the fields that stretch for miles. I can't believe I've been sat on here for an hour without having a fag. All the carriages on this train are nonsmoking. The only thing that has taken my mind off it is the arse on the cute ticket collector. He must have walked past me about twenty times.

I stare out at the bleak moorlands. The last time I was out this way was when I was on a training weekend with the army. It looks quite picturesque when you are sat on a warm train, but it is bloody treacherous when you are actually out amongst it. In fact, I can honestly say I have never been so frightened in my life.

Once we had all checked in at base camp, we were given maps and had to all go our separate ways. The exercise was to make it to a certain checkpoint by nightfall. I wasn't very happy about it, as when I joined the army I thought I would be mainly undertaking physical training activities, not poncing around with a compass.

Anyway, I set off feeling pretty confident, but as the day progresses I feel myself getting well and truly lost. It has started to get really dark as well. I'm going to have to give up for today and start again tomorrow – I'm completely knackered.

I look for a piece of flat ground where I can pitch my tent. As I begin to unpack my rucksack, I notice a glow in the distance. As I strain my eyes, I realise that it is torch light coming from another tent. Maybe it is some sort of camp site.

I throw my rucksack back over my shoulder and head towards the light. I climb over a wooden fence and jump into the next field. As I walk across the field towards the glow, I suddenly realise that it is in fact a green army tent. Great, that means I am not the only sad fucker who has got lost. Must be someone from my barracks.

As I approach the tent, I notice the torch light is casting a silhouette of the person on to the canvas. As I look closer, I notice the man is jerking his arm quickly back and forth. Dirty little bastard is having a wank! They say that after a good day's trekking you often feel horny at night. Something to do with your adrenalin, apparently. I bet he is well up for a bit.

My cock suddenly starts twitching in my combats. I quietly slip my rucksack off my shoulders and place it on the ground. I pull open the buttons on my green army pants, still watching the silhouette of the bloke in the tent wanking himself stupid.

Once I have unbuttoned my trousers, I reach inside and flop out my dick. As soon as it is let out into the cold night air, it begins to harden rapidly. I take it in my fist and start to slowly milk it.

Before long, it has reached its full erect length. I quietly walk over to the door of the green canvas tent, still wanking it in my hand. I stand in between the two guy-ropes that are holding the metal frame up. The top of the one-man tent comes up to my stomach. I stand in front of the doorway and reach for its zip.

As I slowly pull the zip down from the top of the doorway, the person inside the tent freezes. They probably wonder what the fuck is going on. I suddenly have a vision of him stabbing me with the bayonet from his gun.

I quickly pull my dog tag from around my neck. I dangle it in through the small unzipped gap of the doorway. Once I am sure he has seen it, I pull it back out and stuff it in my pocket. I grab my rock-hard cock in my hand and slide it in through the gap in the doorway. I imagine the squaddie in the tent staring at my fat, purple helmet as it enters the tent.

Once I have slid my entire length through, I stand still, waiting to see if he is feeling horned up enough to give me a suck. Everything in the tent remains still. An owl starts to hoot in the distance. My nipples begin to grow and rub against the rough material of my uniform jumper. More blood pumps into my cock, making it twitch against the canvas door. I stand frozen to the spot, waiting to feel if I am going to get a nice, warm mouth around it.

I suddenly begin to realise that he probably isn't interested. In fact, he may be totally fucking disgusted. I begin to pull my cock back out of the tent before he discovers who it belongs to. As I continue to pull it out, I suddenly hear his sleeping bag unzip. I hear the groundsheet rustle as the person crawls towards the door of the tent. I stand still, the tip of my knob still inside the tent.

As I picture a rough little squaddie crawling towards my meat, my cock hardens. I suddenly feel a warm tongue come into contact with my throbbing bell-end. I stick the whole of my knob right in through the doorway. As the man begins to get a little more brave, he takes my cock into his mouth. I close my eyes, totally turned on by the experience of having my cock licked by someone I haven't even seen.

I grab hold of the tent's guy-ropes to steady myself as the squaddie moves his mouth right over the length of my meat. I groan quietly, not wanting him to recognise my voice.

I look down at the base of my cock disappearing in through the doorway. I try to imagine what the hungry squaddie's lips look like clamped around my dick. I grab the guy-ropes tighter as he really starts to pump his head up and down on me.

I reach under my heavy army jacket and start playing with one of my nipples. Thanks to the cold night air and the sucking squaddie, it hardens immediately.

I look through the canvas of the tent and see the silhouette of the squaddie on all fours. His arm moves quickly back and forth as he starts to beat his dick off again.

He suddenly pulls his mouth from my knob. I look down at the unzipped door to try and get a glimpse at what he is doing. His large helmet suddenly emerges through the canvas doorway. He must be knelt at the doorway.

I stare at his meaty little cock in the moonlight. I crouch down on my hands and knees and take him in my mouth. I hear a quiet moan drift through the canvas. Once he is completely inside me, he starts to pump his meat into my mouth. I grab hold of my cock and wank it hard as he continues to fuck my face.

As his juicy shaft slides in and out of me, I try to imagine what he looks like. With a nice chunky cock like that, he must be a muscly little fucker.

I carry on sucking him, making him groan even louder inside the tent. I taste the salty pre-come that begins to dribble out of the tip of his dick.

Before I can suck any more pre-come out, he yanks his cock back inside the tent. I kneel at the doorway, wondering what to do next. As I am about to stand up, his hand suddenly reaches out of the doorway and grabs hold of my cock. The squaddie pulls it inside the tent, and I feel something being rolled over it.

Once the squaddie has finished with it, he lets it go. I pull it out of the tent and see that it is now covered with a condom. Jesus, I've heard about be prepared, but that's ridiculous. Who did he think he was going to shag? Some farm hand he bumped into?

I look down at the unzipped door as he pushes his smooth, muscly arse out of it. The canvas flaps of the door open down each side of his arse cheeks. Dirty little fucker wants to get it pumped.

Getting really turned on by the open air and horny situation, I grab hold of my cock and spit on his arse. As my saliva drips down the crack of his arse, I stick the head of my cock into his wet hole.

Grabbing hold of the guy-ropes, I shove myself right the way up him. A loud groan comes from inside the tent. He pushes his arse back on to my cock, wanting it to slide even further inside. I reach through the doorway and grab hold of his waist, pulling him right on to me. My cock spears through him until I cannot go any further.

As I begin to pump myself in and out of him, he groans even louder. I reach under him and begin wanking his chunky little cock off for him.

'Turn the torch off,' I whisper, not wanting him to see what I look like.

I hear him stretch across the groundsheet, and the tent is plunged into semidarkness, the only light coming from the moon. I grab hold of his legs and throw him over on to his back. He lands on top of his sleeping bag, legs in the air. I crawl through the canvas doors of the tent and stand over him, my head rubbing on the tent wall.

I kneel in between his legs and pull them over my shoulders. My cock finds its way to his gaping hole all by itself. His dilating passage sucks my meat straight back up inside him, without me having to do any work. I can tell that this one has been fucked plenty of times before. I bet he is the barrack bike. I've probably even fucked him before now.

As I lean over him to get my cock further up him, I feel him wanking his cock against my stomach. I grab hold of his ankles and start pumping him really aggressively. The whole tent moves back and forth as my back pushes against the canvas. I look down at his smooth white body in the moonlight. From what I can make out, he looks fucking cute.

He reaches forward and clamps one of his hands around my nipples. As he squeezes on it with his fingers, I feel my spunk beginning to rise. I keep pounding his arse, staring down at him wanking his cock.

Wanting to come all over his face, I pull my dick out of his arse, rip the condom off, and straddle his torso. I sit down heavily on his muscly little chest. I rip my heavy army shirt off, and he reaches for my bare chest. I start slapping my rock-hard dick around his face. He groans loudly, trying to catch my meat in his mouth.

I feel his hand banging into my arse as he continues to wank himself off. I grab my dick really tightly and pump it back and forth, wanting to cover the squaddie's face with my fuck juice. As he yanks on my right tit, I feel my balls release a gallon of spunk. My piss slit opens, and I fire a round of cream out of my weapon. I watch my thick semen slap him right in the face, splashing over his lips and chin. Another spurt of come shoots out and smacks into the canvas wall of the tent behind him. He leans behind and wipes it off. He rams his spunk-covered fingers into his mouth.

As he rolls my spunk around in his mouth, he starts to groan. I feel his hot come smack into my back as he wanks his cock off behind me. Spurt after spurt of thick juice hits my back and then slowly trickles down my skin.

I sit on his chest, totally exhausted. That has really finished me off. My semihard cock lies on his chest, spunk still leaking out of it and covering his nipples. I realise that I have now got to go and put my fucking tent up.

I pull my leg over his chest. 'Better go and pitch up.'

'You're all right: stay in here,' he says, in his thick Birmingham accent.

I stare down at him, just about making out the whites of his eyes in the moonlight. I wouldn't mind bedding down with this one tonight. It would save me having to stick up my tent in the pitch black.

I reach out of the tent and pull in my rucksack. I take my sleeping bag out, and we zip it together with his. We crawl inside them, and he turns his back to me. I put my arms around him and nestle my cock into the crack of his arse. Fuck, this feels good. The distant owl hoots, and I feel my eyes begin to close.

Sun streams in through the unzipped door of the tent. I open my eyes and look down at the shaved head that is fast asleep on my chest. I suddenly remember where I am. I study the squaddie's features. He looks quite young and is very good-looking. I don't think I have seen him before, though. I breathe a sigh of relief when I realise that he is not from my barracks. That will save any future embarrassment.

I try to wriggle from underneath him, but he suddenly wakes up. He smiles at me, obviously impressed with what he can see.

'I'd better get going,' I tell him.

'In a minute.'

He slowly moves his head down inside the sleeping bag. As he disappears from view, I suddenly feel his warm mouth around my flaccid cock. I lay my head back on the groundsheet and grab the tent pole behind me as my cock quickly grows. Sex in tents has always really turned me on. I think it is because I used to enjoy getting fucked when I was on scout camp.

I close my eyes as he starts really sucking my now fully hard meat. I suddenly hear the zip of the tent being pulled all the way down. I quickly open my eyes and sit up. A head suddenly moves into the tent. Shit! It's my sergeant major.

'Dalson! You should be up and moving by now,' he yells.

I pray that the squaddie who is sucking me off has the sense to stay where he is. No such luck. Before I get a chance to hold his head down, he has stuck it out of the side of the sleeping bag to see what's going on.

The sergeant major stares at him in horror. 'Dalson! Back to the barracks – now!'

Birds fly out of the tops of the trees, frightened by the sergeant major's yell. Shit, I am for it now. Shagging always seems to get me into trouble.

The automatic doors at the end of the train carriage suddenly glide open. I snap out of my daze and realise that I am back on the warm train and not still out on the moors.

I turn to face the person walking along towards me. It's that horny ticket collector again. He walks slowly down the aisle, pretending to check the tickets from the people who got on at the last stop. However, he knows full well that absolutely nobody got on.

'Tickets,' he shouts in his thick Geordie accent.

I check him out as he gets nearer. He is about my height, but even more stocky. He has smooth, olive skin, bright-blue eyes and a jet-black, flat-top haircut. His uniform shirtsleeves are rolled up, revealing the Newcastle United tattoos on his lower arms.

He slowly gets nearer my table, staring at me out of the corner of his eye. As he walks past my table, he grins at me cheekily. Now, he is either extremely friendly or basically just dying for some cock.

As he carries on along the carriage, I check out his arse in his tight uniform trousers. The design of them isn't meant to be tight, it's just that his arse and thighs are so chunky, they cling to the material. I can even make out the outline of his underpants.

He presses the button on the automatic doors at the end of the carriage, and they slide open. As he steps through them, he looks back at me. Our eyes meet, and he grins at me once again. He wants me bad!

★

Three coffees later, and I'm still dying for a fag. Haven't even seen the ticket collector to help me take my mind off smoking. He must have given up. Well, he can't exactly cop off when he's working, can he?

Sod it, I'm going to light up in the loo. I'm not going to last another hour. I walk down the aisle, getting thrown across the carriage. I walk through the automatic doors and into the space where the carriages join. I push open the door marked TOILET and step inside. I slam the door behind me and turn the lock.

I lower the toilet seat and sit down on top of it. I take my fags out of my pocket and light one up. I take a huge drag, savouring every moment. Boy, did I need that. I lean back against the Formica surface and take another long drag, relaxing more by the second.

Suddenly there is a loud knock on the door. Who the fuck is that? I look around the ceiling to see if there are any smoke detectors. None in sight. It's probably some impatient old granny desperate for a slash.

I throw the lighted fag down the loo and turn the lock on the door. I pull open the door to reveal the ticket collector stood outside the toilet.

He holds his ticket punch up to me. 'Ticket please, sir.'

'You've see mine,' I remind him.

'No, I haven't, sir,' he says suggestively.

The brazen little bugger is actually coming on to me, is he? I think he must really want it. I look over his shoulder to see if anyone from the carriage behind is looking. The only person who can see the toilet door from their seat is an old lady, and she's snoring her head off.

I grab hold of his shirt and pull him into the toilet, slamming the door behind. He passionately grabs hold of my T-shirt and pulls it over my head. I grab his uniform shirt and rip it open; buttons fly in all directions. As his shirt falls open, it reveals his muscly little chest and big, red nipples.

He thrusts his head towards my nipples and starts chewing on them. As he sucks and licks them, he reaches for my trousers and begins to rip them open. He's a randy little fucker, this one. I wonder if he does this with all the passengers he fancies.

His warm mouth suddenly slides over my hard cock. Fuck, that feels good. He certainly knows what he's doing. He begins to pull on my tits as he slides his mouth up and down over my meat. I grab his head and pull him further down on top of it.

He sits on the loo seat and pulls my trousers down further. He lifts my hard dick and starts to lick my balls. They gradually become drenched in his saliva. As he continues to suck away on my sacks, he unbuttons his trousers and pulls out his long, thin dick. I stare at it, amazed that it is the complete opposite of his body proportion. He starts tugging on it with his signet-ring-covered hand. It grows even harder as he pumps it aggressively with his fist.

I pull his mouth off my balls and shove my cock back down his throat. The train suddenly jolts, and I fall on top of him, forcing my meat even further down his throat. He gags as my bell-end smacks into the back of his mouth.

I pull myself up straight again. He lifts himself up further and begins to lick my six-pack stomach. His tongue slowly works its way up my body until it reaches my hard pecs. He begins to run his tongue all over them, teasingly missing my nipples. I look down at his handsome face. His thick, black flat top digs into me as his tongue continues to wash my chest.

My fully erect nipples stand out to attention, eagerly awaiting servicing from his tongue. He grabs both of our dicks and starts wanking them as he continues to lick my hard chest.

Fed up with waiting for him to lick my tits, I shove his head on to my nipples. He starts sucking on them, like a baby desperate for its mother's milk.

He suddenly stops wanking his own dick and grabs hold of my balls instead. He squeezes them tightly, still wanking my meat off with his other hand. He cups my balls in his hand.

'Come over my cock,' he says, staring at me.

I force his head back down on my hard tits. 'I'll come over your arse first.'

I turn him round and push him over the sink. He stares at me in the mirror that is situated above it. I grab hold of his chunky, hairy arse, rubbing my cock all over it at the same time.

'Got anything?' I ask, desperate to ram my erection up his hairy man-cunt.

He shakes his head. Shit, I really wanted to get inside the horny bastard. I start slapping my hard dick across his hairy arse. He grabs his cock and starts wanking it, watching me looking down at his arse in the mirror.

'Come on mate, soak my hairy cheeks,' he says in his thick Geordie accent. He obviously wants me to come as soon as possible: the driver's probably wondering where he's gone.

He thrusts his arse back against my cock. I really just want to ram my cock up his arse and ride him bareback. I wank my cock even harder, imagining my raw meat sliding up his hole. I reach around him and grab hold of one of his large nipples. I suddenly feel my spunk shooting up through the inside of my shaft. It spills out of my dick and covers his hairy crack. I start to rub my spunk all around his chunky arse, as more and more of my spunk continues to shoot out over him.

His pumping arm action gets faster, and he begins to groan. He turns around and wanks his dick even faster, aiming it directly at my spunky helmet. He suddenly throws his head back as his fuck juice flows out over my cock. I start to rub his spunk into my cock and balls as he keeps pumping out more of his semen. As soon as he has wanked every drop out, he gets down on his knees in front of me. He wraps his mouth around my spunk-covered cock. He groans in ecstasy as he begins licking his own spunk off my semi-erect dick.

His tongue moves down to my big balls as he licks every trace of spunk off those as well. I look down at him licking me like a dog. He is a real spunk-lover, this one.

Once he is sure he has lapped up every trace of spunk from my dick, he stands up and stuffs his cock into his pants. He looks down at my cock and starts to reach for it. There is a sudden knock on the door. Realising he should be on duty, he quickly tucks in his uniform. He tries to do up his shirt, but a few of the buttons are missing.

I stick my cock back into my trousers and unlock the door. The little old lady that had been asleep in the next carriage stands waiting. She smiles at us both as we walk out, not even questioning what two men were doing in the toilets together.

I walk behind him down the aisle of the train, staring at his chunky arse. I imagine my thick come soaking through his underpants. I sit down at my seat and watch him disappear from view. I look out of the window, grinning to myself. Newcastle could turn out to be better than I had imagined.

Fourteen

I've now picked up my new car. It is nowhere near as flash as the last, but I suppose it gets me from A to B. In fact, it got me here a lot quicker than I thought it would. I am sat in the car park of DCA Warehouses. They are a company who rent out storage room in their warehouses. I wouldn't have thought there was much money in it, but the Boss reckons the owner is loaded. So, it would be a good contract to win.

Towering over the car in front of me is the largest warehouse I have ever seen in my life. Floodlights shine down the side of the concrete building. I have thirty minutes to kill before I go in to have my first Northeast appointment. What can I do? I hate having time to think. I seem to always end up thinking about the Boss back in Manchester. I cannot believe I screwed up big time. I have only been here a week, and I am missing him like mad already.

To get me through it, I sometimes tell myself that it just was not meant to be. Other times I want to drive back to Manchester and tell him to just fuck me. Even when I try and have a wank about different people, I always end up thinking about the first time he fucked me at my interview.

I cannot believe we almost kissed before being disturbed by that courier. If he had not turned up when he did, I know the Boss would have shagged me there and then.

My cock starts to get hard just thinking about it. I look out of the car windows to check that nobody is in sight. Once I am sure that the coast is clear, I unzip my trousers and pull out my semi-erect dick. I suddenly have the urge to shoot it. Whenever I think of the Boss I get an instant hard on.

I grab my dick in my fist and start pumping it. I stare through the windscreen, remembering the day we were together when the bar was being converted. I wonder what would have happened if the courier had not showed up.

The builders and decorators laugh and shout on the floor below. The Boss slowly pulls my jeans down over my trainers. He pulls my leg over the plank of wood that stretches across the two ladders. He lays me face down on the plank. My arms and legs fall either side of the plank and touch the cement floor. He mounts the plank behind me and lifts my arse into the air. He bends forward and starts to lick my muscly thighs. His tongue moves closer towards my twitching hole. I feel his hard, moist flesh circling my ring, getting me ready for his weapon.

I reach out in front of me and grab hold of the plank of wood as his tongue slowly enters my hole. My whole body relaxes as the Boss pushes his hard tongue right the way inside me. I feel the bristles of his goatee beard tickling my arse cheeks. My cock hardens, sandwiched between my stomach and the plank of wood.

He moves his tongue out of my hole and starts wetting up my smooth arse cheeks. He moves his tongue up to the base of my spine and slowly begins to lick his way up my back. Straddling the plank, he starts licking the back of my neck. I feel the tip of his rock-hard cock rubbing against my arse crack.

He starts to bite my neck, pulling my skin up with his teeth. As he continues to bite and lick it, he lifts my arse up into the air. He reaches under me and takes my cock in his huge hand. He slowly starts to wank me off.

I feel his other hand take hold of his own cock and aim it towards my arse. I close my eyes and feel him slide his huge meat up inside me. He reaches under me and grabs hold of my stomach as he tenderly fucks me with his cock.

He starts wanking my cock even faster, making my arse cheeks loosen even more. He slides himself further up me, constantly wanking me to try and get even further in. He leans forward and bites my neck, his hard nipples digging into my back.

He lets go of my dick and wraps both his arms around my torso. I feel so protected in his grip. He continues to bang my arse, his huge balls knocking against my pert cheeks.

I grab hold of my dick and begin wanking it. My balls immediately tighten. The Boss starts pumping me faster, grabbing hold of my tits as he thrusts. Not being able to hold back any longer, I feel my spunk start to rip through my shaft.

I open my eyes and realise that I am sat back in the car park. I pump my foreskin back and forth as my spunk flies out of the end of my cock. It smacks into the car windscreen in front of me and splatters all over the dashboard. I continue to wank it, and stream after stream of thick come covers the windscreen.

Just as I have managed to stuff my cock back into my trousers, there is a loud knock on the car window. I look out and see an old security guard holding a torch. He shines the beam into the car and frowns at me, wondering who I am. Luckily, he does not notice my thick, white come dribbling down the windscreen in front.

I walk along the aisle of a huge factory warehouse. Either side of me are wooden pallets, stacked full of cardboard boxes. Walking in front of me is Mr Mark Gibbson, the warehouse manager. He is about forty, with cropped, balding dark hair. He has a stocky build and is about my height. His smart grey suit looks a bit odd next to the Doc Martens boots that I notice he is wearing. He has a cigarette behind his ear, which I think is a strange thing to do when you know you are having a business meeting. Then again, it could be a Geordie tradition.

He is giving me a guided tour of the huge storage warehouse. This is just one of seven that this company own. It is my first appointment since setting up the office in the centre of Newcastle. Twinny set up this meeting. Remember, he bought that Internet list of prospective clients from the Northeast. So I gather this guy must be on it. I'll just give him a flash of my cock in a bit and hope he signs straight away.

I told the Boss that I would do a few 'list' clients to set it up. But I warned him that I just want to carry on repping without the funny business once we are established here.

I stare at the back of Mark's shaven head as I follow him through the warehouse. The warehouse is dead as it is eight at night. The only person who is around is that doddery old security guard who nearly caught me having a wank. Apparently he just falls asleep every night: that is why so much stuff is disappearing. The scallies just carry it out under his nose. So that means this bloke is definitely looking for a new security company. I'll have to make sure I demonstrate that Sureforce could certainly do a better job than granddad.

We reach a large loading bay. A stationary fork-lift truck stands in the middle of the bay. A stack of waist-high pallets sits on its yellow forks.

Mark places his briefcase down on the pallets and turns to face me. 'So, think Sureforce could cope with a warehouse this size?'

'No problem,' I answer confidently.

'What about the other six?'

'We can take care of those as well.'

I look over at him, not sure whether I should try anything on yet. Oh sod it, I've got to try and get my first Northeast contract signed tonight.

'In fact, I can take care of more than just your security needs,' I inform him.

He frowns at me, not understanding what I mean. I put down my briefcase and begin to pull down my fly. I know that I can be brazen with this one. He must have visited a gay porn site at some stage to be on the Internet list that Twinny bought. So he is definitely going to be interested in a bit of cock.

I finish undoing my zip, and my trousers fall to the ground. 'I thought you might like to take a look at my credentials.'

He stares down at the bulge in my underpants. 'What the fuck do you think you're doing?'

He is obviously a bit shy. He just needs a bit of encouragement. I reach down for my cock and start rubbing it through my underpants.

He glares at me. 'Get the fuck over here.'

What is he playing at? I should be the one taking the lead. I am the one in control.

'Get the fuck over here,' he yells again, in his thick Geordie accent.

I kick off my trousers and slowly walk over to him.

'Get on your knees,' he shouts aggressively.

Who does this one think he is? I'm going to be walking out of this place in a minute.

'Get on your fucking knees,' he repeats.

Realising that I am not going to do what he says, he roughly pushes me down on to my knees. He takes his suit jacket off and throws it on the floor.

He begins to unbutton his shirt. 'So, trying to get my cock hard, are you?'

He rips off his shirt to reveal his stocky, hairy torso. He begins to undo his belt and rips his trousers down. He pulls them over his boots and throws them on the floor. He stands in front of me, wearing just a white jockstrap and his black boots. His cock presses against the thin material of his jockstrap. He looks as if he can be a right dirty bastard. My cock starts to twitch, as I look forward to being ordered around by him.

'Come on then, show me what Sureforce can do. Get me hard,' he shouts.

He grabs my head and shoves it against his jock. I feel his twitching meat through the jock. I start to lick his dick through the material. As my saliva moistens the material, it turns transparent. I stare at his chunky, pink dick through the translucent jockstrap. His meat grows bigger and bigger, stretching the material to its limits. The material of his jock looks so thin, I am sure his massive meat is going to tear through it at any moment.

'Get your clothes off,' he shouts.

I stand up and take my jacket and shirt off. I stare at his thick, muscly legs as I pull my underpants down.

He notices my hard cock flopping out. 'My dick turning you on, is it? Get back down on it.'

He pushes me back down on my knees and pulls his meat out from the side of his jockstrap. I stare at his perfectly formed cock. His helmet is the largest I've seen in a long while. I lunge at it, wanting to take it in my mouth. I clamp my mouth round it, and I start sucking on his meaty flesh.

'Yeah, come on, you dirty fucker, give it a good licking,' he shouts, as he thrusts it all the way into my mouth.

He grabs my head and thrusts forward again, forcing himself further down my throat. I reach around the back of him and grab hold of his hairy arse. I pull him even further into me.

'Like that cock, you greedy little fucker?' he says, slapping my face as I suck him off. 'Look at you getting me hard, you little fucking tart!'

I grab hold of my cock and start wanking it. He continues to slap my face.

'Come on, suck it properly,' he shouts aggressively.

I grab hold of his jockstrap and pull it right down. His cock and balls spring out. I suddenly notice he is wearing a cock ring. His big balls are pulled right through it. I lift them up and start sucking on them like a madman. My saliva starts to drip down them and soak his pubic hair.

'Suck those big balls, you worthless piece of shit,' he yells at the top of his voice.

My cock grows even bigger as I really begin to get turned on by being treated like dirt. He grabs hold of my head and pulls me further down on to his throbbing meat.

'Come on, make me come, fucker,' he shouts.

I begin licking his cock maniacally, getting even more turned on by his dirty talk. He suddenly slaps me across the face, and I choke on his knob as it slams into the back of my mouth.

'Eat it properly,' he yells, slapping me across the face again.

I start sucking him again. Before I have had the chance to go down on it further, he slaps me across the face once more.

'I said eat it properly, fucker!'

Before he even gives me a chance to suck him again, he reaches under my arms and lifts me up. He shoves my head down on his large, red nipples.

'Go on, get 'em hard!' he shouts, pushing my mouth right over the top of one of his tits.

I start licking his soft, fleshy nipple, trying to get it hard with my tongue. I feel it slowly grow in my mouth. I start to pull on the other one with my fingers, trying to get them both to stand to attention at the same time.

He looks down at me sucking on his nipples. 'Eat those tits, boy.'

Once they are fully erect, he pushes me back down in front of him. He grabs his rock-hard dick in his hand and starts slapping me round the face with it. 'Want a piece of cock again?'

He gobs down on his knob and starts rubbing it in. He then shoves it back in my throat and starts pumping. As he begins to really fuck my face, he reaches over to his briefcase and clicks it open. He searches inside for something. He eventually brings out a huge, pink dildo. He holds it at the base and starts slapping me round the face with it. I pull my mouth off his dick and wrap it around the dildo. He begins to slide it in and out of my mouth as I continue to suck on it.

'That's it, get it nice and wet,' he shouts.

He suddenly pulls the dildo out and pushes me down on top of the pallets that are stacked on the fork-lift truck. I fall on top of them, and splinters dig in my back. He walks around the stack of pallets and stands over my face. He leans over me and lowers his cock into my mouth. He starts to fuck my face upside down. As he pumps my face with his cock, he reaches over and pulls my arse up into the air. I suddenly feel him gobbing into my arsehole. His phlegm starts to slowly dribble down my arse cheeks.

He suddenly nudges the tip of the fat dildo against my entrance. As he continues to fuck my face with his cock, he slowly begins to slide the pink dildo up my man-cunt. I try to groan, but find it hard to with a mouth full of cock.

As the dildo slides further into me, he pushes my legs apart to get a better view. I stare up at his stomach and chest as he thrusts his meat right down the back of my throat. My body starts to relax, enjoying having a dick at both ends.

'Come on, eat those cocks up,' he shouts. 'Let's fuck your face and arse at the same time.'

As the base of the thick dildo slides deeper inside me, I feel my arse being stretched apart. He reaches down and touches his own knob, wanting to feel the juicy flesh sliding in and out of my mouth. His pelvis thrusts back and forth, stabbing his weapon deep inside me.

He suddenly yanks his dick out of my mouth and walks around the stack of pallets, still holding the dildo that is inside me. He stands at my feet and stares at the dildo that is two-thirds of the way inside me. He takes his cock in his other hand and starts to wank it.

I look up at him, cock in hand and booted. Feeling really turned on, I grab hold of my cock and start beating it. As it gets harder, my arse cheeks begin to relax, and the dildo is sucked even further up inside me.

Once the dildo is completely inside me, I can feel the base of it rubbing against my arse cheeks. Grabbing hold of the base, he slowly starts to pull it out. My arse allows it to slide out until just the tip of it is still inside me.

Before my arse is allowed any rest, he suddenly shoves the huge rubber length right back up inside me. I start beating my cock as he begins to roughly fuck me with the dildo. Still pumping me with the substitute dick, he reaches into his case and pulls out a condom. He tears it open and rolls it down over his throbbing cock.

Grabbing hold of the base of the dildo, he tears it out of my arse. As soon as the tip falls out, he grabs his own cock and thrusts it right up me where the dildo has just been. As he pumps my arse with his knob, he reaches over and slaps the moist dildo in my face.

'Lick it,' he orders. 'Taste your own fucking arse.'

He forces the fat, pink dildo into my mouth. As I start licking and sucking on it, I start to taste my own man-cunt on it. I wank my cock harder, getting really turned on by this new experience.

He starts pumping my arse and face at the same time. My arse muscles tighten around his meat, not wanting to ever let it go. As he bangs me harder and harder, he suddenly spits in my face.

'Look at you, you dirty little cock-lover,' he says aggressively. 'One in your gob and one up your arse. You can't get enough, can you?'

He starts fucking my arse really hard, the splinters from the pallets digging into my back as he rocks me back and forth.

'Pull on my fucking tits and make me come,' he orders.

I let go of my cock and grab his two erect, red nipples.

He throws his head back as I start pulling on them. 'Yeah, milk that fucking cock with those nipples!'

He pulls the dildo out of my mouth and throws it on to the floor. He takes the cigarette from behind his ear and lights it. With his cock still right up my arse, he takes a drag from it, sneering down at me. He looks down at his cock stretching me apart.

He begins to run his hand through my pubic hair. He slowly moves the lighted cigarette down towards my thick bush of hair. He places the lit end against my pubes. He starts to singe them off with his fag, small sparks running through them like a mini forest fire. I feel the heat next to my cock and balls as the lighted cigarette moves closer. He continues to singe off all of my pubic hair; the spark extinguishes once it reaches my flesh. I wank my cock as I watch him move the fag around my pubes, enjoying this weird experience.

I breathe in the smell of my singed hair as he continues to fuck me hard. He throws the fag down and runs his hand over the base of my hairless cock. I feel his cock throbbing in my arse as he stares down at my singed growth.

I start wanking my knob even harder. Without its usual forest of hair at the base, it looks even bigger than it does normally. He watches his cock sliding in and out of my arse.

He suddenly slaps me hard across the face. 'Tighten that fucking arse!'

I clamp my arse passage even tighter around his meat. My cock grows stiffer: I'm getting really aroused from being dominated. He pulls my hand off my cock and puts it on his hard chest, thrusting his nipples out in front of him.

'Pull on my tits, you little shit,' he spits.

I grab his nipples aggressively and almost tear them from his pecs.

He thrusts his cock further up inside me. 'Look at you with my dick up your arse, you dirty little fucker.'

I keep pulling on his tits, wanting to hear him give me even more verbal. I clamp my arse tightly round his meat, knowing that should do the trick.

'Yeah, pull on those big tits,' he yells. He slaps me across the face. 'Harder, you little fucker.'

I keep yanking on his hard bits of flesh. I spread my legs wider, allowing him to get even deeper. My cock feels like it is going to spurt without me even having to touch it.

'Tighten that man-cunt,' he orders. He slaps me around the face once more. 'Go on, fucking tighten it.'

My balls tighten and my cock throbs hard. I clench my arse cheeks as tightly as I possibly can, feeling his fleshy shaft rubbing against my insides. He pumps himself up me aggressively, not caring if he is hurting me. I stare at him looking down at my arse, just using it for his own pleasure.

He notices me staring at him and slaps me even harder. 'Concentrate on my tits, you little cunt.'

My arse starts to ache from where he has been pumping me so violently.

'It's starting to hurt,' I inform him.

He pushes my hands off his chest and looks down at me. He suddenly whacks me hard across the face again. 'Belt it, cunt!'

I start to see stars from being hit so hard. He continues to fuck my sore arse. Although it is hurting, I still feel really turned on by this rough bloke poking me. I grab on to his tits again, wanting to feel him come inside me.

'Tighten that arse,' he shouts.

I tighten it again. He grits his teeth as his cock really begins to throb inside me. He slaps me again. I black out for a second. I come around to the sight of him really fucking me like a bull. He looks down at his huge meat slipping in and out of me.

'Make me come, you dirty little fucker,' he shouts at the top of his voice. He viciously smacks me across the face again. I begin to see stars and close my eyes, concentrating on feeling him sliding in and out of me.

'Shit, I'm coming,' he yells. 'You made me come, you dirty little fucker.'

He slaps me hard across the face again and again. As I feel him empty his gallon of spunk up inside me, my eyes close. I begin to black out, feeling his hard tits in my hands and his cock up my arse.

Fifteen

I stand on the edge of a steep cliff, looking ahead at the clear blue ocean. Seagulls circle above me. They begin to shriek, as if they were calling me to join them. I look up at the sun and outstretch my arms. I take in a deep breath of air. I close my eyes and wait to hear the seagulls beckon me once more.

I suddenly hear a loud shriek. I slowly lean forward over the edge of the cliff. My feet leave the grassy floor, and I begin to plummet towards the roaring sea beneath me. As I get nearer to the sea, I hear the waves crashing on to the rocks below.

Confidently, I begin to flap my wings, expecting to soar back up into the sky. As I continue to flap my arms rapidly back and forth, I suddenly realise that I am still plummeting towards the lethal rocks below. I start to panic, flapping my arms even harder. Why won't my fucking wings work? I could fly yesterday.

My heart starts beating faster. The sound of the sea crashing against the rocks becomes deafening. Knowing I'm about to plunge headfirst into a huge boulder, I quickly open my eyes wide.

A fluorescent light hanging from a plain white ceiling sits over me. My heart continues to beat extremely fast. I close my eyes. Within seconds I open them again. The fluorescent light is still there. No rocks or crashing waves. I sigh deeply, relieved that I haven't been smashed to smithereens on some boulder.

I slowly begin to lift my head. An intense pain shoots down my neck, and I flop my head back down. I want to know where the hell I am. Without lifting my head, I slowly roll it to the side.

I soon realise that I'm lying in a hospital bed in a private hospital room. I notice someone's booted feet and turn to see who they belong to. Sat in a chair next to the bed is the Boss. He is fast asleep and snoring quietly. I stare at the man I am in love with. He looks so perfect. I inspect every inch of his face. His lips are slightly parted. I just want to lean forward and kiss them. His eyes begin to flutter slightly, as if he is having a bad dream. I stare at his long eyelashes. They would usually look feminine on a bloke, but there is absolutely nothing feminine about the Boss: he's one hundred per cent all man.

He suddenly begins to grunt, and his eyelids flicker open. Our eyes meet. It is the first time I have properly seen his eyes. He is usually wearing baseball caps or shades. But today I can see his piercing green irises clearly. He sits up and smiles over at me. I now realise how much I want this man. Up until now it has mainly just been a lust thing. But it's dawning on me that I don't just want him to fuck me: I want him to make love to me.

He gives me a cheeky wink. 'How's my Matty doing?'

My Matty! If only he knew how much I wanted to be his Matty. I sit myself up, still feeling sore from being knocked around. I groan slightly, and the Boss jumps up to see if he can help. He arranges the pillows until I'm in a comfortable position. From the corner of my eye I notice something on my forehead. I reach up to touch it and realise it's a padded plaster.

'Don't touch that,' the Boss warns me. 'You didn't need stitches, but they said it'll be painful for a while. Just brought you here to get you checked over. They've given you X-rays, and you're fine. Just got a bit of concussion.'

'Where am I?' I ask.

'Newcastle General,' he informs me. 'I found you unconscious in the warehouse. Someone had rung the office and left an address.

We're going straight back to Manchester today. All your stuff is in my car.'

'How come?' I ask, confused about what he is doing there.

'I found out that Twinny set you up,' he explains. 'The northeast list was taken from a well-dodgy sadomasochist Internet site. Not that they all are, but this one was. He knew you would come a cropper sooner or later. I got here as soon as I found out. Sorry, I just didn't realise how much he had it in for you.'

I look down at the bedcover, realising that I could easily have suffered worse injuries than this.

'Don't worry, he's history,' the Boss continues. 'That's why I'm taking you back to Manchester. I want you to be my new right-hand man.'

I look over at him, not knowing what to say. I've got him at last. Twinny is well and truly out of the picture.

'I want you to just work in the office, no more repping,' he says, smiling as he talks. 'You can live in the flat over the bar. Means I'll get to see more of you then.'

I wonder if I could still possibly be dreaming. Well, five minutes ago I was plummeting towards a rocky beach; who's to say this is real?

The Boss stands, walks over to the window and looks out. 'Matty, I want to offer you a partnership.'

OK, now I know it definitely must be a dream. How do you wake yourself up? He turns to face me to gauge my reaction. He sees that I am totally gob-smacked.

'It's for real,' he reassures me. 'So, what do you say?'

'Yeah, definitely,' I answer, not needing any time to think about it.

'So you're happy about becoming my partner?' he asks.

I nod.

He walks over and sits on the edge of the bed. He looks deeply into my eyes. 'In every sense of the word?'

Forgetting that my neck is injured, I lean forward in an attempt to kiss him. I freeze as a stabbing pain shoots through my neck. I lean back against the pillow. He reaches over and tenderly touches my neck, as if to soothe it.

He looks out through the glass porthole in the door to check that nobody is around. Once the coast is clear, he slowly leans forward. I close my eyes as his huge, rough lips touch mine. His goatee beard rubs into my chin as he kisses me passionately. His hard tongue knocks a path through my lips and enters my mouth. I cannot believe this is happening. Gazza told me that he never kisses guys, just fucks them. He must really have the horn for me.

He pulls his lips away from mine. I open my eyes to see him staring at me. He moves his huge hand down the side of my smooth face.

'You're beautiful,' he says quietly.

I grin, feeling like I'm about to blush for the first time in my life.

'I'm gonna get that bloke sorted for injuring my Matty,' he says. 'I want to look after you. I want to make sure nobody ever touches you again.'

Fuck, sounds like he's fallen for me as much as I've fallen for him. But this only happens in Hollywood films between famous actors. We're just two Salford scallies.

I bring my arms out from under the bedcovers and grab hold of his shaved head. I pull him towards me, wanting to taste him again. He begins to kiss me passionately. We slide our tongues roughly into each other's mouths. He wraps his arms around me and holds me tightly, so tight that I wince with pain.

He releases me slightly. 'Sorry. I've got to be careful: you're still going to be a bit sore.'

'Fuck it,' I say, as I grab hold of him and smack my lips against his.

My cock grows rigid. As his tongue wraps itself around mine, I imagine him inside me again. I know he's going to make love to me this time, not just shag me like he did before.

As we continue to kiss, I start rubbing his growing dick through his tracky bottoms. I grab hold of it, feeling it in my hand for the first time. I've had it up my arse and have seen it when he was shagging Twinny, but I've never actually touched it before.

I reach for the waistband on his tracky bottoms, eager to get to his meat. I want to feel the actual flesh of his shaft. I've waited so fucking long for this moment.

I bury my hand down through his underpants and grab the already throbbing meat in my hand. He sighs as he continues to passionately kiss me. I stretch my fingers right around his huge girth. His cock is so fat, the tips of my fingers don't actually touch my thumb.

I pull his tracksuit trousers down with my other hand, and pull my mouth off his. I want to get a proper glimpse of his meat before I shove it in my mouth. The navy-blue fabric stretches down to reveal his throbbing piece of man-meat. I stare at it in wonder. I pull the foreskin right back to see the whole of his fat purple helmet. His balls are huge and shaved. I imagine he's got a good load stored up in there for me.

I can't quite believe I'm actually holding his dick in my hand for the first time. It is everything I imagined it would be. It felt tight up my arse when he first fucked me over a year ago, but I never imagined it to be this big.

I look out through the window in the door to check nobody is about. I slowly move my mouth towards his juicy helmet. He touches the back of my head, indicating just how much he wants me to suck it. As my lips move closer to his dick, I look up at him. He is watching my every move and touches my lips with his fingers. I open my mouth slightly, preparing to fit his bulging head in it.

Suddenly, the door bangs open. A nurse walks in backward having pushed it open with her back. The Boss quickly stuffs his cock into his tracky bottoms and covers his huge bulge with the *Sun*. I fling myself back against the pillows just as she turns around.

'How are you feeling, Mr Dalson?' she asks, struggling with a pile of perfectly folded sheets.

I smile at her, secretly wanting to smash my bedpan over her head. 'Fine.'

She begins to change the sheets on the empty bed opposite. The Boss grins over at me. I sigh in frustration. Am I ever going to get his cock in my mouth?

★

The nurse eventually finishes making the bed opposite. She gathers the old sheets up and carries them out of the room. She suddenly remembers something and pops her head back around the door.

'I'm afraid we're a bit short-staffed today,' she informs me. 'You're gonna have to ring if you need anything.'

She disappears out of the room.

I stare at the ceiling, eagerly awaiting the Boss's return. He has gone to get some ice cream – I had a sudden craving. I reach under the covers and start playing with my cock. I imagine that his fat meat is in my hand again.

The door opens and in strides the Boss. He puts a huge tub of ice cream down on the bedside table. I stare at his crotch, which is directly in line with my face. Fuck, I want that cock bad. I won't be able to keep my hands off it when we're driving back down the motorway. I want to taste it now; I can't wait till we get back to Manchester. He'll probably have to go straight off to see his bird anyway.

I pull my bedcovers back to reveal my muscly brown legs sticking out of the bottom of my white hospital gown.

The Boss frowns at me. 'Where do you think you're going?'

I ignore him and climb out of the bed. I grab hold of the curtains that hang from the curtain track that is screwed to the ceiling above the bed. I pull them along the tracking, and the large curtain completely circles the bed. I turn to face the Boss, completely shielded from prying eyes.

'They're short-staffed,' I say, grinning cheekily.

'So?' the Boss replies.

'So, we won't be disturbed,' I whisper.

I grab hold of his face and pull his lips towards mine. He responds immediately and digs his tongue into my hungry mouth.

As we kiss passionately, he reaches behind me with his strong arms. He lifts my hospital gown and grabs hold of my bare arse cheeks with his huge hands. He pulls me closer towards him, one of my tight, muscly buttocks in each palm. I reach down the back of his tracky bottoms and pull him closer to me. Our rigid cocks rub together; the only thing keeping them apart is the fabric of his tracksuit bottoms and my hospital gown.

His tongue explores every inch of my mouth, while his hands do the same with my arse. He pulls my crack apart with one hand and rubs his fingers around the rim of my hole with the other.

I pull my hands out of his tracky bottoms and start to unzip his Sureforce bomber jacket. As the jacket bursts open, I realise that he is not wearing anything underneath. I pull my lips from his and stare at his huge, hairy pecs, knowing that I'm going to get a taste of those hard nipples today.

I pull the arms of his bomber down over his huge biceps, uncovering his many tattoos. His chunky gold chain glistens in the bright fluorescent light.

He lets go of my arse and pulls my head down on to his erect nipple. As I start to gnaw on it, I hear him groan in pleasure. I reach down into his pants and grab hold of his rock-hard knob. I start to wank it as I continue to suck and bite his tits.

He reaches over for the tub of ice cream on the bedside cabinet and rips the top off. He pulls my head off his tit and smears a handful of cold ice cream over his erect nipples. He shoves my head back down on one of them, and I begin to move the cold ice cream around his lumps of hard flesh.

He dips his hand back into the ice cream tub and scoops out some more of its contents. Just as I begin to wonder what he is going to do with it, I feel the cold cream being stuffed up the crack of my arse. His huge hands rub the ice cream around my buttocks until they are completely covered. He then scoops out another handful and starts rubbing it around my rim.

I start wanking his cock harder, pulling his foreskin right back. Our tongues wrestle inside our mouths. I relax my arse as I feel one of his ice cream-covered fingers slowly worming its way inside.

I rip his tracksuit trousers down until they are gathered around his knees. I lift up the front of my hospital gown until our rock-hard cocks are touching. He pulls my arse towards him until our cocks are really rubbing against each other. I grab hold of his meat and push it down under my balls, until it is in between my thighs. I reach around to my arse cheeks to feel his huge helmet poking out through the crack of my arse.

He grabs hold of my cheeks tightly and starts to thrust his cock backward and forward between my thighs. He leans his head against the side of mine, and pushes it to one side. He lunges forward and practically takes a bite out of my neck. As he continues to thrust his cock, he bites and licks my neck. My knees go weak, and the only thing that stops me from falling is his firm hands on my arse.

He moves his tongue under my chin and starts gnawing on the other side of my neck. His ice cream-covered finger slides further up my hole. I relax my arse muscles completely, allowing him to get another two fingers in. He starts fucking me with his hand, ripping my neck apart in the process.

I reach over for the tub of ice cream and scoop out a load on to my hand. I pull his cock out from between my thighs, and smear the ice cream all over it. His body tenses with the coldness of the ice cream touching his tender bell-end. Wanting to taste it, I lean down and take his meat in my mouth. Ice cream covers my lips as I slide my mouth up and down over it. He thrusts his pelvis back and forth, fucking my face good and hard. I move my mouth right down over his shaft, touching the base of it with my lips.

He suddenly tears his fingers out of my arse and pushes me down on to the bed. He kicks off his trainers and pulls off his tracky bottoms. I lie back on the bed wanking my cock, staring at my perfect man. If I saw him in the bar, I'd think he was a right scally gangster. I can't believe someone so rough-looking wants my cute arse.

He stands over me, wanking his cock. He grabs my hospital gown with his other hand and yanks it off. He stares down at my smooth, muscly chest. I run my hand over it, stopping at one of my nipples. I seductively start flicking it with my fingers.

Not being able to control himself any longer, he dives on top of me. My skin tingles as I feel his huge, naked body on top of mine. Our torsos rub together, and our hard tits meet. He pins my arms behind my back and thrusts his tongue into my mouth. He rubs his cock firmly against mine as we kiss passionately.

We have both gone past the stage of worrying about somebody

walking in. What the fuck could they do, anyway? Throw a bucket of cold water over us?

I struggle to get my arms free of his grip and stretch them around his muscly back. I pull him down further on top of me, wanting him to crush me with his weight. His free hands begin to wander down my body and tunnel under the base of my spine. Cradling the arch of my back, he lifts me up and moves his other hand next to the crack of my arse, where it belongs. His fingers begin to circle my rim again. I think he wants to fuck me nearly as much as I want him to.

'Fuck me,' I whisper in his ear.

He groans, and his cock twitches, turned on by the thought of being inside me again. He may fuck some of the other Sureforce bouncers, but I know he's going to make love to me.

He pulls my legs apart and kneels up in between them. He scoops some more ice cream out of the tub and rubs it around the rim of my arse. I stare at his flexing muscles as his hand moves backward and forward along the crack of my arse. His huge cock stands proudly out in front of him, twitching in midair.

He suddenly grabs hold of my thighs and pushes them up into the air until he's got a bird's-eye view of my man-cunt. He groans as soon as he catches a glimpse of it. He moves his head towards it and gobs right at my arse lips. A string of green phlegm smacks me directly in the ring.

He lunges forward and begins to lick around the rim of my arse. I throw my head back in the bedclothes, groaning in complete ecstasy. Once he has circled my arse a few times, he thrusts his hard tongue right up inside me. I feel the spiky hair of his goatee beard digging into my arse as he eats me like a hungry bear.

I grab hold of my cock and start beating it, wanting to relax my arse even further. I spread my legs wider, wanting him to get his tongue deeper inside me. I feel his saliva-soaked tongue edging further and further up my hole. I reach down between my legs and grab the back of his head. I pull his face right against my arse, rubbing the back of his shaved head frantically.

'Fuck me,' I shout loudly.

He pulls his tongue out of my arse and picks up his bomber

jacket from the floor. He reaches into one of the pockets and pulls out a condom. He rips it open with his teeth and gobs inside it. He sticks it over his throbbing helmet and pulls it down over his shaft. As his dick is considerably above average, the condom only covers half of his veiny meat.

He grabs the base of his rubber-covered cock and spits down on it. He rubs the saliva up and down the shaft, making sure it's as hard as he can get it. My arse twitches like mad as I lie on the bed watching him wank.

Grabbing hold of my calves, he suddenly throws my legs over his shoulders. He leans forward and begins kissing me again, plunging his tongue into my welcoming mouth. He moves his cock under my balls until it's rubbing against my entrance.

I stop wanking my dick, as I know I am going to come if I carry on. He pushes my head to the side in an aggressive yet tender way. He starts biting and licking it again, knowing exactly where my weak spot is.

As he continues to gnaw at my neck, he grabs hold of his cock and positions the tip right at my entrance. His throbbing helmet nudges against my arse lips, knocking to come in. My arse contracts, wanting to suck his meat straight up inside it.

He starts to move his tip around the rim of my arse teasingly, staring me right in the eyes. I reach down and touch his cock, wanting to feel it slip inside me. He starts to nuzzle his cock between my arse lips. His huge helmet slowly enters my hole. I grab hold of his tits, wanting him to grow even bigger in me. He leans forward and thrusts his tongue down my throat. As his tongue digs into every corner of my mouth, he begins to slip his cock right inside me.

I grit my teeth as his thick shaft parts my arse to its limits. With one last shove, his whole cock disappears inside me. I grab hold of his muscly arse, wanting to keep him inside me for a while. I've wanked about this moment all year; now I'm going to make it last as long as I can.

Desperate to fuck me, he pulls his cock out of my cunt until just the tip is left inside me. He sits up and grabs hold of my thighs, lifting my arse further into the air. He suddenly shoves his meat right back up my arse. Grabbing my thighs tightly, he starts to pump me like a raging bull.

'Fuck me, Boss,' I shout, wanting him to stab me even harder.

He starts banging me harder than I've ever been banged before. He stares down at his fat cock sliding in and out of my hole. Pre-come oozes out of my end, signalling that I'm nearly there. I know he could make me come without having to touch my knob.

'Harder, Boss,' I yell, not caring if he rips me apart.

'Carl,' he pants in my ear. 'My name's Carl.'

I stare at him lovingly, feeling closer to him than he's ever let any man feel before. I know for a fact he's never let any of the Sureforce team know his real name – not even Twinny. I know I've got him now. I know he is mine. He may have to go off and shag a bird from time to time, but I know I'm his boy. I'm his Matty.

'Fuck me, Carl,' I shout at the top of my voice.

He begins to pump my arse like a piston. I grab the back of his shaved head and pull his mouth down on to mine. I kiss him passionately, not ever wanting to leave this room.

He pulls his tongue out of my mouth and starts to lick my smooth chest. His mouth comes into contact with my rigid tits, and he starts to suck on them to get them even harder. I grab hold of his muscly back that is dripping with sweat.

He kneels up again and looks down at my arse. I pull my legs further apart so that he can watch his knob disappearing inside me. It gets him even more worked up, and he starts ploughing into me in a complete frenzy. I stare at his strong, muscular body. Every bicep on his upper body flexes as he lifts my thighs up higher to get further in. He thrusts out his chest like a proud gorilla. His huge nipples stick out prominently, looking as if they are about to squirt something all over me.

Suddenly, the door of the room creaks open.

'Hello, are you decent, Mr Dalson?' calls the nurse.

'No!' I shout in a panic. 'Give us a minute.'

'OK,' she answers.

The door creaks back closed. Shit, that was a close shave. Carl didn't stop pumping during our little visit. He's more interested in filling my arse. He stares down at my cunt. His cunt. He plunges into me deeper with every thrust.

I play with my hard tits, preparing myself to shoot. My cock bobs back and forth as he fucks me. I feel his huge balls banging on my arse cheeks. He grits his teeth and begins to groan. The thought of him coming makes me release my spunk. My arse clamps itself tightly around Carl's fat cock. My juice flows up through my shaft and flies out of the tip of my cock. It squirts in all directions as my cock springs up and down with each of his thrusts. My man juice is sprayed all over my tits and stomach. Carl reaches forward and rubs it into my smooth skin, concentrating on my erect nipples.

He suddenly yanks his cock out of my cunt and rips off the moist condom. He kneels up straight and pumps his cock with his fist. I sit up and wrap my mouth around his throbbing helmet, wanting to taste my man. He pulls my head right down over his cock and starts pumping it as if it was my arse. I grab his firm arse cheeks and pull him further into me.

I suddenly feel his body tense as he reaches climax. He pulls his knob out of my mouth and starts wanking it. I stick out my tongue and position it under his tip, determined to catch every last drop. I look up at him as his muscles look as if they are about to burst.

'Shit!' he yells loudly.

A thick load of his creamy spunk shoots down the back of my throat, smacking me in the tonsils. As he continues to wank, another stream of hot spunk squirts out and lands on my tongue. I wash the salty liquid around my mouth, wanting to savour the taste after waiting for so long. He continues to pump stream after stream of his thick man juice into me. I greedily drink down every last drop.

Once he is completely empty, he lifts me up into his arms and holds me tightly to his chest. Our hard nipples meet, and he grinds his spunky cock into mine. He squeezes me like he never wants to let me go. I have never felt this wanted in my whole life.

We fall on to the crisp, white hospital bed sheets. We lie on our sides, and he wraps his arms around me. I feel his chest on my back and his semihard cock against my arse. He positions one of his arms around my neck and the other around my stomach. He pulls me close to him, and I feel his breath on my neck. Feeling completely secure, my whole body relaxes, and my eyes slowly begin to close. I know he'll never be mine completely, but a perfect part-time lover beats a second-rate full-time one.

He caringly plants a smacker on the back of my head.

'Partners?' he whispers.

'Partners,' I answer, smiling like the Cheshire cat.

IDOL NEW BOOKS

EASY MONEY

☐ *Published in October*   Bob Condron

One day an ad appears in the popular music press. Its aim: to enlist members for a new boyband. Young, working-class Mitch starts out as a raw recruit, but soon he becomes embroiled in the sexual tension that threatens to engulf the entire group. As the band soars meteorically to pop success, the atmosphere is quickly reaching fever pitch.

£7.99/$10.95   ISBN 0 352 33442 8

SUREFORCE

☐ *Published in November*   Phil Votel

Not knowing what to do with his life once he's been thrown out of the army, Matt takes a job with the security firm Sureforce. Little does he know that the job is the ultimate mix of business and pleasure, and it's not long before Matt's hanging with the beefiest, meanest, hardest lads in town.

£7.99/$10.95   ISBN 0 352 33444 4

THE FAIR COP

☐ *Published in December*   Philip Markham

The second world war is over and America is getting back to business as usual. In 1950s New York, that means dirty business. Hanson's a detective who's been dealt a lousy hand, but the Sullivan case is his big chance. How many junior detectives get handed blackmail, murder and perverted sex all in one day?

£7.99/$10.95   ISBN 0 352 334?? ?

Also published:

CHAINS OF DECEIT

☐   Paul C. Alexander

Journalist Nathan Dexter's life is turned around when he meets a young student called Scott – someone who offers him the relationship for which he's been searching. Then Nathan's best friend goes missing, and Nathan uncovers evidence that he has become the victim of a slavery ring which is rumoured to be operating out of London's leather scene.

£6.99/$9.95   ISBN 0 352 33206 9

DARK RIDER

☐   Jack Gordon

While the rulers of a remote Scottish island play bizarre games of sexual dominance with the Argentinian Angelo, his friend Robert – consumed with jealous longing for his coffee-skinned companion – assuages his desires with the willing locals.

£6.99/$9.95   ISBN 0 352 33243 3

CONQUISTADOR
Jeff Hunter

It is the dying days of the Aztec empire. Axaten and Quetzel are members of the Stable, servants of the Sun Prince chosen for their bravery and beauty. But it is not just an honour and a duty to join this society, it is also the ultimate sexual achievement. Until the arrival of Juan, a young Spanish conquistador, sets the men of the Stable on an adventure of bondage, lust and deception.

£6.99/$9.95   ISBN 0 352 33244 1

TO SERVE TWO MASTERS
Gordon Neale

In the isolated land of Ilyria men are bought and sold as slaves. Rock, brought up to expect to be treated as mere 'livestock', yearns to be sold to the beautiful youth Dorian. But Dorian's brother is as cruel as he is handsome, and if Rock is bought by one brother he will be owned by both.

£6.99/$9.95   ISBN 0 352 33245 X

CUSTOMS OF THE COUNTRY
Rupert Thomas

James Cardell has left school and is looking forward to going to Oxford. That summer of 1924, however, he will spend with his cousins in a tiny village in rural Kent. There he finds he can pursue his love of painting – and begin to explore his obsession with the male physique.

£6.99/$9.95   ISBN 0 352 33246 8

DOCTOR REYNARD'S EXPERIMENT
Robert Black

A dark world of secret brothels, dungeons and sexual cabarets exists behind the respectable façade of Victorian London. The degenerate Lord Spearman introduces Dr Richard Reynard, dashing bachelor, to this hidden world.

£6.99/$9.95   ISBN 0 352 33252 2

CODE OF SUBMISSION
Paul C. Alexander

Having uncovered and defeated a slave ring operating in London's leather scene, journalist Nathan Dexter had hoped to enjoy a peaceful life with his boyfriend Scott. But when it becomes clear that the perverted slave trade has started again, Nathan has no choice but to travel across Europe and America in his bid to stop it. Second in the trilogy.

£6.99/$9.95   ISBN 0 352 33272 7

SLAVES OF TARNE
Gordon Neale

Pascal willingly follows the mysterious and alluring Casper to Tarne, a community of men enslaved to men. Tarne is everything that Pascal has ever fantasised about, but he begins to sense a sinister aspect to Casper's magnetism. Pascal has to choose between the pleasures of submission and acting to save the people he loves.

£6.99/$9.95   ISBN 0 352 33273 5

ROMAN GAMES
Tasker Dean

When Sam visits the island of Skate, he is taught how to submit to other men, acting out an elaborate fantasy in which young men become wrestling slaves – just as in ancient Rome. Indeed, if he is to have his beautiful prize – the wrestler, Robert – he must learn how the Romans played their games.

£6.99/$9.95   ISBN 0 352 33322 7

VENETIAN TRADE
Richard Davis

From the deck of the ship that carries him into Venice, Rob Weaver catches his first glimpse of a beautiful but corrupt city where the dark alleys and misty canals hide debauchery and decadence. Here, he must learn to survive among men who would make him a plaything and a slave.

£6.99/$9.95   ISBN 0 352 33323 5

THE LOVE OF OLD EGYPT
Philip Markham

It's 1925 and the deluxe cruiser carrying the young gigolo Jeremy Hessling has docked at Luxor. Jeremy dreams of being dominated by the pharaohs of old, but quickly becomes involved with someone more accessible – Khalid, a young man of exceptional beauty.

£6.99/$9.95   ISBN 0 352 33354 5

THE BLACK CHAMBER
Jack Gordon

Educated at the court of George II, Calum Monroe finds his native Scotland a dull, damp place. He relieves his boredom by donning a mask and holding up coaches in the guise of the Fox – a dashing highwayman. Chance throws him and neighbouring farmer Fergie McGregor together with Calum's sinister, perverse guardian, James Black.

£6.99/$9.95   ISBN 0 352 33373 1

THE GREEK WAY
Edward Ellis

Ancient Greece, the end of the fifth century BC – at the height of the Peloponnesian War. Young Orestes is a citizen of Athens, sent to Sparta as a spy. There he encounters a society of athletic, promiscuous soldiers – including the beautiful Spartan Hector.

£6.99/$9.95   ISBN 0 352 33427 4

MORE AND HARDER
Morgan

This is the erotic autobiography of Mark, a submissive English sadomasochist: an 'SM sub' or 'slave'. Rarely has a writer been so explicitly hot or so forthcoming in the arousingly strict details of military and disciplinary life.

£7.99/$10.95   ISBN 0 352 33437 1

BOOTY BOYS
Published in September ## Jay Russell

Hard-bodied black British detective Alton Davies can't believe his eyes or his luck when he finds muscular African-American gangsta rapper Banji-B lounging in his office early one morning. Alton's disbelief – and his excitement – mounts as Banji-B asks him to track down a stolen videotape of a post-gig orgy.

£7.99/$10.95   ISBN 0 352 33446 0

---------------✂---------------------------

Please send me the books I have ticked above.

Name   ....

Address   ....

            ....

            ....

            .... Post Code ....

Send to: **Cash Sales, Idol Books, Thames Wharf Studios, Rainville Road, London W6 9HA.**

US customers: for prices and details of how to order books for delivery by mail, call 1–800–805–1083.

Please enclose a cheque or postal order, made payable to **Virgin Publishing Ltd**, to the value of the books you have ordered plus postage and packing costs as follows:

UK and BFPO – £1.00 for the first book, 50p for each subsequent book.

Overseas (including Republic of Ireland) – £2.00 for the first book, £1.00 for each subsequent book.

We accept all major credit cards, including VISA, ACCESS/MASTER-CARD, DINERS CLUB, AMEX and SWITCH.

Please write your card number and expiry date here:

....

Please allow up to 28 days for delivery.

Signature ....

---------------✂---------------------------

WE NEED YOUR HELP . . .

to plan the future of Idol books —

Yours are the only opinions that matter. Idol is a new and exciting venture: the first British series of books devoted to homoerotic fiction for men.

We're going to do our best to provide the sexiest, best-written books you can buy. And we'd like you to help in these early stages. Tell us what you want to read. There's a freepost address for your filled-in questionnaires, so you won't even need to buy a stamp.

THE IDOL QUESTIONNAIRE

SECTION ONE: ABOUT YOU

1.1 Sex (*we presume you are male, but just in case*)
Are you?
Male ☐
Female ☐

1.2 Age
under 21 ☐ 21–30 ☐
31–40 ☐ 41–50 ☐
51–60 ☐ over 60 ☐

1.3 At what age did you leave full-time education?
still in education ☐ 16 or younger ☐
17–19 ☐ 20 or older ☐

1.4 Occupation _____

1.5 Annual household income _____

1.6　We are perfectly happy for you to remain anonymous; but if you would like us to send you a free booklist of Idol books, please insert your name and address

_____

_____

_____

_____

SECTION TWO: ABOUT BUYING IDOL BOOKS

2.1　Where did you get this copy of *Sureforce*?
    Bought at chain book shop ☐
    Bought at independent book shop ☐
    Bought at supermarket ☐
    Bought at book exchange or used book shop ☐
    I borrowed it/found it ☐
    My partner bought it ☐

2.2　How did you find out about Idol books?
    I saw them in a shop ☐
    I saw them advertised in a magazine ☐
    I read about them in _____
    Other _____

2.3　Please tick the following statements you agree with:
    I would be less embarrassed about buying Idol
    books if the cover pictures were less explicit ☐
    I think that in general the pictures on Idol
    books are about right ☐
    I think Idol cover pictures should be as
    explicit as possible ☐

2.4　Would you read an Idol book in a public place – on a train for instance?
    Yes ☐　　　No ☐

SECTION THREE: ABOUT THIS IDOL BOOK

3.1　Do you think the sex content in this book is:
    Too much ☐　　About right ☐
    Not enough ☐

3.2   Do you think the writing style in this book is:
      Too unreal/escapist   ☐   About right   ☐
      Too down to earth   ☐

3.3   Do you think the story in this book is:
      Too complicated   ☐   About right   ☐
      Too boring/simple   ☐

3.4   Do you think the cover of this book is:
      Too explicit   ☐   About right   ☐
      Not explicit enough ☐
Here's a space for any other comments:

SECTION FOUR: ABOUT OTHER IDOL BOOKS

4.1   How many Idol books have you read?

4.2   If more than one, which one did you prefer?

     _____

4.3   Why?

SECTION FIVE: ABOUT YOUR IDEAL EROTIC NOVEL

We want to publish the books you want to read – so this is your chance to tell us exactly what your ideal erotic novel would be like.

5.1   Using a scale of 1 to 5 (1 = no interest at all, 5 = your ideal), please rate the following possible settings for an erotic novel:
      Roman / Ancient World   ☐
      Medieval / barbarian / sword 'n' sorcery   ☐
      Renaissance / Elizabethan / Restoration   ☐
      Victorian / Edwardian   ☐
      1920s & 1930s   ☐
      Present day   ☐
      Future / Science Fiction   ☐

5.2 Using the same scale of 1 to 5, please rate the following themes you may find in an erotic novel:

Bondage / fetishism ☐
Romantic love ☐
SM / corporal punishment ☐
Bisexuality ☐
Group sex ☐
Watersports ☐
Rent / sex for money ☐

5.3 Using the same scale of 1 to 5, please rate the following styles in which an erotic novel could be written:

Gritty realism, down to earth ☐
Set in real life but ignoring its more unpleasant aspects ☐
Escapist fantasy, but just about believable ☐
Complete escapism, totally unrealistic ☐

5.4 In a book that features power differentials or sexual initiation, would you prefer the writing to be from the viewpoint of the dominant / experienced or submissive / inexperienced characters?

Dominant / Experienced ☐
Submissive / Inexperienced ☐
Both ☐

5.5 We'd like to include characters close to your ideal lover. What characteristics would your ideal lover have? Tick as many as you want:

Dominant	☐	Caring	☐
Slim	☐	Rugged	☐
Extroverted	☐	Romantic	☐
Bisexual	☐	Old	☐
Working Class	☐	Intellectual	☐
Introverted	☐	Professional	☐
Submissive	☐	Pervy	☐
Cruel	☐	Ordinary	☐
Young	☐	Muscular	☐
Naïve	☐		

Anything else? _____

5.6 Is there one particular setting or subject matter that your ideal erotic novel would contain?

_____

5.7 As you'll have seen, we include safe-sex guidelines in every book. However, while our policy is always to show safe sex in stories with contemporary settings, we don't insist on safe-sex practices in stories with historical settings because it would be anachronistic. What, if anything, would you change about this policy?

_____

_____

SECTION SIX: LAST WORDS

6.1 What do you like best about Idol books?

_____

6.2 What do you most dislike about Idol books?

_____

6.3 In what way, if any, would you like to change Idol covers?

_____

6.4 Here's a space for any other comments:

_____

_____

_____

_____

Thanks for completing this questionnaire. Now either tear it out, or photocopy it, then put it in an envelope and send it to:

> **Idol**
> **FREEPOST**
> **London**
> **W10 5BR**

You don't need a stamp if you're in the UK, but you'll need one if you're posting from overseas.